THE

BERLIN DOSSIER

THE

BERLIN DOSSIER

Leon Berger

A LOON IN BALLOON BOOK

THE BERLIN DOSSIER
© 2006 Leon Berger

Library and Archives Canada Cataloguing in Publication

Berger, Leon, 1949-
    The Berlin Dossier / Leon Berger

ISBN 0-9737497-1-7

    I. Title.

PS8553.E672B47 2006   C813'.54   C2005-905439-5

Published by: Loon in Balloon Inc.
                     Suite #3-513
                     133 Weber Street North
                     Waterloo, Ontario
                     Canada   N2J 3G9

Cover design by Leon Berger
Interior design by Steve Penner

Printed and bound in Canada by
Friesens Corporation
Altona, Manitoba, Canada

FIRST EDITION
987654321

ACKNOWLEDGMENTS

No amount of historical research can match the power of living testimony and I owe a special debt to the many people who agreed to relive their personal experiences.

In particular, I must mention my friend of many years, Charlotte (Liselotte) Urban, a survivor of the pre-war Nazi pogrom known as "Kristallnacht," with whom I've shared countless hours of conversation. I was also privileged to interview her cousin, Stefan Lesniak, who was on Oskar Schindler's original list.

On a more pragmatic note, I'd also like to offer my appreciation to the enterprising book-lovers at Loon In Balloon who decided, against all odds, to start up a new, independent publishing house and who believe there's still potential in the art of popular storytelling.

Finally, I'd like to express my gratitude to a couple of true literary professionals, Carolyn Swayze and Barry Jones, for their candid, selfless advice.

PROLOGUE

Barcelona, February 1951

My name is Edmund Albert Schaeffer. If I had any friends left, they'd call me Ed, because that's how they knew me back then. Good ol' Ed. Always good for a laugh, always good for a few marks. Of course, that was back when my life still had some meaning. Back before I was forced to confront the most feared individual in the entire Third Reich. Back before I'd ever heard of any damned dossier.

Even now, it's hard to believe. That dossier was nothing more than a stack of papers in a file, inherently worthless, yet it cost me everything I ever valued - and almost cost me my life.

Today, the world I knew is gone and most of my friends are just memories, vanished like ghosts into the fog of war. Now, all that's left is my own solitude, a forlorn existence here in Franco's Spain, where the only warmth comes from the dying rays of a blood-red sun. My face, always a little rough-hewn, has become creased with ever-deepening lines. My hair, once dark and thick, has turned gun-metal gray. My physique, which used to be robust, has finally surrendered to years of wear and tear, exacerbated by a shrapnel wound that still prevents me from sleeping.

What do I do with my time? That's a good question. Mostly, I just sit in this sidewalk café here on the Ramblas and stare out at the passing faces. When I can afford it, I'll take a litre or two of cheap Catalan wine and occasionally, when I can actually get myself together, I write. Why? Probably because it's the only thing I really know how to do. I have a kleptomaniac's collection of old scribbled notes that might eventually, some day, turn into my own account of what happened. The untold secrets. The evil scheming. An epic saga of intrigue and deceit, of love and death, of violence and treachery in the savage cauldron of Nazi Berlin. It would be nice to finish it before the wine destroys my liver.

Ideally, I'd like to be remembered as a journalist of some repute, a dedicated foreign correspondent prying loose the facts and shedding some light on the vile darkness of the Hitler regime. It's a fake legacy, I know. If I'm being honest, I have to admit that, in essence, I was nothing more than a freelance hack, struggling to make a living by feeding tidbits of this and that to the international wire services. Well-researched tidbits, to be sure, but tidbits nonetheless. And in the end, when I finally latched on to the biggest story of my career, I couldn't bring myself to write it because I'd made a promise not to do so. Only now can the truth come out. Only now, when it's all behind me and there's no one left to hurt.

The question is where to start.

The natural place would be my initial arrival in Germany. An eloquently descriptive piece, perhaps, about a Canadian steamer docking at Bremen and a scruffy expatriate descending the gangplank, eager to explore the decadence and confusion that was Berlin. But that was in the late twenties, when I was still more or less free to enjoy it. The serious damage didn't happen until a decade later.

Then how about the time I first met Katharina? Intermission at the Kroll Opera House. Imperious Prussians crowding the bar. And me with a glass in my hand, jostled into spilling my gin and tonic all over the breathtakingly beautiful stranger. No, I don't think I like that either. Focusing entirely on Katharina would be too painful, even after all this time.

Or maybe I'm just trying too hard. If I'm being honest with myself, all I really want to do is relate my own version of events in the hope that it might, somehow, serve to set the record straight - to reveal the truth of what really happened. That in itself would be an accomplishment and, at this stage of the game, it's about all I have the right to expect.

1938

1

Our sordid tale begins with a victim, an aging veteran by the name of Josef Schmidt. He was a German from the north, a "Piefke" as they used to be called, but his murder occurred while he was taking a three-week holiday in the vicinity of Gstaad, Switzerland. He had a cousin living there, a baker if my information is correct, and every day while his cousin worked, Schmidt would lace up his boots, fill a knapsack with bread and bratwurst and go hiking through the high mountain pastures.

He was one of those steely-eyed Germans that you see in old photographs. Stern, stubborn and fitter at sixty-three than most men are at forty. An individual to whom clicking heels still meant gallantry, not subservience. The only part that didn't fit the Kaiser image was his face. He'd lost part of it at Passchendaele, including his left cheekbone all the way down to the jaw line. After the armistice, he'd slowly come to accept the daily difficulties of eating and shaving, and he'd even learned to put up with the headaches, but the one thing he still couldn't abide was the involuntary revulsion in people's eyes when they first saw him. That's why he took his vacations alone like this, as a welcome escape from the pain of human contact.

One morning, after his cousin had gone off to work as usual, Schmidt was standing on the porch finishing his coffee when a car turned into the driveway and slowly negotiated the uneven surface. It was a rare event and, even more unusual, it bore a Berlin license plate. He watched it carefully all the way until it came to a halt next to the woodpile and the engine was switched off.

The silence returned.

"Good morning," said the young driver cheerfully as he clambered out. "Another fine day." It wasn't true that the SS always used terror. Sometimes they used charm.

Schmidt nodded his greeting as the two of them came towards the porch. The one who'd been driving was tall and slightly angular, his hair the colour of straw. His friend was broader and darker with a slight shadow around the jowls. They both wore new-looking outfits of cord pants and Alpine ski sweaters, the kind of conspicuous clothes that tourists might wear.

"We were wondering if you could help us," said the same young man.

Schmidt answered slowly: "If I can."

"Well, actually, we're looking for a guide and you were suggested to us. Some people we met in the village. They said you know this area well."

Schmidt looked from one to the other and said nothing.

"Nice people," the man continued. "Told us how to get here. Told us all about you."

A pause as the old man sipped his coffee. Then, slowly, he responded: "Did they also tell you I'm not from around here?"

"Yes, they told us that."

"So why would you want a guide who's not from around here?"

The young man laughed a little. He had good eyes and an easy shrug of the shoulders. It was a fine act he was putting on. "Well, to be honest, Herr... Schmidt, is it?"

The old man didn't respond.

"To be honest, we'd prefer to have a German national like yourself." He reached into his rear pocket for a wallet and took out a card. Then he handed it up to Schmidt who was still on the porch. "Kiesmüller," he announced. "And this is my colleague, Mannheim. We're with the Technische Hochschule. We're interested in making a film and this, we're hoping, might be one of the locations."

Schmidt studied the card. "What kind of film?"

"A travel documentary... 'Opportunities for Travel in German-Speaking Lands.' It's really just an exercise for the senior students but we've had some success in the past. Dr. Goebbels himself once gave us a favorable review." The young man could still sense the hesitation. "There's a small budget available for local fees and so on. I'm sure that whatever reasonable compensation you care to name could be accommodated…"

Schmidt handed back the card. "For a day?"

"Well, a day, maybe two. Depends how long it takes." A smile. "Depends how good a guide you are."

Schmidt drained his coffee and thought about it. Being proud and unwilling to accept charity didn't alter the fact that train tickets were expensive. And these two young strangers seemed amiable enough. Didn't seem to mind his appearance at all. "Wait here," he said eventually. "I'll get my bag."

Thirty minutes later, Schmidt was dead.

They drove him through narrow lanes to a remote spot, near where the source of the Turbach comes tumbling down from the Giferhorn. The broader man got out first. Then, just as his newly hired guide was stepping out the door, he brought a large piece of rock down on the old man's head with enough force to crush his skull. One blow was enough. The old man crumpled in a heap, blood gushing from the ugly wound. Together, the two young men rolled the body to the edge of the nearby precipice and pushed it over. Who would ever know that death hadn't been caused by a tragic fall?

Except that even remote Swiss villagers can recognize fresh tire tracks when they see them.

The connection was quickly made to the two strangers who'd been asking all the questions, and a hue-and-cry was set up. But of course, they'd long since disappeared. And although several inquiries must have been passed from Berne through to Berlin, nothing ever came of it. No file was ever opened in the German capital, no formalities were ever begun. By that time the Kriminalpolizei, like every other branch of police security, came under the jurisdiction of the SS.

* * *

For the next victim, we must travel to Paris, city of light - chic, debonair and naive beyond belief.

Despite the Spanish civil war, the threat of Soviet-sponsored communism and the recent German takeover of both Prague and Vienna, this was a capital blinded by its own delusions, content to dwell in serene confidence behind its own elaborate façade. In fact, if you'd told the average Parisian shopkeeper that in two short years he'd be watching troops of the Wehrmacht goosestep their way towards the Arc de Triomphe, he'd have laughed in your face. "We have the largest army in Europe," he'd have scoffed. "We have more men, more tanks and more airplanes than the Germans. We have our Maginot Line. What can they possibly do?"

It was all true, all put carefully in place so that nothing should disturb the traditional way of life. Complacency had reached its zenith. French was still the international language of diplomacy and the Republic regarded itself as the guardian of European civilization.

Fittingly, its central seat of government was the magnificently ornate Quay d' Orsay and, to match such status, several of the senior ministers maintained city residences just across the river, on the exclusive Île-Saint-Louis. It was a perfect location, a veritable sanctuary of peace for the privileged class. Narrow, cobbled streets. Elegant houses with tall windows and louvred shutters. Shady courtyards behind high stone walls and locked gates. And around the circumference of the tiny island, mature trees bordering the dark, lapping waters of the Seine.

To capture the real flavour of the place, I always felt the time to see it was on a Sunday morning before anyone was awake. Occasionally, when I used to visit the city, I'd stroll over the Pont Marie, light up a Havana and just let my head drift with the passing clouds. I'd listen to the birds and the chimes of the small church, I'd watch the sun's early rays as they crept over the intricate spires of Notre Dame and I'd dream that I too might one day amass enough funds to purchase an address here.

Now it so happened that among the island's discrete inhabitants was a medical practitioner by the name of Gottfried Bausch.

A leading pulmonary specialist, as I understand, with a clinic situated on the Rue de Poissy over on the Left Bank. He was a man who'd done well for himself in his adopted homeland and he strove to portray his success in both his demeanor and his lifestyle. Most weekdays, for example, he walked at his own stately pace across the Pont de la Tournelle to arrive at his office at around ten - and most evenings, he returned home at about seven, after taking dinner at his usual table at "Le Bijou." In short, he'd become a comfortable creature of habit. And he'd carefully cultivated his manners to the extent that he could, if he wished, be at ease even in the most elevated company.

Yet he had a closely guarded secret, this worthy doctor. As I later found out, he was also an honorary member of the Ausland section of the SD, the chief security division of the SS, and had been for several years. In truth it was quite an elegant operation. The very fact that Bausch was German and didn't try to hide it put him beyond suspicion. Perhaps in lesser circles, he might have been quickly fingered as an obvious spy but in the grandiose strata of the French establishment, such an idea would have seemed absurd simply because it was so obvious. The notion would have been simply too gauche.

Dr. Bausch's regular contact, a certain Friedrich Hahn, was an equally upstanding member of society, a seasoned commercial attaché at the German embassy. Naturally enough, the meeting methodology was a medical appointment that usually took place on the first Monday of each month. During such visits, Hahn would copy down the more interesting snippets of gossip that the doctor was able to glean from his patients and, once back at the embassy, he'd just ship it all off in the diplomatic pouch to Berlin. Nothing to it. Of course, it wasn't terribly valuable as strategic information but it did help to rationalize other rumours that were circulating - which general's mistress had become pregnant, for example, or which member of the cabinet had contracted syphilis from a Montmartre prostitute.

Why Bausch allowed himself to be used like that, I have no idea. He obviously didn't need the money. Of course, it's possible he was a Nazi ideologue, a true believer in Aryan supremacy and the stiff-armed salute, but I doubt it. More probably, he was just one of life's basic survivors whose natural instinct was to play both ends at once. If there was peace, he'd simply be able to continue as ever with his own refined Parisian lifestyle. But if, as he was beginning to fear, Germany went too far and as a German citizen he was forced to return home, then he could arrive as a celebrated agent of espionage, a true hero of the Reich. With credentials like that, he'd be able to set himself up in a fine clinic on the Linden without even skipping a beat.

If that was indeed his plan, he never got the chance to carry it out.

One evening, on September 9th to be precise, he walked home a little later than usual, at some time close to midnight. He'd been to a performance at the Odéon with some acquaintances from the Palais de Justice and was still humming an aria to himself as he walked back across the bridge to the island.

The three men waiting for him had just about given him up. In fact, another ten minutes and he'd have probably made it home.

"Good evening, Herr Doktor."

The voice spoke to him in German. It came from the darkness of one of the stone doorways and, for a moment, Bausch was startled.

"My God, who's that? Hahn, is that you?"

"You're a little late tonight."

"I was at the opera. But what are you doing here at…"

He didn't get to finish his sentence. A metal bar came crashing into his ribcage, doubling him over, followed by a second brutal blow to his head.

The attack was designed to look like a late-night traffic accident. But the police weren't entirely incompetent and a certain Inspecteur Tabac of the Paris Sureté was heard to voice considerable doubts. Since few cars ever cruised around Île-Saint-Louis at that hour, such a theory seemed to him quite unlikely. Unfortunately, there were no witnesses and no one ever found the weapon, so lacking any real evidence, he had no option but to mark it down to a freak occurrence and rationalize its anonymity as the result of some driver scared of losing his license. Although the German embassy was contacted, no one ever thought to connect Hahn, who just went on with his duties as if nothing had happened.

Another successful operation for the SS, this time targeting one of their own.

* * *

It was the final assassination that caused all the trouble, mainly because it took place in the very centre of Berlin.

Yet this was not a Berlin I liked much any more. By 1938, the Nazi metamorphosis was complete and the city that had once been my beautifully wicked girlfriend had changed into a corseted maiden aunt. The vibrancy of artists like Lotte Lenya and Bertold Brecht had given way to the servitude of Werner Kraus and Arno Brecker. This was now the city of thugs and jackboots, of intimidation and lies, all orchestrated by Joseph Goebbels, the intense propaganda genius whose most brilliant creation was the myth of the messianic Führer.

Even the architecture was about to change. Speer's plans called for developing the core into a cross between the Champs Elysées and the Washington Mall. Hitler wanted a grandeur befitting his thousand year Reich and to get it he was prepared to cut out the living heart of the city. The great central rail terminus, the Anhalter Bahnhof, would disappear and a giant swathe would be gouged out from west of Tempelhof almost as far north as the Tiergarten. A living, breathing organism was about to be transformed into a totalitarian monolith. A fascist trophy. And the people who cared were powerless to act. In the new Reich, the demands of the Führer allowed no obstruction. Leni Riefenstahl's film "Triumph of the Will" had been aptly named.

I suppose you're entitled to ask why we all stayed, all the people like me, and the only answer I can offer is a kind of nostalgic affection for what life was once like in that Berlin of ours. You just don't leave the bedside of a patient stricken with cancer, no matter how certain death is going to be. We'd known the city when it was alive and intense - full of its own rude health - and I guess the few of us who were left took comfort in that. We also relished the time we spent in each other's company. We'd all pile into the bar at the Adlon and forget what was happening outside. That's when the stories would start and we were instantly transported back a decade, reliving the hectic and sometimes wild lives that we'd once taken for granted. Of course, the anecdotes became funnier with each telling, to the extent that, even today, I'm not entirely sure whether I'm remembering the facts of my everyday existence or the legends we created while reeking of schnapps.

I guess it doesn't really matter. The overriding truth was that, by that time, Berlin had fallen under the spell of the swastika. Whenever there was a parade, massive crowds lined the streets and buildings were festooned with flags and banners. Children sat high on their fathers' shoulders just to get a glimpse. Veterans on crutches saluted and cried tears of joy at what they perceived to be the glorious resurrection of German pride. And the women! The women would have thrown themselves at the passing Führer if they'd been allowed. It was like a mass ecstasy, almost a national hypnosis. Some of them even fainted. I saw it all with my own eyes and it always made for a good story to send out on the wires.

Yet on other days, average days, it was all frighteningly normal. People still went to work, still looked longingly in the store windows, still put money away each week for the new Volkswagen, the "people's car" that they'd heard so much about. Meanwhile, the U-Bahn burrowed its way across town, carrying the crowds as best it could, and up above, the laden buses and lurching streetcars struggled to find a way through the choking traffic.

It was on one such weekday, on one such streetcar, that the man was sitting. It was Wednesday October 5th and, although the rush period was just about coming to an end, the vehicle was still maddeningly full as it rumbled westbound along the narrow Leipziger Strasse towards the Potsdamer Platz.

His name was Johannes Utz and he was wearing an officer's

uniform of the Kriegsmarine, the German navy. Normally he spent his leave with his wife and two children in his home town of Halle, the epitome of the good husband and responsible father. He even enjoyed gardening on their tiny plot of land. But that was only when he was at home. When he was in town, like thousands of others in his position, he'd found an extra-marital interest. I've no idea who she was but she lived in Wittenau and he was just stopping off on his way to see her in order to purchase some small gift. A few chocolates perhaps, or a modest bauble. Whatever he could afford.

The streetcar lurched to a halt at Markgrafen Strasse and he peered out of the steamed-up window trying to work out where he was. Guessing he must be near his stop, he got up from the seat and edged his way through the packed crowd towards the exit, eventually alighting near the Café Kerkau at Friedrichstrasse. From there, he began walking north towards the Kranzler-Ecke, turning up his collar against the chill of the damp air. He still hadn't noticed the young SS Scharführer who'd been following him discretely ever since he'd arrived that afternoon from his base at Kiel. But then there's no reason why he should. The young man may have been wearing a black tunic but his air was casual and around his neck was a Leica camera. Just another enlisted man on leave, no different from Utz himself.

The evening was already closing in, the heavy nimbus clouds adding to the intensity of the city shadows. As the Scharführer strolled along, he paused briefly to check his camera, a signal to the old car that was slowly trailing a hundred metres behind. Suddenly, with the engine whining in second gear, the car accelerated past the Scharführer and pulled up alongside Utz. Inside were three men in rough clothes who seemed to have had too much to drink. The one in the back rolled down the window and waved a map.

"Hey, sailor boy!"

Utz looked at him and smiled indulgently. He could understand men needing to have a good time. He walked over to the car, prepared to help out. By this time, the man had the map spread out in front of him and was peering at it with the help of the flickering flame from his cigarette lighter. With a slightly rolling gesture, he beckoned Utz to get in.

The moment Utz did so, it was all over.

The man with the map pinned him back and the one in the front passenger seat swung around with a long knife to the chest. There was a look of shock from Utz, a brief moment of delayed reaction before the brain understood that the heart had been pierced and the oxygen supply had ceased. That's when the life drained out of him and he slumped over.

"Come on, move!" said the driver sharply, as the one in the back reached over, opened the door and, with some effort, heaved the lifeless body out on to the pavement.

Some of the people in the street turned, startled at such a scene, frozen into inaction by the sheer speed of it all. Only one person made any kind of response and that was the Scharführer, right on cue.

Afterwards, they'd all distinctly recall the bravery of the young man, chasing the car as it sped away, shaking his fist in angry protest and yelling after them "Damn foreigners!" And the eye witnesses would describe in great detail how he knelt down to try and administer first aid to the unfortunate navy officer. That such things should happen, they would all exclaim with righteous indignation. Must have been saboteurs or anarchists. None had any reason to doubt the Scharführer's claim that they were foreigners.

Of course, the young SS man volunteered his evidence to the police just like any other good citizen. Yes, he believed the car was an Opel. Yes, black and fairly old. Yes, there'd been three of them inside. Yes, in ordinary working clothes. And yes, from the looks of them, they might well have been foreigners.

Then once they were done with him, he took a taxi back to the SD offices on Prinz Albrecht Strasse, where he met the other three for a debriefing session.

2

If public reaction to the Utz incident was limited, the fury within the upper echelons of the police establishment was all consuming. Meetings were held and desks were pounded. Indignant outrage was the order of the day. To a man, they knew perfectly well that such an operation bore all the hallmarks of the SS.

Although they officially served under SS authority, the police maintained the pretense of a separate division with their own uniforms and methodology. And while they could look the other way for book-burning and Jew-baiting, the blatant murder of a pure Aryan naval officer on a major Berlin thoroughfare was clearly going way too far. This they saw as a stain on their reputation and their public credibility.

By the end of the following day, the case had reached the desk of the Berlin police chief, one Wolf von Helldorf, a former count with a grand name but who now found himself languishing in the city bureaucracy. He was a circumspect man, however, and accepted his fate as part of the new era. This was the way things now were and he knew he couldn't launch any protest against an SS operation without inviting retribution, even if it did take place on the streets of the capital. So he decided to do what any self-respecting bureaucrat would do. He shifted the affair sideways. The man had been in the navy? Fine, he concluded, let them handle it. Since they didn't fall under SS jurisdiction, they'd have more independence of action anyway. Or so his theory ran. The case was therefore assigned a priority code and transferred through the appropriate channels to the OKK, the navy high command situated on Bendlerstrasse.

But by 1938, even the navy didn't want to incur the open wrath of the SS, so the docket was shuffled around various in-trays until it was conveniently forgotten. The matter might well have ended there, except for one man who recognized the name of the deceased and couldn't bring himself to ignore it.

We pick up the story on October 11th.

* * *

At about five-thirty on that lifeless gray afternoon, a slightly tarnished Mercedes drove sedately through the quiet, upscale streets of Zehlendorf in southwestern Berlin and turned into the driveway of a large house on Betazeile, its heavy tires crunching on the gravel.

The department chauffeur was an older man, long retired from active service, and his passenger waited patiently until the door was opened. As always, the two dogs sprang out first, a pair of squat brown dachshunds that accompanied him everywhere, their tails constantly wagging at the sheer joy of being alive. A moment later their beloved owner emerged wearing his omnipresent overcoat on top of two thick sweaters. He rarely wore uniform, a habit that was only tolerated because of his unusual function.

"Thank you, Franz," he said as he stepped out wearily. "That'll be all for tonight."

"Yes sir." The chauffeur slammed the door. "Rough day, sir?"

The diminutive fifty-one-year-old allowed himself a half-smile. "They're all rough days, Franz. Especially Mondays."

"Yes, sir, but today's Tuesday."

"That's right. So however bad it was, it wasn't as bad as yesterday, was it?"

"No sir." Franz Meichner had been the department's driver long enough to get used to the little man's intellectual conundrums. "Usual time in the morning?"

"Why not?"

Meichner watched his boss walk up the few steps and saw the prematurely white hair disappear through the front door. Then he returned to the car. He had his observer's report to file to the SS, a despicable task he'd been pressured into performing, but at least after that, he could have the rest of the evening free.

* * *

The dogs were happy to be home, sliding around on the polished wood floor, and the man followed them in.

"Erika?"

"You don't have to yell, I'm right here," answered his wife as she emerged. She was a slim, intelligent woman, dressed today in one of her best city outfits, a sober gray skirt and jacket enlivened by a broad strand of South Sea pearls. "I only just got back myself." She was about the same age as her husband but slightly taller, with calm brown eyes and a conservative disposition, full of middle-class common sense. She needed it to put up with his eccentricities.

She helped him out of his coat and scarf but he insisted on keeping both his sweaters.

"I'm cold," he complained.

"You're always cold."

"Where were you today, anyway? I called you twice."

"At my sister's. I told you I was going. You never remember anything."

That's not true, he thought, but he had no wish to start an argument. He remembered everything perfectly but only if it held any interest for him. Meanwhile, his wife was busy giving him his instructions for the evening.

"Hurry up and take your bath if you're having one," she told him. "They said they'd be here at eight."

He mumbled a grunt and then ignored her by shuffling off into his study, where he poured himself a good shot of his favourite malt scotch and slumped down into the well-worn, green leather armchair by the window. He always drank it neat, just like the Scots themselves, and he savoured it respectfully as he took his first sip. The dogs had scampered off to the kitchen for supper, leaving him completely alone. He had a few things to think about.

His name was Wilhelm Canaris, his official rank was Admiral and, for the last four years, he'd been in charge of the Abwehr, the combined military intelligence unit. But the position was a lot more grandiose on paper than it was in reality.

As difficult as it may be to appreciate now, the Abwehr's role before the war was neither respected nor completely understood within military circles. If it had been, they'd never have handed it to a representative of the Kriegsmarine, Germany's least important branch of the armed forces - and even then, they'd never have given it to Canaris, a man who'd been shunted aside by the brass at OKK as being unfit for high command. Although brilliant and intuitive, he was just far too unorthodox for their hidebound structure.

As evidence, consider the amazing story of his escape as a POW during the Great War, as told to me by a reporter from the *Frankfurter Allgemeine Zeitung* when we shared a beer one evening...

The year was 1915 and Canaris was serving as a junior officer aboard the cruiser "Dresden." They were off the Pacific coast of South America when they were engaged in a firefight by a couple of British destroyers. Outgunned, the German ship refused to surrender and, following a running battle, the captain was finally forced to scuttle his vessel. After they were rescued, Canaris was interned along with the rest of the crew on a small island near Chile. Not wishing to spend the rest of the war there, he made the decision to chance his luck. He was pretty good at languages so he disguised himself as a local, rowed across to the mainland and simply slipped away into the night. To get back home, he first hitched four hundred kilometres south to Osorno. Then he crossed the Andes by horseback to Neuquen, Argentina, catching a dose of malaria on the way. From there he jumped a train for another eight hundred kilometres to Buenos Aires, where he was somehow able to fix himself up with a fake Chilean passport and board a Dutch steamer bound for Europe. Even then it wasn't over. Before the vessel arrived in neutral Amsterdam, it was stopped in British waters and held for inspection. But he kept his nerve and made it the rest of the way, arriving in Hamburg two months after his initial escape.

It was on board that Dutch ship where he first tasted scotch and, as he sat in his study staring at the rich, amber liquid, he found it difficult to prevent his thoughts from wandering back. In many ways, it was a simpler time.

"Willi!" said his wife with some annoyance. "They'll be here soon."

He looked at her but said nothing, then turned his head towards the window. A few seconds passed. It had started raining and the foliage outside was dark and blurred.

"He finally did it," he said quietly. Any trace of good humour had vanished by that point and he looked every bit his age. "He finally got Johannes Utz."

His wife sat down on the chintz sofa that filled the space between the high oak bookcase and the fireplace. She was still holding a checkered dishcloth that she'd been using to wipe her hands. The shock she felt was considerable. "You always said he would," she replied quietly.

"I said it but I didn't really believe it." He paused for a moment, then chose to correct himself. "No, that's not true. I did believe it. I just didn't want to admit that I believed it."

"And what about Johannes? Is he dead?"

"Oh yes, he's quite dead. Stabbed through the heart. Our dear Reinhard doesn't make mistakes like that."

"When did it happen?"

"Last Wednesday. I only saw the report today. Good old navy efficiency."

"And you're sure it's Reinhard who's behind it?"

"Am I sure? What do you mean am I sure? He's gone through the entire list, every last one. Three in the last five months alone... Schmidt, Bausch and now Utz."

"I know but…"

"But what?"

"I don't know. I thought that with Johannes…"

"He'd make an exception for old times' sake?"

She didn't reply and there was a long silence. Eventually she said: "Is there any family?"

"Wife, two kids, a couple of animals. Same as me."

Erika looked at her husband, immediately struck by the power of the implication. Her hands gripped the dishcloth a little more tightly. "What will you do?" She watched him slowly get to his feet.

"Take my bath," he replied as he walked stiffly towards the door with the drink still in his hand.

* * *

Erika Canaris left her husband alone for half an hour, then went upstairs and tapped gently on the bathroom door before entering. She found him soaking in the tub, lost in the complex universe of his own thought processes. His body looked pale and vulnerable.

He didn't even look at her. "Reinhard..." he said, repeating the name that was uppermost in his mind. It was almost as if he were speaking to himself. "I could destroy him, you know. I could crush him in one day. In one hour."

She sat down carefully on the side of the bathtub, noticing the empty scotch glass next to the sink. "But you won't," she replied.

"I might."

"No, you won't. You can't."

"Is that a challenge?"

"No, Willi, it's a plain and simple fact. And anyway..."

"Anyway what?"

"I'm not sure what the point would be. He's far more useful to you alive than dead."

He smiled but it was without warmth or humour. "Interesting," he said. "We're not talking about friendship any more. We're not talking about playing the violin together. We're not talking about Sunday afternoons sailing on the Havel. Now we're talking about how *useful* he is."

With a sudden heave, he got to his feet, splashing his wife a little. She stood up too and handed him the large towel from the rail.

"It's always so damn cold in this house," he said as he began drying himself, trying to get some circulation going.

"Willi..." she said, drawing the word out to its full length. "Tell me something."

He looked at her thoughtfully. He could almost predict what she was going to say.

"If Reinhard was your son," she asked him, "would you still want to crush him?"

"My son? How could he be my son? We're only seventeen years apart."

"You know what I mean."

"No, I don't know what you mean." He was becoming impatient and starting to flush. "The man's dangerous, can't you see that? How much more proof do you need? Do you know what they say about him over there at Prinz Albrecht Strasse? Do you?"

"No, what do they say?"

"They say the temperature of a room drops five degrees when he walks in."

She didn't reply.

"Now let me ask *you* a question," he went on. "Suppose he'd killed one of *us*. One of us here in this house."

"That's nonsense and you know it."

"Nonsense? Is it? Try telling Frau Utz that it's nonsense." He handed her back the towel and pulled on the blue bathrobe that had been hanging behind the door.

"How will you deal with it?" she said. "I mean officially."

He glanced at her. "Officially, I'm not required to do anything. It's up to Bendlerstrasse."

"Will you say anything?"

"I don't know." A pause. "I haven't decided."

"You think they'll be able to trace it back to him?"

"To Reinhard? Personally?" Again, the empty smile. "I doubt

they'll want to try something like that. Even they're not *that* stupid."

He opened the door and ambled along the hallway towards the large master bedroom. After unplugging the bath, she followed him, arriving just as he was combing his thin white hair in front of the dresser mirror.

"So if you don't do anything yourself," she said, continuing the conversation as if there'd been no interruption, "nothing will ever happen."

"That's right," he replied, "nothing will ever happen."

He threw off the bathrobe and began getting dressed. She'd already laid out the suit, shirt and tie she wanted him to wear. Since he didn't much care what he put on, he usually just went along with her suggestions.

"What time are they coming?" he asked her again. He'd finally become conscious of the guests who would soon be arriving: Reichsmarschall Hermann Göring and his buxom new wife, the former film actress, Emmy Sonnemann.

"Eight o'clock. I told you."

"I loathe those people," he said under his breath.

"So why did you invite them?"

"Because it was expected of me, that's why."

Gently she began helping him with his shirt buttons and then the cufflinks. "I've seen you like this before," she said matter-of-factly. "You get upset and somehow it always ends up with me taking the brunt."

She was about to fasten his tie too but he took it out of her hands and put it back on the rack. He didn't feel like wearing a tie tonight, no matter how grand the guests. But she immediately took it down again, placed it around his neck and threaded it neatly under his collar. This time he acquiesced. It was like a well-worn routine between them.

"I don't want to stay up too late," he said as her fingers knotted the silk with a practised ease. "Let's get rid of them early if we can."

3

It was on the same night that a cadre of SS officers was attending a private function in a very august setting.

Webelsberg Castle, near Paderborn in Westphalia, was named after a medieval tyrant called Webel von Buren who built it as a defensive fortress against incursion by the Asiatic Huns. It was an austere place, complete with several wings and a deep crypt. In Hollywood, it would have been considered a great set for a Douglas Fairbanks flick.

It had been bought for the SS by Heinrich Himmler not long after he inaugurated the service and came to be regarded by him as a kind of spiritual retreat. Despite his bland, colourless personality, he'd managed to develop some quirky ideas about German history. One of them was that the Teutonic knights under his twelfth century namesake, Heinrich I of Saxony, had lived a chivalrous, Camelot-like existence and, against all odds, had saved the Rhineland from the despicable Slavs. In his mind, the cult of the SS was a latter-day rebirth of this heroic medieval tradition and he saw Webelsberg as the perfect place for the myth to be resuscitated.

Ideally, Himmler would have liked the castle's echoing stone walls to be used only for solemn ritual, for cleansing meditation and for communion with ancestral spirits. But this evening, it was being used for none of those things. This evening, a five-piece band was playing and some forty members of the SS fencing club, together with their wives and girlfriends, were holding their annual awards ceremony. The only reason Himmler had approved such an activity was because he felt that the sport was honorable and vaguely in keeping with his general intentions for the place.

He himself was not present, however. He had no interest at all in physical activity and usually deferred such matters to his more dynamic subordinate, Gruppenführer Reinhard Heydrich, wunderkind of the SS and, prior to that, the naval protégé of Wilhelm Canaris. Only 34 years old, Heydrich had just recently been named to head up the RSHA, the newly formed Reich central security office, and it was he, not Himmler, who would be hosting tonight's gala.

Everyone was in full dress, the SS banners were elegantly draped and there was an air of restrained reverence for the occasion. The castle did that to people. Only later, after the wine had flowed a little, would the atmosphere become more convivial but, for the moment, they were content to dance, pausing only to have their champagne glasses refilled by a platoon of roving, white-jacketed waiters. They were all waiting for the guest of honour to arrive.

As the band finished up another medley, a pleasant-faced young man mounted the podium to make an impromptu announcement. His name was Walter Schellenberg and, despite his boyish charm, he was able to command a certain respect amongst the assembled elite thanks to a prominent dueling scar on his chin. To add even further to his reputation, the story emerged that one time during an inspection, the Führer himself asked about the scar. Keeping a straight face, Schellenberg replied that he cut himself shaving, a witticism that Hitler evidently found highly amusing.

Of such things were SS legends made.

Schellenberg held up his hands for silence. "Ladies and gentlemen," he said. "I'm happy to inform you that dinner won't be delayed for much longer. We've just received word that the Gruppenführer will arrive within the hour. When he does, I promise you I'll be the first to volunteer the fact that I'm starving."

There was some laughter and the music resumed. Schellenberg jumped neatly from the stage and, after a comment or two, managed to sidle his way out of the hall without being noticed. He was on his way to a pre-arranged rendezvous upstairs. But instead of taking the sweeping front staircase, he went the back way through the servants' corridors and bounded up the narrow stone steps two at a time as far as the second floor.

Quietly, he knocked on a stout wooden door. Then, without waiting for a response, he turned the iron handle and stepped inside. The room was broad and well appointed with an oak-beamed ceiling, heavy tapestries on the walls and a handsome canopy bed.

"You're late."

The voice came from the far side where a former nobleman's dressing room had been converted into a sumptuous, Roman-style bathroom.

Schellenberg turned to see Lina Heydrich, the Gruppenführer's wife, standing in the doorway. She was of average size with fine, sandy hair, a well-formed bone structure and alabaster skin. She was not especially pretty, at least not in any obvious way, but she could be sensual when she wanted to be and this evening, to his pleasant surprise, she was wearing a black leather SS coat, high boots and a standard issue cap with a shiny peak. In her hand was a glass of gin. But the coat had been deliberately left open and, she was wearing nothing at all.

"And good evening to you," he replied.

"How long do we have?" she demanded.

"Less than an hour."

She swept back the coat and put a hand provocatively on her bare hip. "Then you'd better move fast, don't you think?"

In response, he walked over to her but she stepped aside, directing him into the bathroom with a simple nod of her head. He knew what she wanted. He entered, closed the door behind him and immediately began to undress as deftly as his fingers would allow.

Lina Heydrich waited for him outside. She sat down on a chaise longue, crossed her legs and sipped her drink. This was the part she enjoyed the most, even more than the sex itself. Here, *she* was the one giving the orders and controlling the situation - not like at home where her husband was insisting more and more that their sessions together include his own penchant for sexual sadism.

Despite herself, she couldn't prevent her mind from going back to the last time it happened, their most recent wedding anniversary. After having dismissed the servants for the evening, he closed in on her right after dinner. First, he ripped open the expensive gown she'd bought for their special evening together, then dragged her by the arm out to the tiny gardening shed behind the house. There he tied her to a wooden beam with a length of sailing rope and then, from an old drawer, he took out a centuries-old cat o' nine tails which he informed her had once been used on a Portuguese slave ship. Ignoring her cries, he began to lash her, slowly and methodically, not satisfied until her white flesh was raw and beading with tiny droplets of blood. After that, he cut her loose, threw her down on a rough woolen blanket and raped her right there amongst the tools and the potted plants. When he finished, he just left her where she lay, weak and shaking, while he went out on the town.

For weeks afterward, she thought about filing for divorce. It wouldn't have been easy given her husband's status but her family, the von Ostens of Fehmarn, was not without influence and even an SS Gruppenführer was required to be circumspect about such matters. While the Third Reich had become a haven for every kind of depravity, it was well known amongst the Nazi establishment that the Führer preferred to maintain a puritan face for his regime, especially when it came to the sanctity of marriage. It was why his own mistress, Eva Braun, was never officially acknowledged and never once appeared with him in public.

In the end, however, Lina dismissed the idea of terminating her marriage because, for her, it simply wasn't a valid option. If she left her husband, that would defeat the whole purpose of their alliance, the grand vision to which they were both committed. In her own way, she was as ambitious as he was himself and she wasn't going to let some squalid sexual perversion, no matter how painful, get in the way of their future achievements. Much easier, in her view, to deal with the issues on a separate basis. If he wanted to play his nasty little games, no problem - as long as he did it with someone else, some poor slut from the Spittelmarkt who needed the money.

As for Lina Heydrich, she had her pride - and her way of maintaining it was to indulge in her own secretive adventures like this one here tonight, entertaining but essentially meaningless. This was her private means of revenge, a diversion that allowed her to reverse the roles, to *give* the orders instead of taking them. She knew that Walter Schellenberg would have to obey because he had no choice. If he didn't, his career would be finished and perhaps even his life. One word from her to her husband, just a mere hint that the Brigadeführer had been anything but perfectly correct towards her, and she knew the young officer would be lucky to escape a firing squad.

In front of her, the door opened and she brought her mind back to the reality of the moment. Schellenberg was now completely naked and she viewed him with a long, cool gaze that took in every centimetre: from the gleaming gray eyes to the broad smirk; from the almost hairless torso all the way down to the ripe and prominent erection.

"Already at attention," she said. "Good, very good. Now you may kneel."

He did as he was told, quietly and obediently. Then she put down her drink, stood up and slowly paced her way over. Taking her own good time, she slipped off her leather coat and moved even closer to him, her legs apart, still wearing her peaked cap and her high boots. Her light, bushy groin was tantalizingly close to his face but she knew he wouldn't dare begin until he received her command. This was the way it should be, she thought, and she reveled in the power, teasing him and tormenting him until she herself chose the moment. She could feel her entire body warming, as if preparing itself for his tongue, her nipples gently extending and her juices beginning to flow.

Then, when she was good and ready, she closed her eyes and whispered: "Now, Brigadeführer... you may do your duty."

* * *

Downstairs in the great hall, the band was playing a Strauss waltz in celebration of the "Anschluss," the annexation of Austria, when Walter Shellenberg and Lina Heydrich slipped back into the party. While he once again returned surreptitiously by the back stairs, she arrived a few minutes later from the front, greeting people openly as she made her way through. Her excuse for being away was that she'd had a bad headache and, in fact, many inquired how she was feeling now. "Much better, thank you," she replied to each in turn, an enigmatic smile on her lips.

It was not long before the music came to an abrupt halt and a round of applause broke out as a tall, lithe, but slightly broad-hipped man made his entrance. His blond hair was thin and brushed back, his icy blue eyes had a distant gaze and his long, Nordic face was expressionless. At a hidden signal from Schellenberg, the band struck up the Badenweiler march and the crowd gathered around to line the route to the podium.

Their Caesar had arrived.

Yet Reinhard Heydrich was no flamboyant imperialist. He was a thin-lipped Machiavellian and an accomplished achiever, in terms of both his physical prowess and his calculating, cutting intellect. He knew very well that the adulation he received was facile and self-serving but he also knew it was based on the most primitive fear and, as such, it was well suited to his purpose.

He strode confidently up the steps to the podium and took out a sheaf of notes. There were no friendly words of greeting, no apologies for being late. It was his personal style to launch straight into his prepared speech, his staccato voice attacking the audience with its delivery. Addressing the general theme of the evening, he touched on the necessity for personal fitness, recalled the grandeur of the Berlin Olympics two years previously, which he personally had helped to organize, and then spent a few minutes quoting the Führer about how the SS must train their minds to be agile, their hearts to be eager and their bodies to be hard as steel.

When he finished, there was another round of applause and it was the wily Schellenberg who was, as ever, the first in line to shake his hand. Only once the fuss of his arrival was over could Lina Heydrich lead her husband away into a quiet corner, protected from eavesdroppers by a heavy pillar. She demanded news. She hadn't seen him for over two weeks and she'd never dream of inquiring about his progress by telephone. She never knew which switchboards were monitored.

"So? How did it go?"

He understood exactly what she was talking about but, for a moment or two, he didn't answer. Instead he just gazed at her with those cold eyes. "Utz was the last," he said eventually, his voice almost inaudible.

She immediately picked up on the past tense and breathed a short, self-satisfied sigh. "When? How?"

"You didn't see it in the *Beobachter*?"

She shook her head.

In response, he reached into the top pocket of his tunic, took out a small newspaper clipping and began to read: "At 18:35 on Wednesday evening, an officer of the Kriegsmarine was murdered on Friedrichstrasse by three assailants reputed to be foreigners. All three made good their escape in a black Opel automobile. Police are keeping a close watch on the borders."

She listened quietly, then looked at him. "Do you think Willi knows who's responsible?"

Heydrich nodded as he put away the clipping. "Probably."

"What do you think he'll do?"

"Willi?" He smiled at the thought of his old friend and mentor. "I'll tell you what he'll do. He'll brood. Then he'll talk it over with Erika and then he'll brood some more. And by the time he's ready to do anything..." He left the sentence unfinished, its meaning already obvious.

"Do you still need the dossier? I mean, if they're all dead."

"Of course I need it."

"How will you get it?"

Heydrich just looked at her. "I'll get it," he replied calmly. It was all he needed to say. His will would become reality.

A waiter happened to pass within striking distance and Lina Heydrich reached out to steal two of the fine, fluted glasses from his tray. She handed one to her husband. For a few moments they just stood there, silently accepting their mutual dislike and wedded only to the vision of power to which their marriage was now completely dedicated.

"To the next Führer," she declared, raising the glass. Then she drained it. "And God help the Reich."

4

Reichsmarschall Hermann Göring was late for his dinner appointment but that was nothing unusual. Hitler called him a Renaissance man and Göring invariably did his best to live up to it.

When he finally arrived, his giant bulk was garnished in full regalia, his elaborate, self-designed uniform like something from a comic opera and his pompous chest full of ridiculous ribbons. He was a big man, big in every direction, and getting bigger with each passing year. His face had grown jowly and his frame had developed so many rolls of extra fat that even his tailor, perhaps the best in all Berlin, had begun to sigh in frustration. And standing proudly beside him, arm-in-arm, was his new wife, Emmy, the former film actress. Her mighty cleavage was swaddled in fur, she had a fortune in gold jangling on both wrists and wore a suffocating overdose of perfume.

It was all Wilhelm Canaris could do not to burst out laughing when he saw them. But he managed to contain himself and say politely: "I'm sorry. If I'd known it was full dress, I'd have done the same."

Göring chuckled amiably. "It's only because I just came from the Chancellery, otherwise I wouldn't have bothered."

It was a lie and Canaris knew it. Göring always dressed flamboyantly and he often liked to say he'd just come from the Chancellery. He liked to collect titles too. Hermann Göring was not only Marschall of the Luftwaffe, he was also Minister-President of Prussia, President of the Reichstag, Head of the Air Ministry, Commissar of the four-year plan, National Hunt Master and heaven-knows-what-else.

In fact, if ever a man had profited from the Nazi cause, it was him. In addition to all those government positions, Hermann Göring also had directorships in half a dozen major corporations who were more than gratified to have his name gracing their annual reports. Amongst them were the giant automobile manufacturers, Benz and BMW, who, aside from other considerations, were generous enough to supply him with complimentary personal transport. All in all, it was said that his income each year totaled a million Reichsmarks and, despite the preference in some quarters to regard him as nothing more than a buffoon, the truth was that Hermann Göring was nobody's fool and never had been. Beneath all the posturing, there was a layer of substance and that was the real reason the industrialists and the financiers sought him out, counting on him to be a savvy, moderating influence on the more extreme and dogmatic Hitler. In other words, Göring was a man with whom they could do business: hence his palace, Karinhalle, named after his first wife; hence his vast hunting estates; hence his requirement that everyone he dealt with, from corporate chairmen to his own ministry officials, had to remember his birthday each year with as large a gift as they could afford. Even Canaris felt obliged to render such tribute. Nobody forced him. It was all merely because Hermann Göring, in his own gross vanity, expected it.

By the time the valet had taken the guests' coats and the canine welcoming committee had been ushered back into the kitchen, the small group had already been standing in the hallway exchanging small talk for several minutes. At last, Göring slapped his host on the shoulder from his vastly superior height and said: "So Willi, are we going to die of thirst?"

Full of apologies, Canaris led them into the study where he himself had already taken his first drink a couple of hours previously. "What can I get you?"

"Oh, I don't know. Some of that fine smuggled scotch you keep tucked away, perhaps?"

"My God, I should be more careful," replied Canaris. "You're even better informed than I thought."

Göring laughed out loud and settled with his drink into one of the big armchairs, which he seemed to fill completely. The other three did likewise.

It was Emmy Göring, almost spilling out of her décolleté, who said: "A toast. Someone propose a toast."

Erika Canaris was endless in both her patience and her diplomatic polish. "Good idea," she said. "Hermann, your choice."

With some effort, the gargantuan figure sat forward in his chair. "Ah now, this is a serious matter," he said. "I'm from the school that considers toasting an art. All right, let's do this military style. We'll each make a suggestion, then we'll review the possibilities and select the most appropriate for the occasion. Agreed?"

They all agreed. He was in full flow.

"So," he continued. "I'll begin. I propose a toast to... Olga Techechowa!"

"Hermann!" said his wife in mock protest. The lady he mentioned happened to be another actress who'd enjoyed some success recently. Even though Emmy had chosen to give up her career to be the wife of one of the most important men in Germany, it didn't mean she was immune from jealousy when the mood took her.

Her husband, however, was well pleased with his taunt. "You don't like that? Fine, so you suggest one."

"Me, no, I couldn't."

"Absolutely, you must, I insist."

Emmy Göring looked embarrassed, then her attitude changed as she came up with a suggestion. She couldn't help giggling a little as she said it. "To the Führer!" she exclaimed. "Because he has such sexy eyes!"

"Emmy!" said Erika, reacting as if she were shocked. But that just made the other woman giggle some more. "All right," she said, "I've got one. I propose a toast to the British. May they run out of champagne so they can't launch any more ships."

Hermann Göring slapped his thigh. "Bravo! So, Willi, it's up to you. It'll have to be good if it's going to beat that."

Canaris tried to hide his sigh. He wasn't sure he could make it through an evening of this. "Give me a minute…" he said, trying to buy himself some time. Then he had an idea and said: "I propose a toast to… Blomberg's wife. I hope she was worth it."

There was silence for a moment then a great, rip-roaring guffaw from Göring. It was a good one, all right. Werner von Blomberg had, until recently, been Minister of War. However, the previous January he'd chosen to marry an attractive woman who was young enough to be his granddaughter. But very soon, mysterious rumours began circulating that she'd once been a prostitute. When Hitler saw photographs of her naked with another man, he called on Blomberg to resign in order, as he said, to preserve the honour of the Wehrmacht. Of course, the affair was a frame. Hitler wanted to create a new high command structure with himself as commander-in-chief but he knew he'd face opposition from both Blomberg and the generals. It was trouble he didn't need and so, instead of a confrontation, he simply had Reinhard Heydrich's SD create the photos and quietly pass them through to an SS stooge in the Kriminalpolizei called Nebe. This man duly presented them to his boss, von Helldorf, who sent them on to Göring's own Reichstag office and then to Hitler - who put on a good show of being outraged when he saw them. In the end, everyone gained except poor Blomberg whose career was finished. Heydrich got his kudos. Nebe and von Helldorf in the police department both received commendations. Göring received a promotion to Reichsmarschall. And Hitler was able to form his new OKW military command structure with himself positioned exactly as he required, at the very apex.

The toast that Canaris had proposed was therefore an outstanding success with Göring but the two women professed not to understand.

"Well," said Erika, "if you two boys are going to make private jokes, then we girls have no alternative but to go into the kitchen and make jokes of our own. What do you say, Emmy?"

It was a rhetorical question because she'd already stood up and had her hand outstretched. Emmy Göring glanced at her husband but his face was still full of mirth so she did as she was asked and the two women left the room deep in conversation about some new recipe for strudel that Erika had discovered. Her voice faded as she disappeared down the hallway with her guest waddling along beside her.

Hermann Göring stared after his wife's bulging buttocks for some time and then turned back to Canaris. "Great girls, eh?" he said. "We're very lucky men, you and me, Willi. Very lucky."

Canaris raised his glass in agreement and they drank like German men are supposed to once the women have left. Then as Canaris was busy organizing a refill, he said: "The other day you mentioned you wanted to talk about something... Something of concern to both of us." It was the prime reason he'd extended the invitation.

"Yes..." said Göring thoughtfully, but he clasped his fresh scotch and just stared at it.

A minute passed, then two, during which time Canaris sat down again and made himself comfortable. Then the dogs came padding in, having made their escape through the open kitchen door and he tickled them each around the ears.

"You think I've changed?" said Göring eventually.

For Canaris it was an awkward question. "In what way?"

"Oh, I don't know... People tell me I've changed but I don't think so. You know, despite all the trappings, I'm still basically the same simple soldier I always was."

Canaris didn't say anything. Some simple soldier, he thought. Through a masterful combination of opportunism, greed and sheer luck, the man had become richer than many small nations.

Meanwhile, Göring was going on: "And because of these humble beginnings, I find I may not have... Well, to be straight with you, Willi, I don't think I have the shrewdness of some of the more political in-fighters, you know what I mean?"

"Yes," said Canaris. "I know exactly what you mean."

"Yes, I'm sure you do, I'm sure you do. You've been a victim of it yourself. Men like you and me... we're sometimes too honest, too direct for our own good. We do our duty. We follow orders. We do what's right. But others..." He shrugged. It was a heaving, melodramatic gesture. "You see," he was saying, "the fact is that in this Reich of ours, power is what's important. It's all anyone seems to care about."

Canaris went on sipping his scotch and fussing with the dogs, waiting for his guest to come to the point. Outside it was already pitch black and, for the first time, he noticed a patch of moonlight through the thick clouds. Must be clearing, he thought casually.

Göring swirled the drink around in his glass and made a squeaking noise by circling his pudgy finger around the rim. "The fact is," he added, "that the practical application of power is through control of the security apparatus."

Canaris looked at him. He was starting to get a feel for the direction in which this little chat was heading. Göring had once had functional control of both the Gestapo and the Berlin SA, the brown-shirted stormtroopers, but that was back in the early days. By 1938, they'd both fallen under the auspices of the SS and, for Göring, it was obviously a touchy subject. He could have all the titles in the world but without the physical authority to back them up, they were for ceremonial purposes only - and that meant they were of no real consequence. Even his beloved Luftwaffe fell under the final authority of the OKW.

"You're still Minister-President of Prussia," said Canaris, doing his best to sound reassuring. "You've still got the state police."

"A bunch of village idiots in uniform. I can't do anything with that."

"And you've got the Forschungsamt. I'd give my right arm to have an organization like that."

"In name only, Willi, in name only."

The Forschumgsamt was a civilian agency of covert intelligence whose functions included wire-tapping, cryptology and the dissemination of information to the ministries. To all intents and purposes, it was run day-to-day by a capable, pragmatic man called Schapper.

"Anyway," the Reichsmarschall said, "you're avoiding the central issue. You and I both know that if real power lies in the control of security, then it lies in hands other than mine."

Canaris nodded sagely. It was a valid assessment and he was just about to reply when his valet, the venerable Otto, came to announce that dinner was about to be served and that the ladies would join them in the dining room.

The meal, consisting of onion soup, garnished roast lamb and a rich dessert of black cherry tort, turned out to be a major triumph. The conversation, however, was nothing more than pleasantries and platitudes, as it had been over drinks, and Canaris found his thoughts constantly drifting away, trying to understand what this evening was all about - and to anticipate what Göring really wanted to say. By the time the dishes had been cleared away, the decision had been taken for the women to take liqueur in the salon while the men went back to the study.

On their return, Otto arrived with a tray of coffee and a decanter of Louis XIII cognac and they settled into their comfortable chairs once again. Göring was effusive in his praise of the cuisine and continued until Otto was out of the room. "Now then," he breathed contentedly, an outsized snifter resting in the fleshy palm of his hand. "What were we talking about?"

"I believe," replied Canaris, "we were talking about security."

"Security, yes…" Göring nodded slowly. Then as if discovering a whole new train of thought, he said: "You know, I've always admired the way you handle Heydrich like that. Very clever, Willi, very clever."

Canaris nodded at the direction the conversation was taking and perhaps should have predicted it. He knew that Heydrich was the crux of the matter, for Göring as well as for himself. "Reinhard's just a convenient acquaintance," he said, making it sound as casual as he could. "There's nothing more to it than that."

Göring's expression showed that he understood but wasn't buying any of it. "You're too modest, Willi. You're not just his friend, you're his mentor."

"Mentor? I hardly think so."

"Don't give me that."

"It's an amusing thought, Hermann, to see me as Svengali and

Reinhard as my Trilby, but I'm afraid it's completely false. As I said, our connection is merely a convenience."

"All right, all right, have it your own way. But let's compromise by agreeing that it's a damn useful convenience."

"Fair enough, I'll grant you that. Sometimes it is."

"But it's not going to stay that way, I'm afraid."

Canaris looked over at his guest and wondered exactly what was going on in that enormous head. How much did he know? Or suspect? He decided the best thing to do would be to play it out, especially since his own brain was beginning to get a little fuzzy. The scotch, then the wine at dinner and now the cognac. He had to be careful what he said. He put the glass down next to him. "How do you mean?" he asked.

"How do I mean? I should have thought it was self-evident."

"Well, if it is, I'm afraid I must be uncommonly stupid."

Göring rubbed his eyes with his forefinger and thumb. "Look," he said, without even trying to feign his frustration. "What's the most important decision the Führer has to make over the next year or two?"

Canaris looked at him. "Whether Poland is worth invading?" he suggested.

"No, no. Far more important than that."

"Whether *Russia* is worth invading."

It was a droll reply but Göring missed it altogether. He was too involved with his own agenda.

"Willi, you're overlooking the obvious," he said. "The most important decision he has to make is who to name as his successor."

Canaris said nothing.

"Look," said Göring again. "You can't deny that all too often he wanders in and out of the crowds like a fool, correct?"

"Well, he certainly seems to leave himself open."

"Exactly. Now, imagine what would happen if some crackpot, some anarchist or Jew, were to get his hands on a pistol or a grenade."

"Assassination."

"That's right, and then chaos. Total, mass confusion. Everything would be thrown back ten, maybe fifteen years. I'm telling you Willi, there needs to be a plan in place. We need to know who becomes Führer after Hitler, it's as simple as that."

"What about Hess?"

"Hess…" repeated Göring dismissively. As far as he was concerned, Rudolph Hess was nothing more than a lightweight, one of Hitler's old pals who was kept around out of sheer sentimentality.

"So what are you saying?" asked Canaris.

"What am I saying? I'm saying that sooner or later, the Führer's going to have to nominate a real successor. And who do you think that's going to be?"

"You."

Göring smiled ruefully but didn't answer.

"You mean it won't be?"

"Not necessarily. As I said before, the real power lies in other hands."

"So who are we talking about? Himmler?"

In response, Göring just looked at him with an expression suggesting it wasn't the right answer at all.

Canaris paused to drink some of his coffee. It was almost cold but it was still the best antidote to the evening's indulgence of alcohol and he drank most of it in one gulp. So, he thought, the Reichsmarschall has seen the light. At last he's found the courage to talk about it out loud to a relative stranger, someone far removed from the inner coterie. Canaris decided that such courage was worthy of acknowledgement. "Reinhard," he said softly.

"Yes... your good friend Reinhard."

"But you can't just dismiss Himmler out of hand."

"No, but the Führer can. And maybe he will. He's perfectly capable. You said it yourself, Willi, when you made that toast. If he can do it to Blomberg, he can do it to anybody."

That was true enough, thought Canaris. In effect, the Führer had come to the realization that he could do just about anything he pleased, if not one way, then the other - as long as Reinhard

Heydrich was there to arrange it. "You think that's what the Führer wants? To get rid of Himmler?"

"Nobody knows that but the Führer himself. But one thing's for sure. When the Führer dies, and I mean *whenever* and *however*, there'll be a vacuum, am I right? Even if he goes peacefully in his sleep. A vacuum at the very heart of Germany. Now, put yourself in his position. Are you going to risk ruining everything you've worked for at such a time? Are you going to allow chaos? Or are you going to see to it that order is maintained?"

"And you think Reinhard's the one to do that?"

"Under those circumstances, who else would he choose? You know what the Führer calls him? 'The man with the iron heart.'"

"Yes, I know, but we're talking about Reinhard... He can't speak, he can't lead..."

"No, but he can keep control. He can prevent the whole thing from falling apart."

"There has to be more to it than that."

"There does? Why?"

It was a question Canaris couldn't answer and, almost for the first time, he was beginning to see the full scope of this. He'd been thinking long and hard about Reinhard's ambition and where it could lead but even he hadn't fully realized how easily all the pieces might fit into place.

"So what are you trying to say?" he asked.

"What I'm trying to say is that whatever hold you have over him now will vanish in the wind if that ever happens."

"Who said I have a hold over him?"

"Willi, please."

For a second or two, Canaris didn't respond. There was no further point continuing with the pretense. "I'm not sure where all this is taking us," he said.

Göring looked at him squarely. "Then let's spell it out, shall we?" He put his glass down on the low table in front him and leaned forward, causing the great rolls of fat under his chin to crease up. "Reinhard Heydrich as Führer will be a nightmare for all of us. You know it and I know it. There'll be no talk, no discussion, no way for intelligent men to agree or disagree. It'll just be orders, a pyramid of power with Heydrich at the top passing his commands down through the SS. And the rest of us? We'll be nowhere, Willi, nowhere at all. The moment we question anything, we'll be gone, marched off to the camps like so many Jews."

Canaris was about to reply but Göring interrupted him.

"No games, Willi. Forget the games. Time for a little honesty between old friends. Now look…" He took a breath. "I know you have something on him, you needn't bother denying it. Oh, don't worry, don't worry. I'm not going to ask you what it is."

"So what *are* you going to ask me?"

"I'm going to ask you to come to your senses. As I say, I don't know what you've got but listen to me, Willi, listen carefully. If you're ever going to use it, the time is now. Believe me, the time is right now because once he's named successor, he'll be untouchable."

Canaris gazed across at the man opposite him. He saw the predatory gleam in the eye, the flush on his face. He could almost feel the adrenaline coursing through those clogged veins, a return perhaps to the Göring of old, the celebrated air ace who won the coveted Blue Max as leader of the famous Richthoven squadron during the Great War. It was the one medal on the man's chest that actually meant something.

Without thinking, Canaris glanced at his watch. Nearly midnight already. "You may well be right," he answered as he placed his own glass down. There was nothing else to say and, as a way of ending the conversation, he climbed up stiffly out of the chair. Beside him, the dogs stretched themselves and he felt like doing the same thing. "Another cognac perhaps?" he asked politely, but he was very much hoping his guest would take the hint and decline.

* * *

It was late. The evening's guests had finally departed and Canaris found himself alone again in his study. Erika had already gone upstairs, exhausted by the stress of the evening and the endless tedium of keeping the vapid Emmy Göring company. Somewhere in the back of the house, Otto, Maria and the rest of the domestic staff were still active, still clearing up the remnants of dinner. But here it was peaceful. He petted the dogs and thought about pouring himself another drink but, in the end, decided against it. Instead, he walked over to the wall safe that hung behind the Vermeer print.

After dialing the combination, he pulled open the metal door and took out what appeared to be an ordinary-looking manila file, except for one thing. It was completely unmarked. There was no official stamp to say *"Geheim"* (secret), and no department code. It could have been anything, even something personal - a folder of travel receipts, for example, or love letters from an old flame – but it was nothing like that. Canaris took a breath. Then he opened it to reveal, on the inside front cover, a standard photo of his good friend and protégé, SS Gruppenführer Reinhard Heydrich.

For a long time, Canaris stared at the familiar image, looking intensely at the narrow face, at the thin blond hair, at those remorseless, piercing eyes. Even to the people who knew him, the man was chilling. Then slowly, page by page, he began to read again the detailed personal testimonies of all the innocent people who'd been killed, merely for what they knew about him - the real truth about the man with the iron heart.

It was the complete dossier on Reinhard Heydrich, the file Canaris had guarded so carefully all these years. But he had to ask himself, to what purpose? To keep in his safe? To preserve for his own amusement? Göring was right, thought Canaris. If he wasn't prepared to use it, then why did he need it? Why did he keep it? What was it all for? Another conundrum.

And that's when his thoughts were interrupted by the arrival of his valet. Hurriedly, he closed the file cover.

"Will there be anything else tonight, Herr Admiral?" said Otto. He too had been a navy man and liked to use the title as a mark of respect.

"No," replied Canaris, "thank you."

"Then if you don't mind…"

"No, not at all."

The old retainer gave a brief nod, turned and was gone.

Canaris looked at the dossier that was still in front of him but he didn't open it again. He just locked it back in the safe and then went wearily upstairs to the bedroom. By the time he climbed into bed, his wife had been asleep for nearly an hour.

As usual, his feet were freezing and, as usual, he woke her up. She turned to look at him. "So?" she said.

He swallowed his habitual sleeping draught, then leaned back, resting his head on a high pile of pillows. It felt good.

"Maybe I should just get it over and done with," he said softly.

"Reinhard?"

He gave a nod that she had to strain to make out in the darkness.

"Is that what Hermann wants you to do?"

"Yes, unfortunately."

"Does he know about the dossier?"

"He knows I've got something but he doesn't know what."

"You're sure?"

"Who can be sure of anything?"

"So what did you say?"

"I said I'll think about it."

"You're not serious?"

"So what should I have said? Yes or no?"

"And what *will* you do?"

"Like I said, I'll think about it." He closed his eyes before adding: "You know *why* Göring is panicking like this?"

"No, why?"

"Because he's afraid. He thinks the Führer might soon decide he doesn't need Himmler's services any more."

"What?"

"And if that happens, he thinks Reinhard will automatically become the Führer's heir-apparent."

"He said all that?"

"Yes."

"He's out of his mind."

"No, I don't think he is."

"You mean you agree with him?"

"I think I'm beginning to."

"The Führer would never do something like that."

"Wouldn't he?"

She turned over on her side. "I refuse to believe any of this," she said, her voice trying hard to sound skeptical. "Hermann Göring as Führer perhaps. That I can see. He's insufferable sometimes but he's a war hero. Or even Hess. Even *that* I could understand. But Reinhard? No, it's ludicrous. He has no popular appeal, none at all. People wouldn't accept it."

For a while, Canaris didn't say anything. He just looked at her, trying to make out her prone figure. He was recalling Göring's rationale, that the first ability Hitler would look for in any successor would be the power to maintain order, not so much amongst the people as amongst the ruling elite. Between the Wehrmacht, the SA, the Reichstag and the Chancellery, they'd tear themselves apart. Without a strong leader, they'd be like a pack of competing wolves, so why not give it all directly to the SS? Why not just hand it all on a plate to Reinhard Heydrich? People wouldn't accept it? People would have no choice in the matter. This was now a thousand year regime and people would have to take whatever was handed down.

"I don't think it's ludicrous at all," Canaris replied, but it was too late. His wife was already back asleep and all he could hear was her steady breathing.

5

The British Embassy in Berlin was located in a fine old building on Wilhelmstrasse, just a few steps from Ribbentrop's foreign ministry. As a free-lancer, this had become part of my regular beat but, not being worthy of any interviews with His Britannic Majesty's ambassador, I had to make do with lesser forms of life.

One of these was a cultural attaché called Nicholas Brent-Alderton, a stocky Englishman with a round face, red hair, and a lilting Somerset accent. He'd only been in Germany a couple of years - a relative newcomer, or "March Violet" as some of us called him.

This expression deserves an explanation. The Berlin dialect was full of caustic slang and insider jokes, so after Hitler came to power, a "March Violet" became the term given to the many thousands who became instant Nazis, all those people who thought it might be an opportune time to jump belatedly onto the bandwagon. However, by calling Brent-Alderton by the same name, we in the ex-pat colony were by no means implying that he was a sympathizer. It was just our way of saying that he wasn't one of us, a holdover from the previous era.

Anyway, on the afternoon of October 18th, this supposedly respectable member of the diplomatic profession was quietly swearing at me in the upstairs backroom he called his office.

"You're a bloody menace, Schaeffer," he was saying, "a pure, bloody menace. I go out of my way to cough up some good, useful stuff, Lord knows why, and you go blabbing about it all over town."

"I didn't blab about it. I exchanged it."

"Same bloody thing because it's out there now, isn't it? So

much for confidentiality. No wonder your own people want nothing to do with you."

"Really? Wherever did you get that idea?"

"Don't play the innocent with me. You're *persona non grata*, my lad, and well you know it." He always called me "lad" even though we were both about the same age. Something to do with his idea of status. He really could be a pretentious ass when he felt like it, which seemed to be most of the time.

"I'm still here," I replied, "and I'm not starving yet."

"No, but your time's running out, believe you me."

"You know what, Brent…"

"And that's another thing," he fumed. "My name is Brent-Alderton, got it? Some people call me 'mister' and a few call me 'sir' but nobody ever calls me Brent, understand? And if you ever do it again, I'll wipe your bloody nose on the pavement."

I suppose the grin on my face didn't do much to help my cause. Meanwhile I thought I detected the scuffle of tiny feet gathering to listen just beyond the door. "You're not doing a whole lot for your career," I replied. "Whatever must they think of you down in the typing pool?"

"Screw the typing pool."

"Is that an order?"

He smiled but it was his own brand of smile: frozen and completely fake. "Why don't you just do us both a favour and get out, all right? Go and get your bloody gossip somewhere else."

At that point, he picked up the phone to call embassy security, so I decided to follow Shakespeare's advice - something about discretion being the better part of valour. I got to my feet and a few rays of weak sunshine caught my face. "Look at the nice day we're missing," I said. "Children like us should be playing outside."

Stupid, I know, but I couldn't help myself and, as I emerged into the corridor, I could hear his voice calling after me.

"You're supposed to wait for bloody security."

I didn't respond and just kept walking. He was right about one thing, though. I never did follow the required protocol and that's exactly what landed me in trouble with what he called "my own people" - in other words, the official representatives of my native land, the great dominion of Canada.

Although I hadn't been home in many years, I was still a citizen and I was still expected to salute the flag and all it stood for. The only problem was that I'd committed one unforgivable sin. I'd been overheard talking somewhat negatively about our own Prime Minister, the honorable William Lyon Mackenzie King. Since he hailed from my own home town of Kitchener, Ontario, I felt I had the right to make a knowing comment or two but, unfortunately, it didn't work like that. The gentleman who overheard me just happened to be a close personal friend of the aforementioned Mr. Mackenzie King so, free speech be damned, I wound up on the embassy's black list. It's not that I had my passport revoked, or anything as drastic as that, but the word went out that I was to be given no professional assistance whatsoever - no information, no interviews, nothing. I also knew that if any misfortune were to occur to me in Germany, my Canadian countrymen wouldn't exactly fall over themselves rushing to my aid.

By the time I descended to the lobby, the guard on duty, Alfred, had been alerted and was waiting to show me the door. But that's when I saw her again. Katharina Vollbrecht. The woman from the Opera House. Tall and elegant with chestnut hair that flowed to the collar of her impeccable cashmere coat. I'd memorized her face, her name and even her background. I knew, for example, that her family was from the Schleswig-Holstein region of Prussia and that they'd made their fortune breeding horses for the Kaiser's army. I'd taken the trouble to find out as much as I could in the hope that some day, somehow, I'd manage to meet her again. And suddenly, remarkably, here she was! But she wasn't alone. She was standing with the ambassador himself, Sir Neville Henderson, chatting and laughing as if they were old friends. I decided to delay my exit.

Since Alfred didn't want to cause an ugly scene any more than I did, he allowed me to linger in the lobby a minute or two until they left the building. I was desperately hoping that Sir Neville would be whisked away in his liveried Rolls and that he wouldn't feel obliged to give her a lift - then, believe it or not, it actually happened. The scenario actually played itself out right in front of me like a dream coming to life. Henderson must have been desperately late for something or other because once he was on board, the limousine just drove off through the gates, leaving her there alone on the embassy steps. My chance had arrived. I could feel fate giving me a shove.

I stepped out through the high doors and that's when she turned to see me, her eyes registering some kind of vague recollection.

"La Traviata," I said, reminding her. "At the Kroll. Second intermission. I was the fool with the gin and tonic." I'd accidentally spilled it all over her evening gown and then used that as an excuse to introduce myself.

"Yes…" she replied, "I remember now." Her voice was educated and refined, pure Prussian landowner, and although her recognition was friendly enough, she managed to maintain a certain distance, a discreet reserve that suggested she wouldn't pass the time of day with just anyone. "I'm sorry, Herr…?"

"Schaeffer," I replied with as much confidence as I could. "And you're Fräulein Vollbrecht. A pleasure to meet you again." We shook hands.

"How are you?" she asked me.

"Fine, thank you. And you?"

"Yes, thank you. I'm fine too."

So far, a less than sparkling conversation. But the breeze was flicking the tips of her hair and wafting her subtle fragrance in my direction. I recognized it as the same intoxicating Chanel she'd worn last time. I made up my mind. Caution be damned. If I didn't take the chance, I knew I'd regret it, so I launched headlong into my story.

"As a matter of fact," I said, "it's fortunate us meeting like this, here at the British Embassy. I'm currently writing an article on Anglo-German relationships and I was wondering if you'd honour me with an interview. It wouldn't take up much of your time."

"You're a journalist?"

"Yes, didn't I mention that?" I searched my wallet for a business card but couldn't seem to find one at that moment. She didn't seem to mind.

"And your subject is Anglo-German relationships?"

"That's right."

"I see." She looked directly at me. "Does that mean professional or personal relationships?"

I'm not sure if my momentary lapse was evident. I could have sworn she was toying with me. "It depends," I replied, attempting to recover. "The concept is to see how deep the ties really are between the continent's two great powers."

"Really? Well, I'm not sure the French would agree with you on that."

"You're right," I told her, offering what I hoped was a modest shrug. "But I don't sell my articles in France."

"So where *do* you sell them?"

"Oh... England, America, Australia. Sometimes India or Singapore. Depends on the topic."

"And how about Canada? Isn't that where you're from?"

I was surprised she could tell. Back in Ontario, my ancestors were immigrant farmers from Saxony, at least on my father's side, so I learned German from an early age. Besides, I'd been in Berlin so long that I'd picked up the accent. Few people could ever guess my origins.

"I'm interested in visiting Canada," she was saying. "Do you happen to know the foreign minister, Herr von Ribbentrop?"

"No... No, I'm afraid I don't. Not personally."

"He was telling me about Canada, how it's so beautiful. He traveled there a great deal when he was a wine merchant, did you know that?"

"Yes, as a matter of fact I did." I'd written it up in a background piece when he was first appointed to the ministry.

"Excellent," she said. "Then we have a place to start. Perhaps you could tell me more about Canada and in return I could tell you about Anglo-German... what was the word you used?"

"Relationships."

"Relationships, yes." She gave me a gentle half-smile, as if to tell me that she really was making fun. Then she floored me by saying: "You know, if you'd wanted to invite me to dinner, all you had to do was ask."

I just looked at her and laughed. "How about Horcher's?" I said.

"Fine, but I'm afraid my schedule is a little busy this week." She opened her purse and took out a small leather diary. "May I suggest a week Saturday?"

"If I can get a table, certainly."

"Talk to Fritz and use my name. Is nine too late?"

"Nine is perfect."

She nodded briefly, put her diary back and closed her purse. "I look forward to it."

Then she simply walked off towards the busy Wilhelmstrasse, leaving me stunned at this unexpected success and a little overwhelmed by my own audacity.

6

For many people, I suppose the phrase "secret intelligence" conjours up images of furtive intrigue - invisible inks, suitcase radios, hidden codes - a whole shady subculture unto itself. Except that, for the most part, the life of a pre-war operative was technical publications and shipping timetables. Hardly the stuff to make anyone's pulse quicken. And in the case of the Abwehr, the joint military intelligence organization led by Admiral Wilhelm Canaris, it was exactly that kind of mundane information gathering that represented ninety-nine percent of their day-to-day effort.

It was a strange, offbeat kind of operation, just like the man who ran it. In fact, anyone looking back today can't help but get the feeling that it was all incredibly amateurish. Basically they were over-extended and under-funded, and whether they actually accomplished anything of any real significance, either before or during the war, is very much open to debate.

Their offices were situated on a tree-lined street called Tirpitzufer on the north bank of the Landwehrkanal, just west of Potsdamer Strasse. From outside, the graystone buildings looked just like any other row houses, very ordinary and very respectable. The interior, however, was a maze of interlocking rooms that connected all the structures, an intricate warren of narrow staircases and angled passageways with offices that had been converted out of old dining rooms, leaky bedrooms and drafty sculleries. Some of the corridors led all the way through the back to connect with the OKW military headquarters building on Bendlerstrasse but Canaris discouraged their use. He wasn't keen on too much familiarity with the senior command, an attitude of mistrust which stemmed from their past antagonism towards him.

Within the walls, however, activity was incessant. Telephones rang, typewriters clattered and mimeograph machines churned out endless reports. And in the basement, teleprinters with their bulky lengths of pneumatic tubing were forever sending out obscure coded messages to distant parts of the globe.

To help him cope with it all, Canaris had recruited a subordinate by the name of Hans Pieckenbrock, an army colonel from an old military family in Essen. He was an urbane, well-educated man, a little younger than Canaris, and between them, they'd tried to make sense of their burgeoning administrative duties. By the fall of 1938, they were in the throws of reorganizing the entire structure into three basic branches: espionage, sabotage and counter-intelligence. Pieckenbrock himself was in charge of the espionage section and they'd set up an entire network of field posts all over the continent to try to match the increasingly complex political situation.

The real question was whether any of it really mattered. Did anybody use the information they gathered so carefully? Did anybody even listen to what they had to say? These were the perennial questions Canaris asked himself, an ongoing existential crisis that he just couldn't seem to resolve.

In normal periods, it was Canaris' style to just drift in and out of the office as he pleased and hardly anyone, including his two hardworking secretaries, ever knew whether he was just coming in or just going out. But the second half of October was no normal period and, during that time, he was constantly in his office with his door firmly closed in order to prepare his detailed budgets for the following year. Without budgets he had no operation and without an operation, he didn't have much of a career left.

Nevertheless, budgeting was a job he despised and he welcomed any respite. It came just before midday on Wednesday the 19th when he heard the tap on the door. It opened slowly and he saw Pickenbrock's head peer around.

"Morning, excellency." He'd taken to calling Canaris "excellency" after the fashion of senior officers under the Kaiser. It was an affectation, nothing more. "Thought I'd look in to try to relieve you of your misery for a while."

Canaris sat back from his crowded desk with a sigh. There were dozens of folders scattered around, with an ancient adding machine in the centre that he used to spew out calculations in any number of currencies. The exchange rates, in particular, drove him to distraction.

"I was thinking about lunch," said Pieckenbrock. "Interested?"

"Lunch?"

"The meal you eat between breakfast and dinner. How about it?"

Canaris rubbed his hand over his face. He could still see numbers dancing before his eyes. "Might as well," he said. "Any particular reason?"

"Well, we could dine lavishly just for the hell of it... but I was really thinking we could maybe order something from the kitchen and discuss the Malta analysis."

"Yes, Malta, right..." said Canaris wearily. It was a topic they'd been putting off for weeks. He glanced at his watch, then at the depressing piles of paper in front of him. "All right, give me an hour to finish this and I'm with you."

The door closed and Canaris tried to return to his worksheets. But his concentration had been disturbed so, instead of diving back into it, he got up, opened the door to his small balcony and stepped outside. With his dislike of the cold, it was an unusual thing for him to do at this time of the year but he felt he needed to breathe. And to think. The situation with Reinhard was beginning to get to him; not just the death of Johannes Utz but also the warning from Hermann Göring. It wasn't just personal any more, it had become highly political and that was adding enormously to the pressure.

Farther along the street, a small horse-drawn wagon had spilled its load and there were breadrolls cascading all over the pavement. One or two had even fallen into the canal. Not surprisingly, an entire flock of greedy gulls had descended and the driver of the wagon wasn't sure whether to wave his arms in the air to scare them away or to bend down and pick up the food. Canaris might have found it comical if he hadn't been so distracted.

The sight of the birds reminded him of the early days in Kiel when he used to take the dogs out along the fishing wharves. Not the current dogs, of course: his previous pair, a couple of small, wire-haired terriers that liked to run and play. He was just a Lieutenant Commander back then and Reinhard Heydrich was merely a cadet - but even then, the youngster had shown potential way beyond his years. He was intelligent and capable, and it wasn't long before they'd developed a very real friendship despite the difference in their ranks.

Their conversations seemed to last for hours, the topics ranging from naval affairs to sports to politics. Especially politics. As early as 1925, Reinhard had taken a keen interest in a little known rabble-rouser down in Munich called Adolf Hitler, who'd just been released from Landsberg prison where he'd written his personal manifesto, *Mein Kampf* (My Struggle). On his emergence, Hitler found that his writings, as well as the passionate speeches he made at the show-trial, had earned him the undisputed leadership of his party, the National Socialist Democratic People's Party - or "Nazi" for short. Their slogan was "Deutschland Erwache" (Germany Awakes), and to the young Heydrich, their ideas represented a new optimism that hadn't been felt since before the Great War. The conflict itself was bad enough, losing an entire generation of young men in the muddy trenches, but then, after the armistice, there'd been hyper-inflation, mass unemployment, violence in the streets and a series of governments that just couldn't cope.

Hitler found a ready audience for his message but he couldn't convince everybody - especially not the conservative military establishment to which Canaris and Heydrich belonged, who regarded Hitler with disdain. They called him the "Bohemian corporal" and to them he was just an upstart who should be kept in his place. That didn't dampen Heydrich's enthusiasm, however. It only served to encourage it. As he rose rapidly through the ranks, he became ever more arrogant and impetuous, to the extent that he began to attract a certain amount of critical attention. At one stage, after expounding his opinions in the officers' mess, he refused point blank to curtail his remarks and a hearing was called for insubordination.

Canaris could still recall the proceedings vividly. Heydrich had been so confrontational, so downright arrogant, that the tribunal deliberately trumped up extra charges just to threaten him. Still, he refused to show them the respect they felt they deserved, so they went ahead and dismissed him from the navy. Canaris could still remember the look of sheer incredulity on the young man's face when they brought down their verdict.

That's when Canaris stepped in with his own proposal. One evening, over dinner with their wives, he quietly suggested that Reinhard should accept the dismissal in good grace and consider joining the SS. He'd heard that Himmler was looking for someone to head up the newly formed security division and he thought that Heydrich, with his training, his bearing and his impeccable Nordic features, might be well suited to the position.

After some discussion, Canaris made the recommendation to Himmler through a personal channel and Heydrich was finally awarded the position at Party headquarters in Munich. In one stroke, Canaris had managed to maneuver a friendly contact into the very heart of the expanding Nazi organization. At the time, he congratulated himself but he had no idea what he'd just created.

Down in the street, the wagon driver had gathered up his fallen loaves as best he could and was back on his route, his blinkered horse clip-clopping into the distance. Canaris went inside and closed the door. He was chilled but at least his head was now clear and he sat down amongst the organized chaos of his office to consider his options. On the wall opposite was a series of framed photographs of himself at various stages of his career. As a youngster in Dortmund with his very first dog, a schnauzer. On board the training ship "Braunschweig" in the Baltics. At the Nürburgring racetrack, shaking hands with Dr. Porsche. At the Roman Coliseum with Count Spreti. Also one taken here in Berlin with Erika, the two of them looking relaxed and happy as they strolled along the Ku'Damm. Finally his eyes came to rest on a shot of him with Reinhard on the deck of the sailboat they rented two summers ago.

They were standing together, smiling for the camera, their arms wrapped around each other's shoulders, the best of pals.

Of course, the real problem was that despite everything that had happened since then, Canaris still had a soft spot for the man. He couldn't help it. There was a genuine bond between them and, despite his own better judgment, he was still inclined to give his friend the benefit of the doubt.

It was close to one o'clock when Pieckenbrock reappeared with a large tray of sandwiches and a pot of coffee. "Lunch is served, excellency."

Canaris watched him setting it out. Ideally he needed to think about the problem some more, to confront his own feelings towards Reinhard, to allow time for a solution to percolate through. It always did in the end. Unfortunately, Canaris didn't have that time because, even as he was sitting there, events were beginning to crowd in on him.

* * *

The catalyst occurred not at the Abwehr but at the Canaris family home in Zehlendorf.

It took place at about two in the afternoon when Otto Drexl, his longtime valet, heard a tapping noise coming from the French windows. Beyond the terrace was the extensive lawn and, beyond that, the copse of apple trees. The crop hadn't been good that year.

Drexl knew exactly who it was and leaned against the salon door to close his eyes for a moment, a vain attempt to try to shut it out. The SS had arrived as arranged and he was about to commit the worst crime of his life. The tapping sound came again, more insistent. Drexl was alone in the house, as he'd arranged. The rest of the staff, both permanent and temporary, had been given the day off.

For a brief minute he thought about his son, the communist, collecting clandestine funds for the International Brigade which was still fighting its losing battle against Franco's fascists in Spain.

Since Nazi Germany had sent help to Franco with the infamous Kondor Legion, such behaviour was considered traitorous and Drexl couldn't help recalling what the SS said they'd do to his son should his own help not be forthcoming. And the threat was not only to his son. It was to the entire family - uncles, aunts, cousins, everyone. Once a subversive was discovered, they told him, everybody around him became suspect. For the sake of state security, they'd all have to be questioned, incarcerated and perhaps even executed.

Once again, Drexl closed his eyes and took a breath. Then he walked slowly into the conservatory and opened the glass-paneled doors. The young SS officer was wearing an impatient frown at having been kept waiting but the pleasant features and boyish dimples belonged unmistakably to Brigadeführer Walter Schellenberg.

"About time," said Schellenberg abruptly.

Drexl looked at him with a combination of disgust and despair. But all he said was: "This way." Then he led the intruder across the central hallway to the study. "Behind the picture," he said in a tired voice.

"Combination..." said Schellenberg holding out a gloved hand. "Come on, come on."

Drexl reached into his top pocket and pulled out a slip of paper. The safe was an old installation and, even though his mind wasn't exactly nimble any more, his employer had opened it enough times in his presence for him to have memorized the sequence.

Schellenberg snatched the paper and the aging valet sat down heavily in one of the armchairs, a gesture of resignation.

* * *

Otto Drexl was still sitting in the same armchair when Maria, the household's Italian cook, finally returned from her day off. His eyes were open but he was just staring straight ahead and there was a large, dark stain on the front of his shirt. She put her hand to her mouth but she could hardly muffle the involuntary scream.

The bullet had pierced his chest from an elevated angle at very short range, traveling through his body and right through the upholstery to become embedded at the base of the back wall. Once Canaris had prized it out with a pair of household pliers, it confirmed what he'd already suspected. It was of standard SS sidearm calibre.

Like Maria before her, Erika Canaris was in a state of total shock when she got back and had to be helped up to the bedroom. Otto had been with them fourteen years.

Canaris went through all the motions of calling the police and suffering the indignity of having a dozen men tramping around his home for more than three hours. They asked questions, they analyzed angles, they measured the dirty footprints on the living room carpet but, of course, they could draw few conclusions. Rest assured though, they told him, they would be proceeding with all due haste to solve this vicious crime and bring those responsible to justice.

"Yes, thank you," said Canaris as he finally ushered them out the door. "I'm sure you'll do all you can." Then he went back into the study and poured himself a large scotch. The body had been removed but the blood-stained mess was still there and he knew he'd have to call in a specialized firm to steam-clean it all away, otherwise Erika would never set foot in here again. But even if they made it like new, there'd still be the memory of what happened. A murder right here in his own study, his sanctuary. They couldn't eradicate that so easily.

Whoever it was had taken everything in the safe. Some money, about a thousand marks. A great many private papers, although most were replaceable - passports, birth and marriage certificates, wills, share deeds, that kind of thing. And they'd taken some jewelry too that was of sentimental value to his wife.

But none of that meant very much to Canaris. He knew perfectly well that the robbery was just a cover. What they'd really come after was the dossier - except it hadn't been there. It was still locked away in his official department satchel. The day before, he'd removed the file from the safe so he could take it to the office and personally mimeograph the contents. But it wasn't a complete coincidence. After the death of Johannes Utz and the warning by Hermann Göring, he'd thought it would be a wise precaution and, obviously, he'd been right. Whether by luck or by judgment, the fact was that he still had the damn thing in his possession - the complete dossier on Reinhard Heydrich, witness testimony and all. The only question in his mind was what he should do with it.

He swallowed back the scotch and poured himself another. The more he thought about the whole affair, the more incensed he became. His home had been invaded and his valet was dead. This was exactly what he told Erika might happen. His close friend and protégé had finally betrayed his trust.

He recalled how he'd boasted to Erika that he could crush Reinhard in an hour but that just didn't seem to hold up any more. If he committed himself to a full and open revelation of the dossier's contents, he knew with certainty he'd be signing his own death warrant and probably that of Erika too. He was afraid of that. In fact, if he was being brutally honest with himself, he was now afraid of Reinhard. If the man was willing to arrange the murder of Otto right here in Canaris' own study, how far would he be willing to go?

Canaris took a deep breath to steady himself. He knew he couldn't just succumb to the fear. He wasn't built like that. In his younger days, he'd hiked half way across South America to escape his fate. Surely, he thought to himself, he could overcome this current situation. There had to be a way. And if he couldn't expose Reinhard directly, then the trick would be to find a less obvious solution.

* * *

The following morning found Wilhelm Canaris acting strangely normal, the way a man does once events have forced him into a definitive course of action. It had taken a long evening of worry but he'd finally made up his mind. Then one telephone call to a very private number and it was arranged.

His driver, Franz Meichner, arrived for him just before dawn and they found their way through the suburbs of southeastern Berlin until they were close to the Wannsee, its surface just about visible through the trees. There'd been a mix of rain and sleet overnight in the city but out here there was already a thin covering of wet snow, an early harbinger of the winter to come.

The car slowed to a crawl and turned left onto an unpaved road. On one side was the forest, many of its branches already bare. On the other was a broad fenced pasture that contained a pair of horses, old and thick-limbed after a decade of hauling coal wagons around the streets of Spandau. They stood there unmoving, like gray statues, totally undisturbed by the car's presence.

A kilometre along the open track, they finally arrived at the prescribed coordinates. This was not the section of the lake near Schwanenwerder where Canaris and Heydrich had sailed together in years past; this was the narrow part where a tiny spit of land juts out towards Pfaueninsel. Once they were close enough to the promontory, Meichner brought the big car to a halt. There was nobody around and he left the engine running so they could keep the heater on while they waited.

Canaris looked at his watch. "What time do you have, Franz?"

"I have seven twenty-six, sir."

"Really? I have seven twenty-three. Who's wrong?"

"With respect, I believe you are, sir."

A short grunt was the only response and they sank into silence as the minutes passed. Outside, the mist was beginning to lift but very slowly and its teasing revelations only seemed to aggravate the sense of claustrophobia.

Eventually, the car they were expecting appeared through the haze, its headlights trying to cut through the heavy air. It was a Mercedes, the same model, but newer and more pristine. Obviously, someone with a much larger departmental budget. After it had rolled to a stop, the driver jumped out smartly to open the rear door and the occupant stepped out into the snow. Canaris did the same thing and found himself face-to-face with the man he'd come to meet, Heinrich Himmler, Reichsführer of the SS and the man to whom Reinhard Heydrich officially reported.

Despite the high rank and fine uniform, Himmler always seemed to look like an ordinary government clerk. He just had that way about him. Although he was of medium height - several centimetres taller than Canaris - he projected a far more modest demeanor with his soft, bland face, his wire-rimmed glasses and that infuriatingly permanent half-smile. Did he really appreciate the idiocy of the world around him or was it just a mark of his own insecurities? Canaris was inclined to think the latter.

"Good morning, Admiral," said Himmler in his usual restrained voice. He stamped his feet slightly in the cold.

"Good morning, Reichsführer," replied Canaris. "Pleasant weather."

Himmler was gracious enough to acknowledge the humour and they shook hands. "Should we walk a little?" he asked.

Canaris would have much preferred to sit in the warmth of one of the cars but, since he was the one who'd called this urgent meeting out here in the middle of nowhere, he felt it his duty to oblige. He therefore took his leather satchel from the back seat and fell into a slow, rhythmic step alongside the Reichsführer. Underfoot, the ground was soft and the mud welled up through the light snow cover, staining the virgin white. Out on the frigid lake, a motorboat was puttering its slow way along the shore line, its sound carrying far in the early stillness. It seemed like even the birds weren't awake yet.

"Thank you for coming," said Canaris.

"I must say your call sounded intriguing. A matter of some importance, I presume."

"Of course, otherwise I'd never have disturbed you. It's also, shall we say, a little delicate."

"Then we must take great care to be discrete."

"As you say."

"And the topic?"

"Yes, the topic..." Canaris was hesitant, then seemed to come to a decision within himself. "Well, to be straightforward, the topic is our mutual friend, Reinhard Heydrich."

Himmler allowed his eyebrows to raise precisely one millimetre. "Yes, the Gruppenführer. I suspected as much."

"You'll no doubt remember our first conversation about him. When was it, seven years ago?"

"May 1931, to be exact. You were most effusive in your recommendation as I recall. Quite convincing, I might add."

"And I think, at this stage, I can safely say I was proven correct in my assessment."

"I would certainly agree. But forgive me, Admiral... Did you call me out here for a personnel review?"

"No... no, not exactly. It's just that there's something else I feel you should know."

"Something else? You mean about the Gruppenführer?"

"Yes."

"I see," he replied. "And may I ask why you've decided to tell me this now, today? Why not tomorrow, for example? Why not yesterday? Why not seven years ago?"

Canaris gave him an empty smile. "Things change," he said simply.

Himmler considered this for a moment. His nose and cheeks had already taken on a reddish hue from the cold. He gave a single nod as if the answer was acceptable. "I understand," he said. "Things do indeed change. So what else is it that I need to know?"

Canaris unilaterally stopped walking, unfastened the satchel he was carrying and removed a sealed envelope. It contained the dossier he'd been saving all those years. "Perhaps you should take a look at this," he said, handing it over.

7

I never found out what kind of leverage Reinhard Heydrich used on Canaris' aging driver, Franz Meichner. In the world of the SS, suspicion was a cheap commodity and guilt was easily manufactured. The clandestine files, which contained vast quantities of information - and disinformation - about millions of ordinary people, had been transferred along with the entire SD division to Heydrich's RSHA and were now housed at SS headquarters on Prinz Albrecht Strasse.

And it was here that Meichner was brought on the night of October 20th.

He was escorted into a large office on the top floor by Heydrich's adjutant, Oberführer Karlheinz Oehring, and told to sit down on a hard-backed chair. The only light in the room came from a desk lamp. Oehring then pulled back the old man's arms and handcuffed his wrists tightly so that the rough-hewn chair bit into his back. There was no word of explanation for this treatment and Meichner didn't ask for any. The general standard of SS hospitality was well known.

Oehring then left, leaving Meichner sitting in front of a large oak desk. Behind it, nestled in the shadows, was Heydrich himself, still writing out lengthy notes in that spidery scrawl of his. It was only after several minutes that he spoke.

"Tell me again what happened," he said as he continued to write. The tone was very efficient, very matter-of-fact.

Meichner was over sixty, a veteran who'd seen his share of action but, still, he could not hide his anxiety. He'd already given an account as best he could so he was wondering if he'd made some mistake the first time. He told himself he should try to be more careful.

"Well…" he began, his voice breaking slightly, "like I said, I drove the Admiral out to the Wannsee…"

"What time was that?"

"We arrived just before seven-thirty in the morning. The Admiral and I checked our watches."

"I see. Go on."

"Well, a few minutes later, another car arrived."

"What kind of car?"

"Grosser Mercedes, black, seven litres… 1937 model." Meichner knew all about cars. He took professional pride in his work as a driver.

"And who was inside?"

"Just Herr Himmler and his driver."

"How did you know it was Herr Himmler?"

"I saw him when he got out."

"You knew him by sight?"

"Yes."

"How?"

"I'm sorry?"

"How did you know him? Had you seen him before?"

"Well, no, not personally…"

"So how did you know it was him?"

"I don't know, I just did. I mean I knew his face… I've seen it in the papers. I like to keep up with the news. As a matter of fact, I was telling the Admiral…"

"All right, continue."

Meichner was trying very hard not to get flustered. The pain between his shoulder blades didn't help. "Well, the two of them began talking. I remember they shook hands… then they walked off and…"

"What were they talking about?"

"Not much. The weather, I think. That's why they walked off. They didn't want us to hear their conversation."

"Who is *us*?"

"Me and the other driver."

"Why did they walk off?"

"Like I said…"

"They could have just remained in one of the cars and sent you two to the other."

"I suppose they could… but they didn't."

"When they walked off, were they carrying anything?"

"The Admiral took his briefcase… well, not so much a brief-case, it was smaller with buckles…"

"A satchel."

"Yes, a satchel. He often carried it."

"Did it have a lock?"

"Yes, he always kept it locked."

"And the Reichsführer? What was he carrying?"

"Nothing. He was carrying nothing."

"And his hands. How did he hold them?"

"I don't understand."

"How did he hold his hands as he walked?"

"Behind his back."

"All right. What happened next?"

"Well, not much. Like I said, they walked off. I could hardly see them. It was misty…"

"Were you inside or outside the car?"

"I got back in."

"Why?"

"I'm sorry?"

"My question is clear. Why did you get back in?"

"Well, I don't know. It was cold… and damp…"

"Are you sick?"

"No, nothing of importance. For a man my age…"

"So why did you get back in the car? You just said it was misty. It didn't occur to you that you'd be able to see more if you stayed outside?"

"No… I mean… I didn't think…"

Heydrich looked up at him for the first time, the pen still in his hand. "You didn't think?" It was a direct accusation.

"I'm sorry, Gruppenführer."

Heydrich screwed the top back on his fountain pen, put it down on his papers, then sat back with his fingers pressed together. The classic inquisitor.

"What happened next?"

Heydrich's face had retreated once again into the shadows and Meichner found this even more distracting. His body felt clammy and sweat was beginning to trickle down his temples. He just wanted to go home to his wife, to be out of there. He hated the SS, hated the way they treated him, hated what he was being pressured to do.

"Herr Meichner," said Heydrich, a slight edge now to his voice. "I asked you what happened next?"

Meichner gave himself a mental shake. He had to stay alert. "Well... after a few minutes, I think I saw the Admiral open his briefcase and give something to Herr Himmler."

"You saw or you *think* you saw?"

"No, I saw it."

"Even though it was misty."

"Yes... The Admiral stopped to unfasten his briefcase..."

"His satchel."

"Yes, his satchel. Then he took something out."

"And what was that?"

"A file of some sort."

"A file. You're sure?"

"Yes."

"Did you get out to check?"

"Well, no..."

"Why not?"

"Well, because..."

"Was your window open or closed?"

"Well..."

"Open or closed?"

"Closed. It was closed."

"So you couldn't hear anything?"

"No, but..."

"But what?"

"But..." Meichner felt himself breathing quickly and tried to steady himself. It was difficult. "Even if it had been open..." he said, "they were too far away. I wouldn't have heard anything."

"How do you know?"

"Well, I..."

Heydrich just looked at him. "Meichner, you're incompetent." He made it sound like a statement of fact. "What did the file look like?"

"Look like?"

"Yes, look like. Colour, size..."

"It was beige, like a beige folder, you know, ordinary."

"What's ordinary?"

Meichner just shook his head. He didn't understand. He was doing his best but he just didn't know what the man expected of him.

"What's ordinary?" said Heydrich again, still in the same tone. "What's an ordinary file? When did you ever see Abwehr files before?"

"The Admiral..."

"The Admiral shows you his files?"

"No, of course not."

"So?"

"I mean, he has them... he reads them... in the car while we're driving. I see him in the mirror sometimes. He reads files while we're driving."

"How thick was this one? How many pages?"

"I couldn't really see..."

"Two millimetres? Four? Six? Eight?"

"I'd say maybe four."

"Maybe?"

"No, four. It looked like it was about four."

"So he took out the file. Then what?"

"He gave it to Herr Himmler."

"He gave it to him."

"Yes."

"Meichner, I want you to be sure about this. The Admiral gave the file to the Reichsführer."

"Yes."

"You saw this clearly."

"Yes."

"Even from a distance. Even though it was misty and you were inside the car with the window closed."

"Yes."

"And then what happened?"

"Then they walked and talked some more."

"How long?"

"I think about fifteen minutes."

"A long time to be outside in that weather."

"The Admiral was cold when he came back. He asked me to turn up the heat."

"Did you get out?"

"Get out?"

"When he came back to the car. Did you get out to greet him? To open the door for him?"

"Well, yes, of course. The other driver too, for Herr Himmler, I mean."

"You never spoke to the other driver?"

"No... Well, I don't know him and..."

"And what?"

"Nothing."

"And what, Herr Meichner?"

"Well, he's... you know..."

"No, I don't know."

"He's SS."

"And you don't like the SS?"

"I didn't say that."

"You don't trust us?"

"No, I... I didn't mean that."

"What were they talking about? When they came back. When you got out of the car. What did you hear them say?"

"Not much. Just the usual."

"The usual?"

"Well, goodbyes and so on."

"Did they make any plans to meet again?"

"No, I don't think so."

"You don't think so?"

"No… not that I heard."

"And what else?"

"Nothing… nothing else."

"And when the Reichsführer got back into the car... Was he still holding the file?"

"Yes, he carried it under his arm."

"You're absolutely sure."

"Yes."

"After that, you drove the Admiral back home or straight to his office?"

"Straight to his office. Then I called you. First chance I had."

Heydrich remained silent for awhile, then scraped his chair back, got to his feet and strolled deeper into the darkness at the far end of the room. For a minute or two, he stood still, gazing through the window at the night beyond. Then, without saying another word, he walked out of the room, closing the door behind him.

* * *

It was early the following morning when the call came through. Erika Canaris took it, still in her robe. "It's for you," she called out, then went back to the kitchen. Her husband was just finishing in the bathroom.

Eventually he came downstairs wearing yet another woolen sweater from his collection. "Yes, Hans… Yes… What? Dammit, when was this? Yes… Yes, I see… Yes, all right, thank you."

He slowly placed the receiver back on the hook and went into the kitchen, trying hard to mask his feelings. The dogs were glad to see him but his face had lost much of its colour.

"What is it?" said Erika. "What's happened now?"

It was brighter that morning, an odd variant in the depressing weather pattern they'd been having of late. "Nothing," he answered. "Office panic. Nothing unusual."

She poured him coffee and watched as he took a sip, scalding his mouth slightly. She wasn't fooled for a minute.

"Tell me," she said to him.

He continued drinking his coffee without touching the hot breakfast she'd set out for him. Normally Otto would have served it but Otto wasn't here any more. Otto was dead. How could he possibly tell her what had just happened to Franz Meichner?

He seemed to drift off and she waited awhile but there were limits even to *her* patience.

"Willi…" she said threateningly.

He looked at her with no expression on his face. "They found Franz this morning. He was floating in the Landwehrkanal, not far from the office."

This time she didn't go into shock, she just sat there, her face blank. "How many more?" she said quietly. "How many more before he's finished?"

Canaris shook his head. "You know what the funniest thing is?" Without waiting for an answer, he went on: "The funniest thing is I didn't even suspect them. Me, the head of military intelligence and I didn't even suspect them. Not Otto and not Franz." He looked at her, another thought having just struck him. "You think we should keep an eye on Maria, just in case?" He was only half-joking.

But Erika wasn't in the mood, even for half-jokes. A gray pigeon landed on the ledge just outside the kitchen window and then, just as quickly, flew off again, as if it didn't care much for the conversation. She watched it absently. "But it has to come to an end now, surely…"

"Why do you say that?"

She shrugged. "What more can he do? He must know by now you don't have the file any more."

"I presume so."

"So what can he do?"

Wilhelm Canaris glanced at his wife. "Who knows?" he said.

"To be honest, nothing would surprise me."

"And what if they still want to be friends?"

"What?"

"Reinhard and Lina... You said that nothing would surprise you. What if they still want to be friends?"

He allowed himself a brief smile but it was empty, devoid of emotion. "Then perhaps we should ask the Wehrmacht to station a Panzer tank on the front lawn."

8

If Reinhard Heydrich had been like most people, he'd have measured risk against reward and might have called it quits right there.

After all, Himmler was not only the supreme commander of the SS, he actually helped create it - Aryan heritage, black uniforms, death's head insignia and all. He was also one of Hitler's closest acolytes, so we might be forgiven for thinking the dossier was safe under his personal lock and key.

But, as we've already seen, Gruppenführer Heydrich wasn't like most people.

* * *

It would have been about seven-thirty on the morning of October 28th that a prim, conservative woman of indeterminate age was walking from the Wilhelmsplatz U-Bahn station across to her place of work at SS headquarters on Prinz Albrecht Strasse. Although her clothes were inexpensive, she was neatly dressed and her hair was pulled back in a tight, tidy bun. As usual, she stopped at the kiosk outside the I.G. Farben building to buy her daily newspaper and as usual she exchanged a greeting with the vendor.

"Good morning, Herr Frühe," she said in what she hoped sounded like a normal voice. "How are you today?"

"All the better for seeing you, Frau Jürgens."

He called her "Frau" even though she was unmarried because she had a certain matronly air about her which demanded that kind of respect.

She took her change and crossed the street, only to be startled by a delivery man on a bicycle who swerved, skidded and then went sprawling across the road. That, in turn, caused the van behind to scrape the side of a double-decker bus and both came to a grinding halt, thus blocking the entire street. The resulting commotion caused some debate as to who was at fault but, by that time, Ingrid Jürgens had pulled herself together and walked hurriedly away. She had a great deal on her mind that morning.

Once she arrived at her building, she made a conscious effort to calm down. She showed her pass as normal at the security desk just inside the staff entrance and proceeded along the corridors to the elevator. As usual, she said "Heil Hitler" to everyone she met along the way. She'd never actually become a paid-up member of the party but the greeting was official procedure at SS headquarters and, as Reichsführer Himmler's senior personal secretary, she felt it was her duty to set the tone.

Himmler himself had been gone a couple of days. He'd been called to a meeting at Bechtesgaden, the Führer's mountain residence near Salzburg, and was expected back that same afternoon. She had a great deal of work to finish before his return, so it was still early when she pushed open the door to Himmler's large anteroom where she had her desk and her files.

According to her regular ritual, the first thing she always did on arrival was check her hair and make-up in the mirror she kept at the right side of her private desk drawer but today she hardly recognized herself. Her face was tense and one of her eyes was bloodshot.

The only thing to do, she decided, was to swallow hard and make the best of it. She knew the call would be coming through at eight and she had to be ready.

* * *

Reinhard Heydrich was also at his desk, a stack of reports still to be cleared. That morning he was having trouble with a major headache, thanks to his previous night on the town.

At eight sharp, his assistant called through from the next office to remind him of the time. "Thank you," he said succinctly, before hanging up and dialing immediately.

"Good morning, Frau Jürgens," he said as pleasantly as his head would allow. "I hope you're well today."

"Yes, Gruppenführer, very well."

He noted her attitude, polite but brusque. "Good. So to business. Have you checked with Bechtesgaden?"

"Yes, I have."

"And?"

"According to Oberführer Wolff, the Reichsführer is approximately thirty minutes behind schedule. They will try to make up some time on the journey." Wolff was Himmler's adjutant.

"Very well," said Heydrich. "You remember your instructions?"

"Yes, Gruppenführer."

"In that case, please repeat them to me."

* * *

Just as he was about to leave Bechtesgaden, Heinrich Himmler was called in to yet another meeting which lasted a further two hours. So instead of making up time on the journey, he was delayed even more and didn't arrive back at his office until close to four.

As usual, Ingrid Jürgens was waiting for him in the anteroom when he got back. Usually the driver called through to her on arrival downstairs so that she could have his favourite herbal tea already brewing when he walked in.

"Good afternoon, Reichsführer," she said as she helped him off with his leather coat and hung it in the closet. "How was the trip?"

"Long," he replied and strode through to his office.

She finished preparing the tea, picked up a pile of papers she needed him to sign and then followed him in. "Something to eat?" she asked him as she poured.

Wearily, he peeled off his glasses and rubbed his eyes. "No... no, thank you." Then, as if noticing something, he put them back on and looked around. "Frau Jürgens... Who was in here today?" His face was a combination of confusion and annoyance.

"No one... except me, of course."

"Did you touch anything?"

"Just the work you asked me to do. Why, is something missing?"

He glanced around the room. "Not the furniture? The pictures? The carpets?"

"Oh that. Well, that would have been the fire brigade."

Himmler turned back and stared at her. "What did you say?"

"The fire brigade. You didn't know? Oh, I'm sorry, forgive me, Reichsführer, I thought..."

"What happened?"

"Nothing. It was just a false alarm. That's why I didn't think to mention..."

"What time was that?"

"It would have been just before eleven."

"So you weren't here?"

"No, Reichsführer. All staff were required to evacuate the building."

"And you're telling me the fire brigade came in here? To this office?"

"Yes... at least, I assume so. They needed to check, to make sure there was no fire, so I assume if they were thorough, they came in here too. Why? Is there a problem?"

Suddenly, without any warning, he strode over to his private safe, the one that was hidden behind the mirror of his private washroom. Ingrid Jürgens was one of the few who knew it was even there. With frenetic fingers, he found the secret lever behind the shelves to release the mirror mechanism. The safe possessed a complex lock that had been built specially for him by a company in Düsseldorf - but, as he'd very much feared, the heavy metal door was now open slightly. He searched the contents thoroughly but the dossier was missing. This was no random robbery. This was the precise, calculated theft of a specific item.

He was furious and his face took on a deep hue as he tried to maintain self-control. "Frau Jürgens!" he called, as he slammed the safe shut.

He was already planning how he'd tear apart the fire brigade, the lock company, the building's security guard, everyone he could think of to find out who had betrayed him. He would interrogate them, torture them, send them to Dachau if he had to, but he would get to the bottom of it... but that's when he sat down heavily in one of his office chairs. He realized that even if he tracked down the culprit and made him regret the day he was born, it wouldn't do any good. The dossier was gone. The damage was done. And although he had no proof, nor even any evidence, there was no doubt in his mind that it was the Gruppenführer who'd ordered it. Who else would have both the means and the motive? Who else would have the sheer audacity even to attempt such a theft?

The only course that remained was to raise the matter with the Führer himself. But that was hardly practical. It would force Hitler into making a decision he didn't want to make, with no option but to choose between them... Himmler or Heydrich... loyalty or dynamism... efficiency or ruthlessness. And when faced with such a choice, who could ever predict what the Führer might decide? Such was the nature of the Reich they'd built.

* * *

It was late when Ingrid Jürgens arrived home at her modest rooms just behind Gertrauden Strasse, one of the older districts of Berlin.

She'd just gone through the most nerve-wracking day of her life and she was thankful it was over. She'd done everything the Gruppenführer had asked and she prayed that, in the future, he might leave her alone. At exactly the right time, she'd set off the fire alarm, then called down to security so they could organize the evacuation and send for the fire brigade. But the Gruppenführer hadn't mentioned that they were going to steal something from the Reichführer's safe, otherwise she'd never have agreed. Never.

When she came in that evening, her mother was sitting in her usual place by the window where she could watch the streetcars that rumbled past on Niederwallstrasse, not far away. She was knitting, as always, her blue veined, arthritic fingers stubbornly trying to manipulate the long needles. It was supposed to be a cardigan for her Ingrid, in dark rose with matching buttons, but it wouldn't be ready for winter. Not this year, nor the one after.

"Is that you, Ingrid?" she called out. "Did you buy the coffee?"

"Yes, Mutti, I bought the coffee. I'll make you some in a minute."

Good coffee seemed to be her mother's sole pleasure. It had to be bought at just the right place, from Braun on the Potsdamerplatz she always insisted, not from that thief, Schweib, who wouldn't know good coffee if it was poured all over him.

Ingrid Jürgens went into the kitchen but instead of putting a match to the stove, she just sat down on one of the wooden chairs and held her head in her hands. Tears began flooding down her face and, for a long time, she just sat there giving in to her misery and self-pity, her whole body trembling at the guilt she felt. Never mind that there were extenuating circumstances. Never mind that Herr Himmler never once returned her glances, never once recognized that she was a woman even though she felt more towards him than his peasant of a wife ever could. And never mind that she needed the Gruppenführer's money just to pay her mother's expensive medical bills. Never mind all that. The fact was that she'd betrayed the Reichsführer's loyalty and for that she could never forgive herself.

"Not too weak," her mother called from the other room. "You always make it too weak."

But Ingrid Jürgens was too upset to reply.

* * *

It must have been about the same time that Reinhard Heydrich returned to his large house on Reifträgerweg.

For him, it was unusually early but he still had the remains of his morning headache and decided that sleep would be the best cure. Besides, he knew his wife wouldn't be home and he was quietly thankful, as he stepped inside, that she wouldn't be standing there with that hypocritical greeting of hers.

He handed his cap, gloves and leather coat to his waiting servant, Hedda, then carried his own briefcase through the wood-paneled hallway into the salon. As he sat down on the broad Ottoman and put his boots up on the coffee table, he allowed himself a rare sigh, a combination of both relief and achievement.

It was done.

He opened the briefcase to take another look at the troublesome file and found his own eyes gazing back at him from the photograph.

Even now, he wasn't entirely sure whether Himmler would take the matter all the way to the Führer. He seriously doubted it. Such an approach would be a gamble and he felt Himmler was far too risk-averse to attempt it. Yet he didn't know for certain and, despite all his calculations, an arrest order could still be forthcoming. After all, a break-in at the Admiral's house was one thing. Even a murder. But daylight robbery from the office of the Reichsführer? That was nothing but an affront. Himmler would surely deduce the truth of it.

With obsessive precision, Heydrich had tracked down the original locksmith and threatened him into revealing the combination. He'd bribed Himmler's own personal secretary into setting the alarm, despite the fact that it was totally against her better judgment. Finally, he'd intimidated a supervisor in the fire marshal's office into taking the file, before ordering the man's neck to be broken, supposedly an accident while falling down a flight of stairs.

And now, at last, the dossier was in his possession. He was holding it in his own hands. He flipped through the pages and, once again, marveled at what he saw. It was all there. His ancestry, complete with a detailed family tree, plus all the key events of his childhood. All with unerring accuracy. Dates, names, details and, above all, the signed witness testimony.

There, for example, was Gottfried Bausch, the doctor who'd first brought him into the world back in Halle. There too was Josef Schmidt, the district clerk who'd altered the birth certificate. And there too was Johannes... Johannes Utz, his best friend at school, the one in whom he'd always confided. Later they'd met up in the navy where they'd both fallen under the spell of a slightly eccentric war hero called Wilhelm Canaris. It was a shame about Johannes. He'd been a good friend.

But he couldn't allow remorse to be a factor. Not remorse, not mercy and certainly not pity. To the Führer, he was "the man with the iron heart" and he felt it both an honour and a duty to live up to the title.

After an hour or so, he heard Hedda scurrying to answer the door. He knew it must be his wife arriving. Carefully, he gathered up the papers and put the dossier safely back in his briefcase. He knew it would be her first question when she walked through the door but he'd already decided not to tell her he had it in his possession. He would be deliberately vague in his response. The simple truth was that he didn't trust her. If she knew he had the file, she might attempt to seize it for herself as her own future leverage and that would be intolerable. In that case, he'd have to eliminate her, too, and once the von Osten family started sniffing around, it could get really messy.

No, he decided, better for both their sakes that she shouldn't know.

9

The following day, Heinrich Himmler cancelled his daily agenda and departed on an unscheduled trip north to Schleswig-Holstein.

Normally he worked in the car but he had a great deal to think about and he spent much of the long journey gazing out at the countryside as it flashed past the window. Towns, villages, isolated farms. Thousands of average rural Germans, he thought to himself, all living their lives totally unaware of the mad frenzy that was Berlin.

As a creature of habit, he was doing the same thing he'd always done when faced with an intractable problem. He was seeking advice. In the past, such advice had most often come from the Führer, especially back during the early days in Munich. However, since Hitler's infatuation with Heydrich made that course of action impossible, Himmler determined he must search for counsel elsewhere. And the person he'd decided to ask was Manfred Vollbrecht.

Yes, that's right, Vollbrecht. The same family name as the woman I'd just invited out to dinner. In fact he was her father. So now you can begin to see how circumstances were beginning to entwine and ensnare me. Good ol' Ed. Just when I thought my luck had started to turn.

As I mentioned, the Vollbrecht family made their fortune breeding horses for the Kaiser's army and, in their heyday, they maintained a stock of five thousand animals with a full staff of over eight hundred, all housed on a superb estate that stretched across several hundred square kilometres. As the *Berliner Zeitung* commented: "What Krupp is to steel, Vollbrecht once was to horse-flesh."

But all that was part of another era. Although the Vollbrechts of Prussia had done very well for themselves, they'd also paid the price. Two of Manfred's younger brothers were killed in the Great War and a third, Erwin, had become mentally unstable due to shell-shock. He was still in the asylum. Manfred himself escaped active duty because of the heart condition he'd had since he was a child, so he was the one who'd always remained behind to run the business.

Eventually he married a handsome Berlin socialite who died giving birth to their only child, Katharina, leaving just the two of them to rattle around the estate's thirty-room mansion. Of course, his daughter had the finest of everything: private tuition, servants, horses, travel, whatever she wanted. But somehow there was always a sadness hanging over the place. In the end, all the riches in the world don't make up for a family missing in action.

By the time Heinrich Himmler arrived in that last week of October 1938, the great Vollbrecht estate had become little more than a giant rustic retreat for a sorrowful old man. Katharina was often traveling, busy in her chosen career of buying and selling artwork on the international market. She'd been left an impressive collection of Dürer drawings by her grandfather and she'd used it as a base from which to start.

As we've seen, she happened to be in Berlin that week but Himmler was still gracious enough to ask after her as he climbed out of the car and shook the old man's hand. It was long and thin, like the rest of him, and not as steady as it once was. In honour of the occasion, Vollbrecht was today wearing a handsome hunting jacket with a brown leather collar over a stiff white shirt and a black SS tie. On his lapel, he'd taken care to pin the silver SS flashes that he'd been awarded as chairman of the "Friends" organization.

Once inside, Himmler was invited to sit in the large conservatory. In deference to his tastes, a fine local blend of herbal tea was served together with platters of home-baked cake and biscuits that were still warm from the oven. Preparations had been feverish ever since the previous evening's telephone call. It was not every day they received such a visitor.

The two men hadn't known each other long, just a few years, an acquaintance which had begun when Vollbrecht offered a minor piece of his property to the SS as a training ground. In return, he was offered membership in an exclusive club known as "Friends of the SS." Then, when the honorary chair became vacant, Himmler had immediately offered it to Vollbrecht, believing that such a respected establishment name could only add lustre to the organization.

However, the notion of going to him for counsel only occurred when Himmler's mind began running through the list of possibilities. It had to be someone with impeccable integrity, total discretion, worldly experience and, perhaps most important, someone who was far removed from all current political machinery. In other words, someone with no vested interest, no agenda of his own. In the end, it wasn't a very long list and Manfred Vollbrecht was soon left as one of the few viable options.

Yet Himmler was still somewhat hesitant, even as the heavy clock ticked away the minutes. Above where they were sitting, a large oil portrait of one of the former Vollbrechts looked down at them, looking distinctly uncomfortable in his stiff-necked Hussars uniform. Himmler knew how the man must have felt.

Eventually, during a gap in the small talk, he decided to broach the matter.

"Herr Vollbrecht… while it's always a great honour, I didn't drive up here to pass the time of day. There's an issue I'd like to discuss with you, if you wouldn't mind. Perhaps some advice you can offer."

Vollbrecht gave a simple nod of his head. He knew it had to be something and was undoubtedly glad, in his forthright Prussian way, that it was finally being addressed.

"What it concerns," Himmler began, "is an incident that took place yesterday at my office. It seems that while I was out, there was a fire alarm and, during the evacuation, a certain item was stolen from my wall safe."

If Vollbrecht was surprised by the admission, he didn't show it. "Something valuable?" he asked.

Himmler thought about it. "I'd say more like something unique."

"Am I permitted to ask what it was?"

Himmler looked across at the other man and came to a decision. "Perhaps I'd better be frank."

"I think that may be best."

"Do you know Gruppenführer Heydrich at all?"

"Reinhard Heydrich? I know his reputation, of course, but I've never met him personally."

"Well, the item that was stolen? It was a dossier concerning the Gruppenführer."

"I see. And I assume the material is... sensitive?"

"I'm glad you appreciate the situation."

"But you can't tell me what it contains."

"No, I'm afraid not. Suffice it to say that the revelation of such material would compromise the Gruppenführer considerably. It would probably end his career... and perhaps even worse."

"I understand. So, obviously, he must be the principal suspect in your investigation."

"Yes... but at this stage, there *is* no investigation."

"Really? That surprises me. May I ask why?"

"It's... difficult."

Vollbrecht was not too sure how to respond. "A serious situation," he said, for want of something better.

Himmler peeled off his glasses and began polishing them on his sleeve, an old practise. "A lot more serious than you could possibly imagine."

Vollbrecht nodded again, just the once, then put his cup down and clambered to his feet with the help of a brass-tipped cane that he always kept beside him. Slowly he tapped his way across to a fading, glass-covered wall plaque on which was mounted a frayed military flag, some faded ribbons and an original map of the Katzbach battlefield as the lines were drawn, a hundred-and-twenty-five years previously.

"That was my grandfather's regiment, the Brandenburg," he said. "On the left flank, Scharnhorst. On the right, Gneisenau. In front of them, Bonaparte, trapped in the city of Leipzig. Terrible rainstorm the day they charged. Terrible. Nobody could shoot because the powder was too wet. You know what Blücher ordered them to do? Use their muskets as clubs. Imagine! They destroyed an entire French battalion using their muskets as clubs."

Himmler listened patiently to an old man telling his war stories. He was prepared to be tolerant.

"You know that Blücher himself charged with them?" Vollbrecht was saying. "Seventy years old. Drove back the French, then stopped to refill his pipe." A gentle smile. "Or so legend would have us believe."

Then, with great effort, he pulled himself away from 1813 and back to the present. Blinking a little, he turned around to face his guest. The morning light from the east-facing window illuminated his face and reflected in the watery blue eyes. He looked tired.

"I suppose," he said at last, "that your problem is the Führer. If you arrest Heydrich, you're not sure if Hitler will support your action."

Himmler was taken aback by the crisp analysis which somehow seemed to make a complex, nuanced problem sound remarkably simple. "What would *you* do in my position?" he asked.

They looked at each other, one generation to another, the past and the present. They had almost nothing in common, the two of them, except perhaps a genuine love for the Fatherland.

Vollbrecht walked slowly back over, taking care not to trip on the splayed fringes of the Persian rug that covered much of the darkwood floor. Then he eased himself back down into his armchair and laid the cane down where he could reach it. Finally, before speaking, he took out a large linen handkerchief and coughed up something into it.

"Did you, by any chance, happen to make a copy of the file?"

"No... no. I didn't have time."

"Does one exist?"

"I believe the man who gave it to me made a copy."

"Excellent. So if you can obtain it, you still have the advantage."

"How do you mean?"

"Forgive me, Reichsführer, if I too speak openly..."

"No, please, by all means. That's why I'm here."

Vollbrecht looked over at Himmler. "I think," he said slowly, "that your strategy may be too defensive."

"Too defensive?"

"Take a lesson from Blücher."

"You think I should club the Gruppenführer to death?" It was a rare joke from Himmler, born of the unusually desperate situation in which he found himself. "And then, perhaps, stop to smoke a pipe?"

Vollbrecht didn't respond to the humour. "What I mean is that you must attack, always attack, and if you can't do it one way, you must do it another."

"Can you be a little more specific?"

"You assume that your only option is to show the dossier to the Führer, then wait for his verdict on who to support. You assume you must passively accept your fate. But if you'll forgive an old German who's been around far too long, I can tell you one thing for certain. Hitler may be Führer but he's not God."

"Excuse me, Herr Vollbrecht, but I hardly think..."

"Forgive me, Reichsführer. I'm not being disloyal, I'm merely stating a fact. All I'm saying is that Hitler is a man like all of us and he makes decisions like all of us... with his best judgment at the time. Can we agree on that?"

A slight shrug. "I suppose."

"Then you must find a way to influence that judgment. Every degree of influence you can bring to bear is another factor in your favour. And if you ask me, the influence in this case can only come from one place... From outside."

"From outside where? Outside the party?"

"No, no, much wider than that. I'm talking about outside the country."

Suddenly a small ray of hope began to creep into the caverns of Himmler's pessimism. Influence from outside the country. German standing in the world. It made sense to him. "This influence," he said. "Are we talking about foreign governments or the foreign press?" he asked.

Vollbrecht considered the question carefully. "Essentially both but, personally, I don't trust governments so I'd have to say the press... and specifically the western press."

"You trust the western press?"

"No, but I do trust their motives. They don't care about diplomacy or propaganda. All they want is to sell newspapers. They're in business, Reichsführer, and business is something I understand."

It was all becoming perfectly clear to Himmler, like a microscope brought into sharp focus. If he quietly released the dossier to the western press, the contents would then become international news. Exposure of that magnitude would severely compromise Heydrich in Hitler's eyes and his position would change completely. From being one of the Führer's key assets, he'd be transformed into an embarrassing liability. And the beauty of it was that the western press wouldn't care if the dossier were a copy. They wouldn't care if there were no signed originals. To them it was just a story, as Vollbrecht said, a way to sell newspapers.

Himmler looked across at his host in a whole new light. "I must compliment you, Herr Vollbrecht. I can see the world of business makes for sound strategic training. But strategy is one thing and execution is another."

"As you say, Reichsführer."

Himmler reached forward to pour himself more tea, then sat back in his chair and there was a period of silence while both men digested the conversation so far.

"The problem," he said eventually, "is that if I expose the dossier, whether it's to the western press or anybody else, I immediately destroy the man's career."

"Isn't that the general idea?"

"If I do that, I deprive the Führer of his talents and I won't exactly be thanked for that. Heydrich is highly capable at what he does. Perhaps even irreplaceable."

"So what are you saying? You not only want your dossier back but also for things to remain as they are?"

"I believe that would be the ideal situation, yes."

"With respect, Reichsführer, that doesn't sound like much of an attack to me."

"Perhaps not. But an attack doesn't always have to be a direct frontal assault."

"No, you're right, it doesn't."

"And I don't really have to expose the Gruppenführer. All I have to do is *threaten* to expose him, wouldn't you say?"

"Well, yes, that might accomplish your goal…"

From the tonality, Himmler knew there was more to come. "You don't sound too confident about that approach."

Vollbrecht thought about it for a few seconds. "How was your working relationship with the Gruppenführer? I mean, up until this happened?"

"Excellent."

"Really? The word you'd use is 'excellent?'"

"I thought him one of my most able deputies."

"Then how do you think he'd feel if you issued him a threat? Do you believe your relationship would continue to be excellent? Do you believe things could ever be back to normal between you?"

Himmler conceded the point. "So… you think I should expose him and have done with it? Just accept the consequences?"

"No, but nor do I think you have to threaten him."

"Is there a third option?"

"Why not get someone else to threaten him?"

Himmler nodded slowly. "An intriguing notion," he said. "Are you volunteering?"

Vollbrecht smiled and shook his head slightly, as if that's not what he meant at all. "I'm not sure I'm up to that. But it would certainly have to be a candidate who's intelligent enough to understand the situation."

"That already limits the selection severely."

"And who can make the threat credible."

"How do you mean?"

"Someone who maintains good contacts with the western press. Someone who has the credibility to threaten exposure."

"A diplomat? An embassy attaché? Perhaps a journalist?"

"Perhaps. But whoever he is, I'd say he needs to be someone who could be easily sacrificed. That is most important."

"You mean in case the threat doesn't work."

"Exactly."

For Himmler, that too made perfect sense. "And... would you happen to know of anyone like that?"

Another shake of the head, this time more definitive. "I'm sorry, I don't get into town too much any more. Heart, you know. But if you wish..."

"Yes?"

"I was just thinking... If you wish, I could ask my daughter."

"Your daughter?"

"She knows a lot of people in Berlin."

"Yes, I'm sure she does. But does she have her father's head for business?"

"Oh heavens, no. She's much better than I ever was."

Heinrich Himmler laughed out loud, an all too rare pleasure. Undoubtedly a result of some of the pressure having been relieved. "Well, this has been most enlightening, Herr Vollbrecht, most enlightening." He got to his feet. "I won't keep you any longer."

"You won't stay for lunch?"

"No, no, thank you all the same. Another time, if you care to invite me again. But today I really must get back."

"I understand," said Vollbrecht as he too got to his feet. It was something of a struggle. "And about my daughter?"

"She's in Berlin?"

"Yes, until Sunday, but I can always reach her by telephone."

"Let me think about it and I'll let you know tomorrow. Would that be acceptable?"

"As you wish.'"

They walked together towards the front door, moving at Vollbrecht's slow pace, and then out to the gravel driveway where Himmler's car was waiting. But they weren't quite done. Not yet.

"Reichsführer... there is one more thing."

The driver was already holding the door open when Himmler turned back. "Yes, Herr Vollbrecht."

"Well, it's a small matter... I'm sorry to trouble you but it's about my brother."

"Your brother?"

"Yes, my brother, Erwin. He's quite sick, has been for some time."

"I'm sorry to hear that. Is there anything I can do? A doctor? A medical facility?"

"No, I'm afraid you don't quite understand. He's not sick physically... "

"I don't follow."

"He's in a mental institution."

"Ah, I see..." This was more difficult for Himmler. A program of euthanasia for the mentally ill had already been initiated as part of Reich policy and, as head of the SS, it was his ultimate responsibility to carry it out. Part of their plan was to shut down all such places. Yet he really was extremely grateful to Vollbrecht for the conversation, not to mention the old man's exceptional contribution to the "Friends" committee. "May I ask how such a thing came about? Was it from birth?"

"No, a result of the war."

"He's a veteran?"

"He was at Verdun."

Himmler stood thinking for a moment. He never liked to break policy even as a favour but if it involved a veteran then he could probably find an excuse to rationalize it. "Let me see what I can do," he said. "Would you be willing to remove him from the institution?"

Vollbrecht hesitated. It was not an easy request but if that were the only way, he'd have to accommodate it. "I could perhaps try to organize some sort of home care."

"Then I'd definitely recommend that as a first step."

"Thank you, Reichsführer."

"I'll let you know about your daughter."

With that, Himmler climbed back in his car and instructed his driver to make haste back to Berlin. The entire visit had taken no more than an hour but, with all the travel time, it had still removed a full day from his agenda.

All in all, he was well pleased with the discussion and congratulated himself on having selected Manfred Vollbrecht to be his counsel on the matter. Yet that didn't obscure one small error he'd made. He'd told himself that Vollbrecht had no vested interest but that obviously wasn't true. The man was anxious for his brother and that was undoubtedly why the advice had been dispensed so freely. Indeed, he thought, that may even have been the reason for the financial largesse in the first place.

Everyone wants something, he reminded himself. It was one of the laws of the universe.

10

Of course, I couldn't afford a restaurant like Horcher's, so why I'd blurted out the name of the toniest eatery in town, I don't know.

Or maybe I'm just deluding myself. Maybe I know perfectly well why I suggested it and the plain answer is ego. I wanted to impress her. She certainly didn't seem like the kind of person who'd enjoy beer and knockwurst at the Sportspalast, so Horcher's it was. One of the most sought-after reservations in Berlin on a Saturday night, packed with its affluent clientele - and me in my one good suit.

Naturally, they didn't know it was my one good suit but when I arrived ten minutes early and presented myself to the highly polished Fritz at the door, I kind of got the feeling that he'd priced my outfit down to the last pfennig. Without the magic of the Vollbrecht name, I think he'd have seated me in the kitchen next to the potato peelings. As it was, he led me beneath the crystal chandeliers to a well-placed table for two from where I could just about take in the entire room, all the way across to the small dance floor on the other side where a slick three-piece combo was offering some gentle rhythms. Most of the tables were already full and I'd already recognized at least half a dozen people whose acquaintance I'd love to have made - junior ministers, corporate vice-presidents, editors, publishers - they all came to Horcher's.

That night, however, I had other things on my mind - like whether I'd over-reached myself and was about to be stood up. But I needn't have worried. At exactly two minutes past nine, she made her appearance. It turned out to be quite an event.

As Fritz led her across the room, she was obliged to stop and say "*Guten Abend*" and "*Wie gehts?*" at so many tables that it took her a full ten minutes to actually reach me. Some people were not only shaking her hand, they were also kissing it. Marlene Dietrich herself couldn't have caused such a stir. When I finally stood up to greet her, I felt that every pair of eyes in the restaurant was watching us - or, should I say, watching *her*. But then no wonder. She looked stunning. She was wearing a classically tailored dress and jacket ensemble in a subtle shade of apricot with coordinated topaz jewelry. I recall vaguely wondering if she had gemstones to match all her outfits.

"Good evening, Herr Schaeffer."

"Good evening, Fräulein Vollbrecht. Do you always arrange for this kind of an entrance?"

She smiled as she sat down gracefully in the chair that the attentive Fritz was holding for her. I noticed that he didn't bother holding mine. Then he threw starchy white napkins onto our laps and snapped his fingers flamboyantly in the air. It was a signal for an elderly waiter to begin making his way over with a pair of beautifully bound menus under his arm. Without even looking, I knew what the prices would be like.

"Would you care for a cocktail?" said the waiter, looking directly at the Fräulein.

"Yes, thank you," she said. "I think... I think I would like to try a Canadian rye whiskey. Do you have such a thing?"

"Yes, Fräulein," he replied but it was evident he wasn't used to a woman like her ordering a drink like that. "How do you take it?"

That's when she looked at me. She had no idea how to take a rye.

"With ice and soda," I offered. "Make it two."

"Yes, mein Herr." Then he was gone, his polished shoes squeaking slightly on the blue and gold carpet.

"Thank you," she said to me.

"Who told you about rye? Herr von Ribbentrop?"

"Yes, as a matter of fact it was."

"And what else did he tell you about my homeland?"

"Well he said it was big."

"Yes, it's certainly big all right."

"And he said that in winter it gets very cold."

"Obviously, a very perceptive man."

For a moment she just looked at me but once she realized I was just teasing, her smile broke out again, even broader this time, lighting up the whole room.

"How long have you known him?" I asked her.

"Oh, a long time. Long before he joined the ministry."

"And what kind of man is he, would you say?"

She thought for a moment. "He has a certain self-regard."

"You mean vain?"

"He can't pass by a mirror without looking at himself."

My turn to smile. "Is he really as effective as they say?"

"Effective? I would have to believe so. Although how much is him and how much is the Führer, I'm not sure."

She was referring to the fact that a couple of months earlier, Ribbentrop and Hitler had successfully managed to negotiate a peace agreement with Britain and France known as the Munich pact. Of course, it was a complete sell-out of Czechoslovakia and would later brand both Chamberlain and Deladier as the worst kind of appeasers - but at the time, the agreement had been hailed by much of Europe as diplomacy of the highest order.

"Do you think the pact will hold?" I asked her.

"Why, don't you?"

"I don't know. Some people say it's just showmanship."

"All politics is showmanship, Herr Schaeffer."

I wasn't sure whether I'd touched a nerve. In fact, I wasn't sure where her affiliations lay. I could see she was politically astute and it would have been all too easy to slip into full-fledged discussion but this was neither the time nor the place, so I just let it go. No sense allowing serious issues to get in the way of an otherwise pleasant evening.

"Ed," I replied, correcting her formality.

"Excuse me?"

"Not Herr Schaeffer... just Ed."

"And I'm Katharina."

I reached across to shake her hand. "Delighted to meet you," I said.

The waiter arrived back with the drinks but since we hadn't even glanced at the menu yet, he just bowed gently and left. Horcher's wasn't the kind of place to hurry you along.

"To Canada," she said as we clinked glasses.

I guess I should have replied by offering a very diplomatic toast to Germany but I just couldn't bring myself to do it, not with the current state of affairs, so I just nodded and asked her instead about the drink. "What do you think?"

"Interesting. I thought it would be like scotch but it has a very different taste. Is this what they drink where you come from?"

"Sometimes, when they can afford it."

"And where *is* that, if you don't mind my asking?"

"Kitchener... It's in southern Ontario."

"Kitchener," she repeated. "I can't really say I've heard of it."

"No reason you should have." I didn't feel like telling her about Prime Minister Mackenzie King growing up there. He wasn't my favourite person in the world and, besides, she probably hadn't heard of him either.

"Any polar bears?" she asked me.

Her expression was perfectly serious but I knew she was joking. I liked her sense of humour. "No," I replied. "And no caribou either."

"I bet you didn't even live in a log cabin."

"No, it was made of brick. But the roof did leak occasionally during spring thaw."

"Ah, finally some romance."

I laughed. "Believe it or not, Kitchener was actually called Berlin at one time."

"Really?"

"Sure. It was founded by German Mennonites. They must have felt homesick, I guess."

"And why did they change the name? Because of the war?"

"Yes..." I replied hesitantly, "because of the war." I could have added that they chose the new name after the commander-in-chief of the British army, just to prove their loyalty to the crown, but I didn't mention it. I realized it might be a touchy subject, considering her family's involvement on the Kaiser's side and I was glad she didn't pursue it.

"Were your parents German?" she asked me. "You speak the language so well."

"Thanks, but only my father. My mother was second generation Irish."

"That's an unusual mix."

"I know. Logic and emotion all wrapped in one."

Again the smile. I loved her smile.

"Are they still alive?" she said.

"No... They died in an accident when I was sixteen."

"Oh, I'm sorry to hear that. I never knew my mother either."

A few moments followed in which neither of us spoke. We just looked at each other with a kind of mutual understanding. But I don't like being maudlin so I just continued my tale.

"I stayed at my cousins' place for a while but I didn't like it too much, so I just left. Jumped a freight train to Vancouver. Took four days to get there! By the time I arrived, I was so hungry, I signed up on a boat just so I could eat. It was only when I got on board that I found out it was actually going to Hong Kong."

"Hong Kong? That must have been a surprise."

"I'll say. I thought it was going to Alaska."

"Did you stay on board?"

"Sure, why not? Signed up for the whole trip. It was a big adventure for a scruffy Ontario kid. After Hong Kong, we went to Bombay, Singapore, Rangoon... various outposts of the empire."

"And when did you come to Germany?"

"Not until much later. First place I washed ashore was Australia. Melbourne, to be exact. That's where I tried my hand at journalism. After that I covered London and Paris, then back to Toronto for a while. It was only in 1928 that I actually came to Germany... My God, it's been ten years already. Hard to believe."

"Ten years," she repeated. She had some nostalgia in her voice. "Ten years ago, I was just finishing my graduate studies... European art history, from the Renaissance to the Impressionists. It was all I lived for." Then a smile, this time much more gentle. "I was still very innocent."

I nodded my understanding. In 1928, we were all very innocent - not necessarily about life, I'd seen enough of that, but about where the world was heading. The crash. The depression. And the rise of military Fascism.

It would have been all too easy at that point to sink into a long bout of melancholy, and I was about to suggest we order some food, but that's when the mood changed without any help from me. The band launched into a popular French melody, which we both seemed to recognize.

"You like Piaf?" I asked her.

"I adore Piaf."

The tiny Edith Piaf, "the sparrow of Pigalle" as they called her, had recently become the sensation of Paris.

"You know what this one's called?" she said.

I shook my head.

"It's called *'Mon coeur est au coin de la rue'* which means…"

"'My heart is at the corner of the street.'"

"You speak French?"

"Canada," I explained. "We learn it in grade school. You know, Québec and all that."

"Yes, yes, of course," she said, as if it were something she should have known. "I see you're a man of many talents, Herr Schaeffer."

"Ed," I corrected.

"Ed," she echoed, as if trying it out. "And do you also dance, Ed?"

"Dance?" I had no idea what to reply. I'd danced a little in my time but I really wasn't very good. Not exactly Fred Astaire. However, before I could say a word, she was on her feet with her hand stretched out towards me. A direct invitation. What could I do but take it and follow her?

She led me all the way across to the small dance floor where a few couples were already swaying their way around. She exchanged a pleasant nod to the bandleader as if she knew him too, then put her hand on my shoulder - and everything else around us just melted away.

Suddenly we were close, very close, just the two of us in our own bubble. I could feel the softness of her lustrous brown hair and breathe the delicate scent of her Chanel. Was I the one leading or was she? I had no idea. We were just moving in unison and I could feel her in my arms being transported by the music, humming softly so that only I could hear. I didn't know who was around us or who might be watching but I didn't care. Let them watch. Let them all be jealous. I just didn't care. I was proud as hell and practically swooning from the headiness of her graceful, sensual presence next to me.

"Is it true you know everyone in Berlin?" I asked her.

"Who told you that?"

"Everyone in Berlin."

This time she didn't just smile, she laughed out loud, right there on the dance floor, and I liked that too. In fact, I was beginning to like everything about her. Something was happening between us, something that was neither tangible nor totally evident but real all the same. I could feel it and I think she could, too. I dared to hold her just a little closer.

The band played another song from their repertoire, then another. It was almost like we'd forgotten about dinner. We were dancing, chatting, laughing, and I just didn't want it to end. We talked about her art for some time. Then music, theatre, literature and even sports. In fact, we made a solemn agreement that if she'd teach me to ride, I would teach her to skate. But none of that mattered very much. Not really. What was important was that I could feel myself becoming seriously involved with the exquisite Katharina Vollbrecht and I couldn't help it. Unlikely as it might seem after such a brief time, I was becoming dangerously smitten. My pulse was racing, my blood was charged and my soul was in raptures. I felt I was the luckiest man in that entire privileged restaurant...

And then it all came to a crashing end.

A tall figure in a black tunic was standing at the edge of the floor, looking directly at us, as if singling us out. We both turned at the same time and found ourselves staring into the stern, self-important face of a young SS officer.

As soon as he had our attention, he came a few paces forward and clicked his heels together on the polished wood floor. "Fräulein Katharina Vollbrecht?"

"Yes?" she replied.

"Excuse me, Fräulein, but may I speak to you in private for a moment?"

"On what subject, may I ask?"

"It's a matter of importance."

He indicated the direction stiffly with his hand. He was trying hard to be gallant but, in truth, he looked as if he hadn't started shaving yet and his actions came off as clumsy and immature.

"Look, Sturmführer…" I began.

"Obersturmführer," he corrected.

"Fine… Obersturmführer… I don't know what it's about but I'm sure that whatever it is can wait until morning."

He turned his full attention to me. "And you are?"

"Never mind who I am. Fräulein Vollbrecht will call you first thing in the morning. Now, if that's all…"

But it wasn't going to be as easy as that and his presence was already causing some unease amongst the other guests.

The officer remained unfazed. "Fräulein Vollbrecht, I'm sorry but I'm going to have to insist. My orders come directly from Prinz Albrecht Strasse. If you'll just step this way…"

With some trepidation, she stepped away from me. Then, obviously deciding that it was better to get this stupidity over and done with as quickly as possible, she strode purposefully towards the lobby. She didn't even say goodbye, which I assumed meant that she'd be right back. The young officer looked at me for a moment, then clicked his heels again and raised his arm, making a crude show of it. "Heil Hitler!" he declared, then turned and followed her out.

I had no idea what to do so I just went back to the table and sat down. A few minutes later, the waiter arrived with the chef's complimentary hors d'oeuvres and I saw a beautifully arranged crab salad looking back at me from Horcher's finest china. Meanwhile, there was no sign of her. Then another five minutes. It was ridiculous. I rose from my chair and strode purposefully towards the lobby but, when I got there, it was empty. There was nobody but the hat-check girl.

Then Fritz appeared. "Can I help you, mein Herr?"

"Did Fräulein Vollbrecht leave?"

"Yes, a few minutes ago."

"On her own or with the officer?"

I could see Fritz was a little reluctant to answer. The black uniform tended to have that effect. "With the officer," he said quietly.

"Did she leave word for me? Schaeffer..."

"No, Herr Schaeffer, no word. Will that be all?"

"No... No, I'll take coffee," I told him and walked as boldly as I could back to the table, trying to pretend there was nothing untoward. But what I really needed to do was clear my head.

I admit I was shaken. Had she been arrested? No, impossible, I told myself. She knew Ribbentrop personally, for heaven's sake. It made no sense. So what else could it have been? For a while I wondered if I should just accept the whole thing at face value. She'd gone with them to talk about some minor matter and, perhaps, if I just sat there long enough, she'd eventually breeze back in and sit down as if nothing had happened.

Another half hour went by but she didn't appear. I'd finished the seafood along with two cups of Horcher's very strong coffee but I didn't feel like eating any more and, since there was really nothing else I could think of to do, I decided to leave.

Having no car, I normally crossed Berlin's haphazard grid of streets by public transport, either bus or streetcar, or for a longer journey I might use the U-Bahn, but on that occasion, I decided to hell with it: I'd take a taxi to my apartment on Prenzlauer Strasse. Compared to Horcher's prices, the cost would be insignificant anyway.

But after a kilometre or so, I changed my mind. "Wait," I said to the driver, "make it Prinz Albrecht Strasse."

He had bad skin as I recall and his cab smelled foul. He looked at me in the mirror. "What?"

"I've changed my mind."

"Not Prenzlauer Strasse?"

"No, Prinz Albrecht Strasse."

"But that's in the other direction."

"Yes, I know."

"I can't turn around here."

"Wherever it's convenient."

"Won't be for awhile."

"Well, see if you can do it before we get to Warsaw, all right?"

I was obviously upset but, as it turned out, the extra ride gave me time to cool off. SS headquarters was not exactly the kind of place where you banged your fist down and demanded to speak to the manager.

11

Since the SS is such an integral part of this story, maybe it's worth taking a short pause at this point in order to demystify it a little.

It was, in fact, a highly complex organization. In all honesty, I wouldn't even comprehend much of it myself except that sitting here, in post-war Spain, I get to meet a lot of the old SS "Schwartzkorps" as they pass through. Barcelona has become a kind of staging post where they can rest up before boarding ships bound for Brazil or Argentina or Paraguay. I've found it takes only a couple of beers and a friendly Berlin accent to get them talking and, once they do, it's hard to get them to stop...

"We could have licked all of Europe," they tell me earnestly, "if only the British had come to their senses in 1940." Or... "if only winter hadn't come so early in Russia." Or... "if only the Japanese hadn't bombed Pearl Harbor and brought the Americans in." There are any number of reasons for the defeat. And then, inevitably, they come to the wish list. "Wish we'd developed the bomb... Wish we'd finished off the Jews..." And so it goes on. "But don't worry," they assure me, "we'll be back. We just have to regroup and re-arm. Rumour has it the Führer's not even dead. Don't worry, it'll be different next time..."

As you can tell, I've heard it all. And I only listen because once they have it out of their system, I get them to answer a few questions. It's how I learned, for example, that the SS was nowhere near the rigid monolith that the world now imagines. In truth, its powers were unclear, its divisional functions often overlapped and there was rampant infighting amongst its ranks. Only its philosophy was absolute and that amounted to one thing and one thing alone

- loyalty to the Führer - even as far as using his actual name in their oath of allegiance. In this regard, it was unique within the Third Reich. A highly trained, highly committed force which, by its own definition, was required to ignore government, ignore policy and even ignore the law in its dedication to one individual. This was the reason it was both so feared and resented by the rest of the Reich establishment.

What exactly did the SS mean to Hitler? Well, looking back at the newsreels, I suppose it's easy to imagine that he was as dominant a figure at the beginning as he was at the height of his power. Everybody remembers the showy pageantry, the torchlight parades, the ranting speeches, the mass rallies of fifty, eighty, sometimes a hundred thousand. But much of it was just propaganda, expertly staged by masters like Goebbels and Speer, and it obscured the real situation. The truth was that, even after Hitler was voted into office in 1933, he still had many enemies, the most serious being those with the force to back up their threats. In essence, that meant primarily the army, known as the Wehrmacht, who followed their generals' orders. But it also meant the SA or Sturmabteilung, the four million brown-shirts who were little more than street thugs and who were intensely loyal to their own commander, Ernst Röhm.

What Hitler needed was a disciplined force that would be loyal to him alone - and it grew out of the seeds of a fledgling unit commanded by the most unlikely of men, the dull and plodding Heinrich Himmler. As it turned out, Himmler was a very smart choice. He was efficient, he was patient and, above all, he was dedicated, just the qualities needed for the careful planning that was necessary in order to seize power. Himmler's only fault was that he wasn't dynamic so he, in turn, recruited the young Reinhard Heydrich who'd been sent to him like a gift by Wilhelm Canaris.

Together, Himmler and Heydrich orchestrated the legal takeover of all legitimate police powers and then, in one brief period of well-organized butchery now known as the "Night of the Long Knives," they eradicated the entire brown-shirt leadership, imprisoning Röhm for the crime of homosexuality and killing off dozens, some say hundreds, of others. The real numbers are still unknown.

Then, for Hitler, there was an added bonus. Since the generals of the Wehrmacht were as uneasy as he was with the idea of four million brown-shirts on the loose, they were actually thankful that he'd managed to bring such an untrained, unruly mob into line - and their thanks transferred itself, if not to trust, then certainly to a modicum of loyalty.

So that's how the SS were key in helping Hitler surmount the twin obstacles and climb to supreme dictatorial power. Meanwhile, he put his faithful war hero, Hermann Göring, in charge of the Reichstag, the parliamentary chamber, in order to rubber stamp everything the SS did and present a public appearance of respectability and legality. In some cases, the laws they needed to justify their actions were even passed retroactively.

As a reward for their commitment, the SS were awarded control over not only the leaderless brown-shirts but also every aspect of internal security, including the Gestapo, with complete discretion over issues of coercion and punishment, including the camps. They were also placed in direct charge of Hitler's policies for racial purity and it was from that directive that their most barbaric crimes of genocide emanated.

By 1938, SS supremacy in the new order was beyond question. They'd become an exclusive elite and they'd developed an aura of omnipotence - which is why, on that night of October 29th, I was justifiably nervous as the taxi deposited me outside their building.

* * *

I'd often seen the place in passing - a sizeable "L"-shaped structure with what could be called a traditional Berlin façade, very much in keeping with its former occupation. Before the SS came and installed themselves, it had been a major hotel, the Prinz Albrecht.

I stood outside, composing myself for a moment or two, and

then walked up the steps, past the duty guard and through the large doors. When I was young, my mother taught me always to stride into a place as if I owned it but, somehow, I don't think she had a place like this in mind.

Inside, the public entrance lobby was as bland as that of any other government building. On one wall was the requisite portrait of Hitler, on the other a giant gilt eagle carrying a swastika in its talons. Directly in front of me, across a well-worn granite floor, was the inquiries counter manned by several uniformed officers. But they all seemed to be busy and a printed sign told me to sit down and wait my turn. There appeared to be several people ahead of me.

It didn't take too long, about twenty minutes, before I was at the desk. The officer facing me was middle-aged, balding and bored. He looked like he'd seen it all.

"Yes?" he said, his voice curt.

"Good evening," I replied cordially. "I wonder if you could help me. I'm looking for a young lady. Tall, brown hair, very classy..."

"Who isn't?"

I forced a laugh. "Her name's Vollbrecht."

"Vollbrecht?" he repeated.

For a moment I could have sworn he knew the name. "Yes," I said, "Katharina Vollbrecht."

"Just a moment," he told me, then went to one of the desks in the back and picked up a phone but his conversation was inaudible. After a few minutes, he came back.

"Your name?" he said.

I didn't see why he needed *my* name but I assumed it was just procedure. "Schaeffer... Edmund Albert Schaeffer."

He wrote it down in a slow, legible script. "Address?"

"Prenzlauer Strasse 76/3."

"Citizenship?"

"Canadian." Sometimes people were surprised when I said that but not this man. His expression remained completely blank.

"Profession?"

"Journalist."

"Employer?"

"I'm freelance... self-employed."

"And this lady you're inquiring about..."

"Katharina Vollbrecht."

"This Fräulein Vollbrecht. What makes you think she's here?"

"Because I was conducting an interview with her at Horcher's restaurant and one of your officers took her away."

"He arrested her?"

"I don't know but he said his orders came from Prinz Albrecht Strasse."

He stared at me for a while, then shook his head. "I'm sorry, there must have been some misunderstanding. There's nobody here by that name."

"Really? Are you sure?"

"Very sure."

I was getting nowhere. I decided to try something else. "Look," I said, taking out my wallet. "I was in the middle of an interview and I just want to find out what happened to her. If I miss the deadline, I'm in deep trouble. I'm sure you understand." I began fingering a few of the notes. "Is there nothing at all you can do?"

Yes, yes, I know. It was a clumsy move after all I've said about the SS. But Germans are no more scrupulous than anyone else and the tactic, crude as it was, had worked for me in a hundred other situations. Greasing the wheel, it used to be called.

The officer looked at me, then at the wallet. Then he said: "Could you step this way please?" He was very polite for a functionary. He lifted the hinged counter flap and I had no real option but to walk through.

He led me past several unoccupied desks and through a doorway to a long corridor painted pale green. It smelled vaguely of antiseptic. On either side were doors with frosted glass panels and he selected one of them. The room we entered was empty except for a badly scratched wooden table and two chairs, one on either side. The only window looked out directly onto another wall.

"Wait here," he said.

After about five minutes, another man came in, slightly

younger but looking more authoritative. I'm not sure what his rank was because it was always difficult to tell with the SS. They made the insignia deliberately obscure, in keeping with their quasi-cult image.

"My name's Graf," he said as he sat down. He took a small notebook from his pocket and flipped through a few pages. "And your name is... Schaeffer?"

"That's right."

"And you're what? Canadian?"

"Yes."

"A journalist?"

"Yes, that's right."

"Do you always get your information by paying for it?"

The question was deceptively casual but I was ready for it. "I'm sorry," I told him, making it sound as convincing as possible. "In my business, it gets to be a habit. I shouldn't have done it, I know."

He offered no reaction. He just reached into his pocket and pulled out a carton of cigarettes. He offered me one but I declined, so he just lit one for himself and took a deep pull. I didn't know why I was getting the kid gloves treatment but I thought maybe it was because I was a foreigner from one of the more acceptable western democracies.

"I don't know how it is in your country," he said, "but I must tell you that here in the Reich there are heavy penalties for trying to bribe an official."

"Yes, I'm aware of that but..."

"And if I were you, I would not confuse the friendliness of this warning with its severity."

"It won't happen again," I assured him.

"No, it won't." The threat was very clear. "Now, who is it that you were looking for?"

The abrupt change in attitude threw me a little. "Katharina Vollbrecht," I told him. Then just to be sure, I spelled it out.

"And what did the desk officer tell you?"

"He told me she's not here."

"And what's your reason for doubting him?"

"We were at a restaurant. Horcher's. An officer of yours interrupted her and led her away. He said his orders came from here."

"Do you have a relationship with this woman?"

I hesitated. "No, not really." I could see he wasn't ready to believe that, so I said: "Officially, it was supposed to be an interview."

"Do you always conduct your interviews at Horcher's?"

I sensed a note of amusement on his part.

"No, I don't," I admitted.

"Well, I can confirm that she's not here." He got to his feet. "Herr Schaeffer, you are free to go. But I suggest that in future, you save your bribes for clerks and taxi drivers."

"The advice is appreciated." By that time I'd have said anything just to get out of there.

He walked me back to the lobby where the desk officer was busy with someone else. Then he escorted me all the way to the door without saying another word.

I stood out on the sidewalk for awhile, just to catch my breath. My heart was still pounding. I was grateful that my fool move with the wallet hadn't caused me more trouble but their denials concerning Katharina weren't exactly convincing. I'd heard far too many stories of people being arrested by the SS and never being seen again.

Whatever the truth, I knew it would serve nobody's purpose by continuing to tilt at windmills. There was nothing else I could do that evening, so I decided to go home and hope that some other approach might occur to me in the morning.

12

Prenzlauer Strasse, where I lived, was an averagely busy street just east of the downtown core. Not far away was the landmark Alexanderplatz and just to the north was the predominantly Jewish area known since the middle ages as Scheunenviertel, or "barn quarter."

The tenement in which I rented rooms was a four storey affair with a narrow entrance that was sandwiched between a cigar store and a record emporium. I was on the third floor but, when I kept my windows open during the summer, I could nevertheless catch a whiff of Liebermann's pungent tobacco blend while listening to the delicate strains of Richard Tauber.

My building was owned by the gentle, slow-moving Asher Feldstein. Like the majority of his community, he was religious without being overly orthodox but he always wore a skullcap and his family's claim to fame was a second cousin who taught at the yeshiva's rabbinical college. Unfortunately, his own son, Yossel, was somewhat less gifted intellectually, a source of some disappointment, but he was big for his seventeen years and willing as hell. And his passion, unusual for a Jewish kid, was piecing together old motorbikes. I remember one time he was out riding and got into a minor accident over on Münzstrasse. At the family's urgent request, I went along to the police station to straighten things out and his father was so grateful that, in return, he cut my rent in half. Refused to hear a word about it because that was the kind of man he was. Gentle, but also proud and a little stubborn.

As a result, I had a convenient place to live, I was paying next to nothing and the landlord was my true friend. In Berlin, this type of luck was considered a miracle. The only drawback, I must confess, was the daily reminder that I lived in a Jewish neighbourhood in a nation that was officially anti-Semitic. Every day, Jews were picked on in the streets, their businesses were closed down at random and their windows were regularly daubed with the most vulgar obscenities. I suppose I could have moved out but, for me, staying there had become an act of... I don't know how to describe it. Was it principle? Solidarity? I'd like to think so but I knew others in Berlin who called it plain stupidity. Maybe in the end, it was just the cheap rent.

Whatever the reason, the night I came home from Prinz Albrecht Strasse, there was a big new sign pasted on the paned glass of the record store. It was in Germanic script and read *"Kaufen Sie nicht bei Jüden!"* It meant: "Don't buy from Jews!" But I'd seen many like it and barely gave it a glance as I hurried into the building, chased by the rain that had just started.

As I passed by the Feldsteins' apartment, I heard the door creak open and there, peering out, was Asher's wife, Rivka, a thin woman with dark, dry hair and wrinkled bags around her eyes.

"Oh, Herr Schaeffer, it's only you."

"Only me," I confirmed.

She smiled in that nervous way of hers, then closed the door as I continued my way up the stairs. Every time I made that climb, I felt more out of shape.

There was nothing special about my apartment. In the living room, an old sofa, a table and four chairs, a couple of lamps, a worn rug. In the attached kitchen alcove, a chipped and tarnished ceramic sink and an ancient two-ring gas stove with a personality all its own. And in the bedroom, a giant double bed with springs that dug into your back if you didn't know exactly where to lie. But the place was light thanks to a couple of large windows and it was reasonably spacious - which, to a born and raised Canuck, made up for a lot.

I threw off my coat, ambled across to the kitchen and put a match to the stove, which was kind enough to light first time. I wasn't in the mood for alcohol so I decided on coffee. I'd had more than enough at Horcher's but I thought that one more wouldn't make much difference. I needed something. When it was ready, I sat down at the table with my tin mug and flipped through some magazine or other. But I couldn't get interested in any of the articles and ended up just staring through the window above the sink. From here, I could usually see across the rooftops as far as the steeple of St. Georg but tonight the heavy rain clouds hid the moon and the vista was as black as an SS tunic.

All I could think about was Katharina and the image blocked out everything else as I tried to recall every detail. The deep brown eyes that were warm and intense. The long, majestic fingers which formed such elegant angles. The ringing laughter that emerged so easily at my jokes. And then there was the smile, that amazing smile that could radiate an entire restaurant. In my mind, we were still dancing very close together, slowly and easily. I could feel her soft chestnut hair and sense her perfume - and I could still hear the song they were playing: "My heart is at the corner of the street."

Because of the coffee, I didn't fall asleep until about three, so it was much later than normal when I finally shook myself out of bed the following morning. The first thing I noticed was that it was still raining. The downpour had turned into a monotonous drizzle but I decided to go out for breakfast anyway. I washed, shaved and put on some comfortable clothes. It was Sunday and I didn't feel like getting dressed up. There are only so many neckties a person should have to wear in one lifetime and I felt like I'd pretty much fulfilled my quota.

First, however, I decided to try and find a number in Schleswig-Holstein. "The name is Vollbrecht," I told the operator, "Manfred Vollbrecht." Since I had no idea where Katharina stayed when she was in Berlin, I figured her father's estate might be the next best thing.

It took several minutes before the operator came back. "I'm sorry, mein Herr, I can't find any number for the name you gave me."

"But he runs a huge estate. There must be a number."

"In that case, it may be unlisted."

"And you can't find out? This is an emergency."

"I'm sorry, mein Herr. If it's unlisted, there's nothing I can do."

So much for the easy way. In truth, it didn't surprise me that a man of that standing would have an unlisted number and I should have expected it. But I was frustrated anyway and I left the apartment in a foul mood.

The clock at St. Georg was just striking ten as I walked over to Werner's café, one of my frequent haunts. It was a small place, tucked away under the arches that carried the S-Bahn over König Strasse and on down towards the Jannowitz Brücke. Werner himself wasn't there but I knew his younger brother, Klaus, and I nodded my greeting as I sat down at a table near the counter. At that time of the morning, right in between breakfast and lunch, the place was only half full and it was better that way. The steamy atmosphere and the constant, permeating smell of sauerkraut sometimes made it difficult to breathe. I ordered eggs, black bread and yet more coffee. Then I sat back in the rickety chair and stared blankly out the front window at the diffused shapes passing in the street. I was trying to think what else I could do, what course of action I could take regarding Katharina.

The food arrived, plentiful as always, just as the lunchtime crowd was beginning to drift in with their wet faces and dripping raincoats. Then, all of a sudden, I had the idea. It wasn't much but it was better than nothing, so with my plate still untouched in front of me, I asked Stefan if I could use the phone. I assured him that Werner wouldn't mind.

I went behind the counter and dialed the office of my favourite diplomat, Nicholas Brent-Alderton. It was Sunday but I knew he often worked weekends to escape his wife. Sure enough, he was right there doing his duty for King and Country. I turned to face the wall so that neither the staff nor the customers could overhear my conversation.

"Would that be Sir Nicholas?" I asked.

When I spoke English, I still had my homegrown accent and he was able to recognize me at once. The answer was abrupt.

"What do you want? I'm busy."

"I'm in a position to do you a favour," I said.

"Your kind of favours I don't need."

"Now, now, be nice. This one's a beauty."

I heard him sigh. "All right, I'll bite. Do your worst."

"Ever heard of a lady called Katharina Vollbrecht?"

"No, should I have?"

"Yes, actually. She's a close friend of your ambassador's."

"What about her?"

"I've a strong reason to believe she's been arrested."

I sensed a distinct change in his tonality. "All right, let's take it from the top. How do you know she's a friend of the ambassador's?"

"Remember the last time I was with you?"

"How could I forget?"

"Well, when I left, they were talking together in the lobby. It seemed to me like they were friends."

"And how do you know she's been arrested?"

"I don't. But like I said, I have good reason to believe it."

"I see," he said with what passed for sarcasm. "Un-named sources, I suppose."

"Something like that." I didn't feel like getting into the details of our rendezvous. Not with him.

"And do these sources also happen to tell you who she's been arrested by?"

"Yes... the SS."

That brought him to a halt. There was utter silence for several seconds, so I just continued: "I'll tell you something else too. She's on first name terms with Ribbentrop."

"Is that right? Some sort of whore, is she?"

The word in connection with Katharina offended me deeply. "You've got a mind like a stinking sewer," I told him, except I said it in gutter German and he didn't quite grasp it.

"Was that another insult?" he asked me.

"Now what reason could I possibly have for insulting you?"

He wasn't sure how to respond so he reverted to his usual condescension. "You think you're so damn funny. Well, listen here, sonny boy, I haven't got all day. What's the great favour?"

"I just gave it to you."

"You did? I'm sorry, maybe I fell asleep while you were talking. I think I missed it."

"Of course you missed it. You work for the British Foreign Office." That was below the belt, tarnishing him with the political stupidity of his own government, but I didn't care.

"Schaeffer, if I've told you once…"

"Look Mister Brent-hyphen-Alderton, if you're too thick to see a blindingly obvious career move when it comes your way, then I'm sorry for you."

I finished with the implication that I was just about to hang up but I waited a moment. He'd backed himself into a corner and I knew he'd have to come crawling out.

"All right," he agreed, "just say what you've got to say and get off the phone."

I smiled to myself and decided to make the most of it. "Fine," I replied amiably. "Here's what I suggest. Call one of your Nazi friends over at Ribbentrop's office and tell him what happened. Let him know the lady is a personal friend of the minister and that he can do himself a good turn if he finds out what's happened to her. I would propose starting the search at Prinz Albrecht Strasse with a man called Graf. If he does manage to find out anything, it'll make him look good. Then he can tell you, so you can pass it on to your boss, the ambassador, which will make *you* look good. Finally, you can pass it back to *me* in order to return the original favour. Got all that or should I repeat it?"

He didn't answer right away but I knew I had him hooked when he said: "What was her name again?"

After a couple more minutes, I put the phone down, finished eating and promptly left. I had some invoicing to take care of as well as some bills to pay that couldn't be delayed any longer so I thought I may as well get on with it. The place was already packed and I had to sidle my way out past a couple of off-duty SS men who were waiting for a table. They appeared to be in good spirits but, then again, there was no reason for them not to be. The whole world seemed to be going their way.

* * *

That night I found the mouse in my bedroom again. I don't know if it was the same one or different but it was there under the wardrobe, its eyes shining and its pink nose twitching. To my mind, it bore a remarkable resemblance to Joseph Goebbels, known within Nazi circles as "The little Doktor," so I'd taken to calling it Doc. I explained this once to Asher Feldstein and I thought he was going to fall over laughing. Before I knew it, the story was all over Scheunenviertel and I half expected the brown-shirts to come calling one night to fumigate both the mouse and me.

But what nobody knew was that I actually talked to the damn thing and I recall that, on that particular night, the conversation consisted of a question-and-answer period in which I tried to examine every facet of my life and all the nuances that made up the subtle shades of my character. I believe the whole dialogue took less than ten minutes as I finished my cigar and got undressed.

Sadly, I came to the conclusion that I was a relic and a misfit. I was also a shallow, one-dimensional, superficial pretender with the gall to imagine that some kind of romantic liaison might possibly exist between myself and a ghost of a woman who, for all I knew, had left to go cavorting with some wealthy baron on a sun-drenched island in the Aegean. Whether the mouse concurred with this assessment, I never found out. As usual, it vanished midway through my discourse.

Then a short time before midnight, I was woken from a disturbed sleep by my dear friend Brent-Alderton who called to say that he had some information already but he didn't want to talk about it over the phone. Since he was scheduled to go down to Munich the following morning, the only time he'd be able to see me would be at the Anhalter Bahnhof, the central rail terminus, at eight sharp. It was either that or wait a week so, of course, I said I'd be there.

"That's more like it," I said as I hung up. But then I realized that if I wasn't talking to the mouse, I was talking to myself and that was even more dangerous.

* * *

I got up early and took the packed U-Bahn across town, surfacing just outside the giant, yellow-brick façade on the Askanischerplatz. The rain had more or less exhausted itself, leaving a high, uniform cloud cover that only served to lock in the damp. I bought a paper in case Brent-Alderton was late and eased my way through the morning crowds to the concourse.

Like any great terminus, the Anhalter was an exercise in organized chaos. Billed grandly as the *"Tor zum Süden"* (Gateway to the South), it presented the traveler with a mind-bending series of signs that pointed the way to ticket halls, baggage services, platforms, cafeterias, bookstalls and public toilets. Adding to the confusion was the echoing noise and the putrid, belching smoke from upwards of a dozen heavy locomotives. In its favour, however, was the fact that with trains arriving daily from all over Europe, it was just about the most cosmopolitan place in all of Berlin. On many occasions I had prior knowledge as to when certain dignitaries would be arriving or leaving and I could often get a good quote as they passed by me on their way through.

The designated meeting point was a small refreshments stall near the east entrance, so I bought a coffee and read the paper until Brent-Alderton decided to show up.

"I don't have long," he said. It was his version of a greeting.

"You want a coffee? My treat."

He looked over at the stall, his expression disdainful. "From here? What are you trying to do, poison me?"

I shrugged. "What takes you to Bavaria?"

He looked at me, as if trying to work out whether I deserved a reply. Then he gave in. "Martyr's Day," he said with some distaste.

"His Majesty's government has decided it comes under the heading of culture."

"Sorry to hear that," I replied. "You have my sympathy."

Each year in Munich, Hitler liked to celebrate the anniversary of the failed 1923 putsch when he and his Nazi marchers tried to take over the Bavarian government. But the local state police opened fire, thirteen of the marchers died and Hitler had used their "martyrdom" ever since as a rallying cry. He also expected the foreign missions to pay homage and, for some reason, Brent-Alderton had become the British Embassy's designated representative.

"Not taking your wife?" I taunted.

He looked at me sideways. It wasn't necessary for him to say anything. He knew I'd seen him hanging around with one of the embassy's debutantes. They were infamous for getting drunk at every party and the booze inevitably made them a lot more raunchy than English young ladies of good pedigree were ever meant to be.

"Well, I hope the weather's good for you," I said, but I couldn't help adding: "Not that it'll matter much in a hotel room."

He glared at me, outraged that I could make such a comment. Against the school code, I suppose. I don't know why I enjoyed riling him so much. It just happened.

"Look here, buddy boy," he said, poking me in the chest with his stubby finger. "At least I get some semblance of respect around here."

"You do? Who from?"

"From the people who matter."

"To me, the people who matter are the editors who buy my stuff, nobody else."

"Oh, do me a favour. You know it strikes me you've actually convinced yourself that you're some kind of legitimate journalist. You're a joke, my lad, nothing more."

"So how come I manage to sell so much?"

"How come? Because it's cheap, that's all. Cheap rubbish. Gossip. Belly-filler for the masses."

"Sure, Brent, sure. And I'm asked to believe that your little junket down to Munich with some embassy floozy is furthering diplomatic relations."

He didn't answer. A man had jostled him in the back and we both suddenly realized how loud we'd been talking. You couldn't be too careful, even when speaking English.

"Look," he said in a much softer tone, "I don't much like you and you don't much like me, and the only reason we're standing here is because I'm a man of honour no matter who I'm dealing with. So I'll return the favour I owe you, then I'll go catch my train. And if I never see you again, it'll be too soon. Have you got that?"

"First intelligent thing you've ever said."

"You want this or don't you?"

"Absolutely. Shoot."

He took a long breath. "All right, so the young lady you were asking about... Vollbrecht... You'll be pleased to hear you were right on both counts. Yes, she's a friend of the ambassador and yes, she's being detained by the SS."

"On what charge?"

"Nobody's quite sure. But... and this is only a rumour, you understand..."

"Okay."

"They say that whatever it is comes straight from the top."

"Who, Himmler?"

"It's only a rumour."

"And?"

He looked at his watch. "And it's been a pleasure as always."

"You mean that's it?"

"What more do you want?"

I didn't know what to answer and he turned to leave.

"Wait a minute," I called after him. "Is anything being done?"

He turned to look at me. "About what?"

"About getting her out?"

He smiled his evil little smile. "I see. Not entirely business, then? A little bit of personal involvement on the side? And you've got the nerve to talk about *me*. You really are a piece of work, you know that?"

With that he walked away, leaving me there like a wounded animal that wasn't even worth finishing off.

I loathed him and his boring career but I was starting to loathe myself even more. A woman I hardly knew was starting to make me feel concerned and protective towards her. Worse than that, I knew how idiotic it was. I'd done what I wanted to do. I'd discovered that she had indeed been arrested by the SS - or, to be more accurate, that she'd been "detained" - and after my own experience at Prinz Albrecht Strasse, that should have settled the matter right there. I should have just turned around and walked the other way.

But my head just couldn't seem to let it go. I was being drawn along by some strange mix of journalistic curiosity, mad infatuation and sheer bloody obstinacy, as Brent-Alderton might have said. It was ludicrous. Did I actually think I could save her from the SS? Did I think she'd be so grateful that she'd collapse into my arms and be mine forever? We hadn't yet spent one full evening together, not even one full hour. How much more presumptuous could anyone be?

13

As I left the station, I looked at the clearing sky and decided on the therapy of a long walk. Instead of taking the U-Bahn, I therefore set off at an easy pace towards the Potsdamerplatz via the peaceful expanse of the Tiergarten, Berlin's great central breathing space.

It was Monday morning and the rest of the world was back to work, so I just about had the place to myself. On each side were dark columns of trees and, beyond, the soaked brown mass of shrubbery. But I wasn't really focusing on the scenery. My head was too full of my own affairs.

If it was true that she'd been detained, then the next question would have to be: why? She couldn't be a common criminal, otherwise they'd have sent a regular police officer. Then someone's political enemy, perhaps. Had she or her father offended someone of importance? Ribbentrop, for example? It was all speculation because sometimes the SS needed no reason at all, except their own arcane calculations. Nonetheless, my mind was desperately trying work it all out and, the more I thought about it, the wilder my projections became.

Without even realizing it, I'd ventured down past the large lake and was considering a detour through the zoo but I didn't get that far. As I arrived at the Tiergarten Ufer, I turned a corner and bumped into my old friend, Traudl Lohse, who was just standing there, casually as you like, lighting a cigarette. It was ages since I'd seen her. She was a well-built, middle-aged woman with uneven, bleached hair and gray-green eyes that were either bright or soulful depending on the moment. Her name was constantly changing to the extent that even she had to think carefully which alias she was using at any given moment - but I knew her from the old days as Traudl and, to all of us who'd been crazy once upon a time, she was something special.

"Hello Traudl," I said quietly.

She turned, surprised. "Edmund?" she said, squinting through the smoke. She was the only one who ever called me that. "Edmund! My God, it *is* you!"

She rushed forward and threw her arms around me. Even through her raincoat, I could still feel the crush of that enormous chest and it took me instantly back to that New Year's Eve party at Cameron's when, as midnight struck, she leaned topless towards every male in the room so we could each lick whipped cream from those magnificent, bulbous breasts. In those days, she'd been the total party animal and, whether it was a few drinks or a full Roman orgy, you could always count on Traudl being front and centre. No evening was ever quite complete without her own intoxicated version of the "Dance of the Seven Veils." But sadly, as with everyone and everything, the passage of time had left her the worse for wear and, these days, she looked her age, especially on a damp Monday morning in Berlin.

"Stunning as ever," I lied, as she finally pulled herself away from me.

"Thank you, Edmund," she said with just a glint of that old fun smile. "You always were such a snake-charmer. Where've you been hiding yourself? How come I don't see you around any more? Did you become a monk or what?"

"I work for a living, Traudl. You should know that."

"So? What kind of excuse is that? Come on, we'll walk. It's too cold just to stand around." She put her arm in mine and led me off in the direction of Friedrichstrasse. The zoo would have to wait until next time. "Tell me all the news, Edmund. I don't get to see too many of the old crowd any more."

"That's because most of the old crowd have already left."

"Sven… Whatever happened to Sven?"

"Last I heard he was back in Stockholm."

"Why, for God's sake? Sweden is such a boring place, like Christmas without the lights. Edmund, you remember that night we all went swimming out near what's-his-name's place? You know, the one with all the money."

"Siegfried."

"Siegfried! That's right! You remember that night, Edmund? That was the night Sven got that little girl Anna pregnant, you remember? Right there in the bushes. We watched. We were witnesses. Whatever happened to little Anna? Did she go to Sweden too?"

"I don't know. I didn't really keep in touch."

"I wonder if she's happy."

"I wonder if any of us are happy," I replied.

She glanced at me and I could see the dark hollows in her eyes. But she was trying hard to be the old Traudl and she smiled again quickly.

"And Ulrich?" she asked. "I haven't seen him around either. Such a handsome boy. What happened to Ulrich?"

"Joined the brown-shirts."

"What, Ulrich? My beautiful Ulrich? Impossible."

"No, it's not. I saw him at the birthday parade. He was leading a large troop."

She was shaking her head as if to say "what a waste" but the words didn't emerge. Instead she just sighed. "What's happening, Edmund? Where are we going?"

"Towards Friedrichstrasse, I think."

She tugged at my arm and laughed. It was good to hear. Then she fell silent and stared straight ahead as we walked. "You know... I recall seeing the Kaiser one time. At the Heidelberg festival. Did you ever go there?"

"Sure."

"I was just a child but there were flags and trumpets and the people stood in line for hours just to catch a glimpse as he rode by in that big carriage. You know, somehow, all those people... they were happy. Today we have flags and trumpets and... I don't know… It's like they're part of a funeral, a huge state funeral. You understand, Edmund? Why is that? Why did people cheer back then?"

"People cheer today too."

"But not in the same way. Back then they cheered and sang, today they just chant slogans. It's not the same."

I let her talk like that for a while. It was as if she hadn't spoken to anyone in a long time. Poor Traudl, I thought. Poor, lonely Traudl. So that's what happens to party animals when they reach middle-age.

Eventually, she came back to life. "So, Edmund…" she declared brightly. "Are you in love?"

I looked at her. She'd always been good at prying loose my secrets. "Does it show?" I asked her.

"All over your face. So tell your Traudl… Who is she? Do I know her?"

"I don't think so."

"Does she treat you well, at least? Does she give you her body?"

You could always rely on Traudl to get to the nub of things. "I don't know her that well," I said.

"Oh, one of those."

"What do you mean, 'one of those?'"

"You know perfectly well."

"No, I don't."

She leaned over and whispered: "Middle class."

I had to laugh. "Finally!" I exclaimed. "Finally, the famous Traudl makes a mistake! I've been waiting years for this."

"She's *not* middle class? No, don't tell me she works for a living. What is she? A shop girl? A hairdresser?"

I couldn't resist answering. "No, she's not middle class and she's not working class either."

She looked at me with eyes wide. "An aristocrat? Edmund, you thief! You stole yourself a big one. That's wonderful news! My advice is to rob her blind, then drop her like a stone."

"Really? And what if it's the real thing, Traudl? What then?"

"Then, my prince, I'm sorry for you. I'll say a prayer and send flowers."

I smiled. "Didn't *you* ever think of getting married? Living with one man?"

"I've always lived with one man."

"I don't mean one at a time. I mean forever."

"Forever? I don't know what that word means."

"Do you know what commitment means? Do you know what devotion means? Do you even know what *love* means, Traudl?"

"No, I don't know what any of those things mean. Nor do you. You just *think* you do. You hope you do. What you don't understand is the price you have to pay."

"And that is?"

"Boredom, my prince, boredom."

She'd been smoking her way through that cigarette of hers. When it was finished, she threw the butt away and reached into her purse for another but the packet was empty and she cursed softly. Since I had none to offer, I couldn't help very much.

We walked on for several minutes, content just to be with each other. It was pleasant to indulge in the fading glow of our own nostalgia. Then, before I knew it, the ugliness of the present intruded without me even realizing it.

"Traudl," I said without thinking, "know anyone in the SS?"

Strangely enough, she didn't even flinch at the question. "How high up in the SS?" she replied.

"As high as you can go."

"May I ask why you're so interested in that bunch of Philistines?"

I thought about telling her, then decided against it. And then I decided I didn't care after all. "This woman..." I said.

"The princess? Don't tell me she's mixed up with an SS man. That's all you need."

"No, no, it's nothing like that. It's just that... well, I think she may be in trouble." Then I just came out with it. I told her Katharina's name, how I met her and a brief version of what happened at Horcher's. I wasn't sure how wise that was but I did it anyway. The intimacy of old friends, I suppose. When I'd finished, there was a long silence.

"So?" she said eventually. "What are you going to do, Mister Mountie? Ride in to the rescue? This isn't Canada, you know. Do that here and you end up in Dachau. Ever heard of it?"

"Yes, thank you. I've heard of it."

"So what else do you need to know? You want my advice?" She glanced around as if we might somehow be overheard. It was a habit many Berliners had developed but we were out here amidst the greenery with no one around. "My advice is just leave it alone," she whispered. "Go find somebody else. No woman is worth the grief."

"I wish I could just leave it alone."

"You've got it that bad? Oh, my dear prince."

"I need to get hold of someone near the top so I can find out what's going on."

She nodded and I thought she was considering it but then she seemed to change the subject completely. "Do you have any money, Edmund?"

It threw me for the moment. "No, not much. Why? You need some?"

She nodded.

"How much?" I asked.

"Five hundred marks."

"That's a lot of spare change. May I ask what you need it for?"

"You don't have a cigarette?"

"No, sorry."

"Look, I can't tell you what it's for, Edmund. Do you have the money or not?"

I felt awkward so I decided to tell her the truth. I don't know why. "I've got just under seven hundred in the bank. If you like, I could…"

She interrupted me. "That's all you've got in the world, isn't it?"

Again, the truth. "Yes," I said simply.

She smiled but it was with a good deal of sadness, perhaps

even resignation. Then she said: "I had it in mind to sell you the information. But I couldn't do that to you."

"Information?"

"Try the old man," she said.

"What old man?"

"Her father."

"You know her father?"

"Sure I know him."

Of course, I might have guessed. A paying customer. How else would someone like Traudl survive? "Where can I find him, do you know?"

"Up north somewhere, on his fancy estate. That's where he usually is. Only comes into town to see me, about all he can manage… and even then he can't do much, if you know what I mean. But I let him think he can."

"I tried calling the estate but I couldn't get through."

"Then try the SS."

"The SS? Her father's in the SS?" I could feel my forehead creasing.

"Just about."

"What does that mean?"

"He's one of those people… what are they called? "

"I don't know who you're talking about."

"Friends," she said, finally remembering. "They call themselves 'Friends of the SS' but they're just a bunch of rich old men who like to dress up in black uniforms and pretend to be good little Nazis. Too much time on their hands, if you ask me. You must have heard of them."

"Yes, I've heard of them. You're telling me he's one of them?"

"Not just one of them, Edmund. He runs the damn thing."

"Really? You sure about that?"

"Edmund, he's a client of mine. Of course I'm sure." She looked at me, then looked away, as if she had all the secrets of the world wrapped up inside her head.

"Let me give you the money," I said.

"No, Edmund."

"A few hundred. What's a few hundred? Think of it as a loan. You pay me back when you can."

She gave me a soft tap on the arm. "Edmund, a lesson. Never give money to a woman. Or to a man for that matter. Never give money to anyone, Edmund. That's my advice. Take but never give. It's the only rule in life."

We walked on, finally leaving the park near the Brandenburg Gate. "I have to leave you here," she said. "Look after yourself, my prince." Then she gave me a sentimental kiss on the cheek, let go of my arm and hurried away, dashing over to buy some cigarettes from a booth while I headed east towards the U-Bahn at Friedrichstrasse.

I was just about to descend into the station when I happened to glance across the street and saw her being helped into a car by a tall man in a leather coat. I could have been mistaken but it all seemed very official to me. Was Traudl being arrested too, just like Katharina? Both of them right after talking to me? What was going on? I didn't know what to do, whether to chase after them and make a fool of myself or just stand there like a zombie and watch.

In the end, I just stood there, not through any decision-making process but through simple inertia. If you must know, I felt like garbage. Both Katharina and Traudl had been taken right in front of me and I'd done nothing. What the hell was wrong with me? And why were my female friends becoming such targets?

* * *

I was considerably shaken up, so instead of continuing down to the U-Bahn, I walked a block to Guiseppe's Italian bar and sat down with a coffee to try and steady my nerves.

I knew that what I should really do was call the operator and ask for the number of the "Friends of the SS" but I have to admit that, after my visit to Prinz Albrecht Strasse the other night, I wasn't exactly looking forward to a repeat of that experience anytime soon. I sat there for some time, staring vacantly at the customers, at the waiters and at the framed scenes of Italy around the walls.

The one nearest to me happened to portray a Florentine equestrian statue - and it suddenly gave me a whole other idea. I got up and went over to the phone.

"Horse Breeders' Association," said the female voice.

"Yes, I wonder if you can help me..."

"I'm sorry but there's nobody here right now. I'm just the telephonist."

"Ah well, actually, I'm looking for the number of one of your members... Herr Manfred Vollbrecht."

"I'm not authorized to give out information. I just take messages."

"Oh, I see. Well, who would you suggest I speak to?"

"The person you want is Herr Gessendorfer but he's not here."

"Do you know when he'll be back?"

"He has appointments all afternoon."

I decided some charm might be appropriate under the circumstances and began by addressing her as *gnädige Frau*, an old-fashioned form of address. "If I might be allowed to explain," I said. "You see, I've just arrived from Canada and the matter is very urgent. I'd be very grateful for any help you can give me."

"Urgent, you say?"

"Yes, very urgent."

"Well, I'm not supposed to tell you this... but Herr Gessendorfer usually takes his lunch at the Café Bauer. He might just be there now if you can catch him."

I knew the Café Bauer. It wasn't too far from Guiseppe's. If I walked quickly I could be there in ten minutes. "That's very helpful, thank you so much."

"Canada, you said?"

"Yes, that's right."

"You know, I always wanted to travel but my husband, well, it's difficult what with one thing and another..."

"I understand. Perhaps one day. Thank you again."

A little rude, perhaps, but I was anxious to be on my way. I put the phone down, paid Guiseppe for the call and was out of there.

The great detective was back on the case.

* * *

The Café Bauer had never been one of my favourite places. The smell was worse than Werner's, the sausage they served was full of gristle and the coffee was nothing but flavoured water.

As I entered through the revolving door, I almost bumped into a waitress who was laden down with platters of steaming food. Flanks of fatty beef, boiled potatoes and black bread, as well as the ubiquitous sauerkraut. "Sorry," I said politely. "Do you happen to know a Herr Gessendorfer by any chance?"

She didn't even look at me. "Back wall, last table," she muttered and then went on her way.

I looked over in that direction and could just about make out a plump, balding man dining alone. I threaded my way across to him.

"Herr Gessendorfer?"

He was in the middle of his meal and, as he looked up at me, his flabby jowls went on chewing like a perpetual motion machine. Then he speared a potato and dipped it in horseradish sauce before loading that too into his face. "That's me," he said flatly in response to my inquiry. His upper lip was perspiring as he ate.

"My name's Schaeffer. I wonder if I might disturb you for just a moment."

"You already have," he replied, his mouth still full.

"May I sit down?"

He shrugged. Then he put his knife and fork down so he could tear off a piece of bread which he also put in his mouth, while I took the chair directly opposite.

"I'm trying to contact one of your members," I told him. "Herr Manfred Vollbrecht. Do you know him?"

"I'm on my lunch break."

"Yes, I appreciate that. But I'm not in the city for very long…"

"What do you want to see him about?"

"Some private family business. It's urgent... Do you know how I might contact him?"

I sat waiting while he dug into his beef, splashing the already stained tablecloth with gravy. The waitress came over and asked me if I wanted anything but I declined. Then I looked back at Gessendorfer to let him know that I was still waiting for a response.

At last, he condescended to speak. "You're too late," he said. "He had a heart attack."

"A heart attack? When was this?"

"Last night."

"Is he dead?"

"He may be by now."

I didn't know what to think or what to say. "Can you give me his phone number?" I asked. "So I can find out for sure."

"I can but it's in the office."

"Well, may I call you there this afternoon?"

"No, I have appointments."

I breathed a sigh. The man was a natural bureaucrat. "In that case," I said, "perhaps you'd be good enough to leave the number with your telephonist and I'll get it from her?"

He considered the request but then seemed to conclude that he didn't care much one way or another. "If you like," he said.

And that was that. There was nothing left to add so I thanked him and left.

He wasn't exactly the nicest individual I'd ever met but he was as good as his word and, when I called through promptly at three, it was ready and waiting for me - the private, unlisted number of the Vollbrecht estate in Schleswig-Holstein. I dialed immediately but the man I spoke to couldn't tell me much, except that yes, Herr Vollbrecht was alive but still on the danger list. No, he couldn't give me any more details. Yes, he could take a message. No, he couldn't assure me that Herr Vollbrecht would receive it. That would depend on his condition which, in turn, would depend on the doctors.

I put the phone down in frustration. I had more questions than answers and I tried to list them in my head. Why had Katharina been detained? Where had she been taken? Did she know about her father? Did *he* know about *her*? Was that why he'd had the heart attack? Somebody, somewhere, knew what the whole game was about but I was totally lost.

My head was once again full of theories but what good were theories? I thought I'd come to a standstill, with no other place left to turn, but that wasn't quite true. There was a whole other avenue to explore and it concerned my friend Traudl. She'd also been taken away in an official car. And that led to a whole other series of questions. Was it just an accident that I'd bumped into her like that in the Tiergarten? After all those years? And how come she just happened to possess the exact information I needed? Was that just coincidence too? In fact, she even admitted that she'd been ready to sell it to me. So if it wasn't an accident, she must have been waiting for me - which meant our meeting was a set-up and that Traudl was in on it too.

Was I crazy to think that way? Was I becoming paranoid? I had to know.

Despite my better judgment, I decided to push further. Although I had work to finish, I decided to ignore it all. I needed to put my livelihood on hold and take this thing as far as I could.

* * *

"Wachter residence," said an elderly voice.

"Yes, I'd like to speak to Siegfried if I may."

"I'm sorry, Herr Wachter is unavailable. Who shall I say called?"

"Go tell him it's Ed."

"Ed?"

"Yes, Ed. Go tell him that if he doesn't come to the phone, I'll start charging him interest on the twenty he still owes me."

"I'm sorry, mein Herr, but…"

"Just go tell him, all right?"

There was a sigh of injustice on the other end but he did as he was told. A minute later I heard a familiar giggle that I recognized from times past.

"Eddie, my dear boy, I thought you'd long since passed away."

"I'm working on it," I replied.

"Where in God's name are you calling from?"

"Berlin, where else?"

"Where else indeed? And to what do I owe this pleasure? I don't hear from you for ages and, suddenly, from out of nowhere, here you are. Next thing I know, you'll be presuming we're still friends."

"I need to see you, Sieg."

The urgency in my voice was unmistakable and he changed his tone.

"Are you in trouble?"

"No, but someone I know might be."

"Well, I'm expecting guests… But all right, come on over, as long as you promise not to annoy them."

"I don't even want to meet them."

"That's even better."

"I mean it, Sieg. What I really need is to talk to you alone."

"No problem, dear boy. I have cognac, I have cigars… If you need to talk, we'll talk."

"Must be nice to have money."

"Yes, it is, very nice. And as you well know, I try to enjoy it as much as I can. When will you arrive?"

"I'll catch the first train tomorrow. You can send Jeeves to pick me up at the station."

"He'll be there."

Needless to say, his valet wasn't really called Jeeves but Siegfried was such a Wodehouse type of character that it was just too easy to make fun. Besides, he was also a self-confessed anglophile. Loved everything to do with England and the English. Wore suits from Saville Row, had specialty foods sent over from Fortnum's and he even rode around in a Bentley.

"Siegfried?"

"Yes?"

"How's everything with you?"

"Oh, you know me."

"That's why I'm asking."

"It's all in the wrist, dear boy, all in the wrist."

I smiled. I hadn't heard that in years. "I'll see you tomorrow," I said. "Do I need to dress up to smoke your cigars?"

"Absolutely. We must safeguard civilization at all costs."

"I'll do my best," I said and hung up. The tension which had been building inside me all day was finally beginning to ease a little. It had been good just to speak to him.

14

It was only a hundred and forty kilometres but it took forever, the train stopping at every two-bit village along the way.

My destination was Magdeburg, famous for the early scientific experiment in which they hitched teams of horses to a pair of giant, vacuum-locked hemispheres just to try and pull them apart. When I was in seventh grade, I had to draw the scene as part of my year-end exam. The drawing was immaculate but it took three-quarters of the exam time and I got a low mark. It wasn't that I didn't try hard at school. It's just that I always seemed to be going off in the wrong direction.

Siegfried's valet was waiting for me in the Bentley as arranged, with a long face and a scornful expression. We took an instant dislike to each other for absolutely no reason and drove the thirty or so kilometres in silence. The only thing he told me was his name, Alois, which happened to be the same as Hitler's father.

It was already mid-afternoon when I finally arrived at the residence. Set well back from the narrow country road, it was a fine stone mansion with two wings, ornate gables and a portico. There were thick vines clinging to some of the walls and the effect gave the place a sense of timelessness and peace. In fact, once the car engine had been switched off, the only sounds I could hear came from the raucous rooks who made their home at the top of the high birch trees and the quiet rushing of the River Elbe that passed close by.

I breathed in deeply. The air was as damp as it had been in Berlin but it was good to be away from the city fumes and the grating hum of traffic. I'd forgotten what the countryside was like.

Alois was obliging enough to take my overnight bag from

the car and I followed him into the house. Almost immediately, a cheerful voice greeted me and a glass of red wine was thrust into my hand.

"Rothschild," said Siegfried in his most conspiratorial voice. "Just don't tell your friends at the Chancellery we're drinking Jewish wine."

"I don't have any friends at the Chancellery."

"Then it's about time you did."

Good old Siegfried. It was refreshing to see that at least he hadn't changed much. He was a big man in every direction, a little younger than I was, with smooth skin and almost no hair on his head. His lightweight afternoon suit flattered his bulky physique and he wore a silk cravat inside his Oxford striped shirt. As impeccable as ever.

"Still trying to be Noel Coward?" I asked him. Coward was a famous wit and *bon-vivant* in British colonial society and I once heard Siegfried perform an excellent rendition of Coward's classic "Mad Dogs and Englishmen," complete with plummy, upper-class accent.

"Noel and I, we're a dying breed," he replied dryly. "But come, you haven't seen the house."

He gave me the grand tour, clearly relishing the fact that he owned such a property - all eight bedrooms, all five bathrooms, the vast kitchens, the extensive gardens, plus the converted stable that housed his three cars. I was very impressed and said so repeatedly.

We carried our glasses around with us so, by the time we got back, we were in need of a refill, which Alois brought to us in Siegfried's oak-paneled study. Outside, the sky was a mottled combination of ever-darkening grays but in here we relaxed in big chairs, lit cigars and warmed ourselves in a general glow of well-being. I never knew anyone who knew how to live better than Siegfried.

But life wasn't all easy, even for him. Without putting too fine a point on it, he was homosexual and, according to the Alice-in-Wonderland world of the Third Reich, that was as bad as being handicapped. Many had already been rounded up and it was only due to Siegfried's money and, more importantly, to his connections that he'd continued to prosper. His personal fortune came from trading commodities - and a newly armed Germany very much needed commodities. Nevertheless, in the past he'd made no secret of his tendencies and his life since the Nazis came to power had been one long balancing act.

"So, my dear Ed," he said, lifting his wine to check the colour. "I gather you came to see me about Traudl."

"Good guess," I replied. "May I ask how you knew?"

"Because no sooner had I put the phone down yesterday than she called me herself."

"What did she tell you?"

"She simply told me you'd be calling and I replied that you already had."

"Did she tell you what it was about?"

"I'd prefer to hear it from you."

"Are you sure you want to get involved?"

"No... but you're here, which means I'm already involved."

I glanced over at him, feeling just a little guilty. "I didn't know she was going to call you," I said quietly. "My idea was to approach it a little more carefully. To give you the choice of helping. I didn't intend to plunge you into it all like this. I know you've got your own problems."

"Thank you, apology accepted. Now let's get on with it, shall we? My guests will be arriving in an hour."

I did my best to give him the whole story, a much more comprehensive version than the one I told Traudl, starting with Katharina at the Kroll Opera House and going right through to Traudl herself being picked up on Friedrichstrasse.

"Was it the SS who picked her up?" he asked me.

"Who, Traudl? I don't know. It might well have been. Why, you think there's a connection?"

"A connection?" He laughed. "My dear boy, you run all over town like a good little journalist but when it comes down to it, you know absolutely nothing."

"Thanks for the insult. Can you answer my question?"

"Eddie, our friend Traudl *works* for the SS."

"Yes, I know. She told me. She said Vollbrecht was her client and that he runs the 'Friends of the SS' organization."

"I don't mean *that* kind of work. I mean, she's an informant."

I don't know why that should have surprised me but it did. Many people were obliged to do the same thing all over Germany. They were either paid or threatened but, either way, they gathered and gave information just to survive. It had become a way of life.

"She actually told you that?" I asked him.

"She didn't have to. I already knew."

"You did? How?"

"The same way I know a lot of things."

Another of his non-answers. I just looked at him but there was nothing more forthcoming. He was difficult to read, my friend Siegfried: or, as Traudl herself once said, an onion with many layers.

"So what *did* she tell you?" I asked him.

"What she told me was that it wasn't exactly an accident her bumping into you like that."

"Damn, I knew it."

"Her instructions were to tell you about Manfred Vollbrecht, no more, no less. After that, you were supposed to take the hint and call him."

"I tried but he had a heart attack."

"Yes, I know. That was the problem. That's where their plan fell apart."

"What plan?"

"Whatever plan they had in mind."

"Siegfried, you're talking in riddles."

"Am I? Then let me make myself perfectly clear. If Vollbrecht's involved, you can be certain that whatever's going on comes right from the top."

"So what are you saying? You think I should just leave it alone?"

"No, on the contrary. I don't think you *can* leave it alone. You don't have that choice."

"I don't? What if I choose not to play their silly games?"

"Ed, please. This is the SS we're talking about. They're not in the habit of playing games, silly or otherwise."

"All right, all right... Warning duly noted. So what's going on? What's it all about? Once and for all, do you know or don't you?"

He drank some more of his wine. "Should we light a fire in here?" he said. "It's a little chilly, don't you think?"

"Sieg, this is important."

"Everything's important, Ed. It just depends how you choose to assign your priorities."

I shook my head in frustration. "I don't need philosophy, Siegfried. I just need answers."

"Answers? What answers? You have all the answers you need. You want me to spell them out?"

"Yes, absolutely. I'm the dumbest guy in the world and I want you to spell them out. Please, go ahead."

"Fine," he replied, totally ignoring my aggrieved cynicism. "Let's list them in order, shall we? First, the SS are behind all this, can we agree on that?"

"I believe we can."

"Good. Second, they're trying to lead you in a certain direction, which you're expected to follow, right?"

"If you say so."

"I do. And third, they want you to contact Manfred Vollbrecht. You see? It's not that difficult."

I gave a long sigh. "But what's the point of it all? That's what I *don't* know. And why all the subterfuge? If they want me to contact him, why don't they just pick me up like they do everybody else and dump me on his doorstep?"

"All good questions, dear boy, but you're asking the wrong person."

"So who do you suggest?"

"Manfred Vollbrecht."

We were going around in circles and I have to say it was annoying as hell. I had to force myself to calm down. "I already told you," I said in a slow, controlled voice, "I can't reach him. He had a heart attack."

"Of course you can reach him," he replied cheerfully. "Just say the word."

"You?"

"Do you see anyone else in the room?"

"How?"

He didn't answer. He just gave me that smug smile, as if to say that with money you can do anything. Another flash of the old arrogance - but I held my tongue. And then, lo and behold, against all expectations, he came right out and said what he was thinking. Maybe I'd known it all along and didn't want to admit it but, whatever the reason, when he actually uttered the words, it hit me like a thunderbolt.

"I hope you realize, Ed, that the lady herself might not be so innocent in all this."

"Excuse me?"

"Don't tell me it didn't occur to you."

"Katharina? No... that's impossible."

"Really? Why is it impossible? Strikes me you don't even know she was truly detained."

"Sure I do, I heard it from the British Embassy for heaven's sake. Brent-Alderton, remember?"

"Yes, so you said. But, as we both know, that's no guarantee of anything."

He was right, of course, and I just stared at him. I didn't know whether to laugh, or cry, or scream out loud. Had I really fallen for the oldest trick in the book? Had I really become enamoured with the woman sent to entrap me? I couldn't believe it. I didn't know how or why she would even do such a thing, yet there it was. If Traudl worked for the SS, then so could Katharina. Especially considering her father. The stark possibility was staring me right in the face.

"What you're really trying to tell me," I said eventually, "is that I should have known. I should have realized a woman like that could never really be interested in someone like me."

"Now don't start feeling victimized, dear boy. That's not going to help at all."

I drained the wine in one gulp. Very disrespectful to a fine vintage but I didn't care. "So... you really think I've got no choice but to go and see Vollbrecht?" I asked him.

"No, I don't think you do."

He offered me an expression of sympathy. It seemed real enough and I nodded slowly. As far as Siegfried was concerned, my course was set, entrapment or not. Everything was pointing in the same direction: good ol' Ed, just a dumb pawn in some twisted SS plot.

But there was still something else rattling around in my head.

"Did she ask you for money?" I said to him.

"Who?"

"Traudl... when she called."

"Yes, as a matter of fact."

"Five hundred marks?"

"That's right."

"Did you give it to her?"

"Yes."

"And may I ask why?"

"Why I gave it to her?"

"No, why she needed it."

"It's... not relevant."

"Okay, I understand. But tell me anyway."

He thought about it for a few moments, then appeared to relent. "You recall her sister, Gerda?"

"Sure," I said. Gerda was younger than Traudl. Of the two of them, it was always Gerda who'd been the more stable and sensible one.

"She needs an abortion," he told me.

"Oh, I see. " So that's what it was all about. "Does that mean Gerda's in the same business as Traudl?"

"Does it matter?"

"No, I guess not."

"One of the few benefits of being like me, Eddie. We have to worry about many things but pregnancy's not one of them."

He giggled in that way of his and I smiled along, just for the sake of doing so. But at least I'd managed to clear up one mystery this evening. As for the rest, it would have to wait because Siegfried was already looking at his watch.

"*Tempus fugit*," he said. "Now I really must go and get dressed."

* * *

His guests for the evening were all from his own special circle. They were a good bunch for the most part, both amusing and affluent like Siegfried himself, and for a while it was entertaining just to be with them. But then as the booze flowed and the jokes became raunchy, it all began to get a little too much for me, so after dessert I respectfully excused myself and left them to it, tramping my way upstairs with alcohol in my bloodstream, smoke in my lungs and Katharina still on my mind.

Did I mention there were cats in his house? In fact there were several of them, all different types. A sleek Siamese, a Persian, a couple of tabby siblings, a half-crazy albino and a fat marmalade the size of a badger. Siegfried doted on them but I sensed that his long-suffering valet, Alois, merely put up with them. It was a strange household, to say the least.

Before turning in, I took a long hot bath in the company of the fat one, the marmalade, who'd taken a shine to me. I enjoyed the soak but, at the same time, I was asking myself some very difficult questions. Like, for example, was Siegfried in on the whole thing too? Did he also have some kind of tacit arrangement with the SS? He was certainly leading me in the same direction so I couldn't just dismiss the notion.

The problem was that the whole thing seemed like a house of cards, just assumption built on assumption. What the hell could the

SS possibly want from me? By the time I lay my head down on the pillow, I'd made no further progress.

I was exhausted but I didn't sleep well. I was beginning to get depressed and I realized that while I'd been hyperventilating all over town, I was fine but out here in the country, my energy was dissipating and a morose case of lethargy had set in. I lay awake and wondered what the hell my life was all about. What was I was still doing in Germany? War was already raging across China and Spain. Would we be next? Was that what Hitler really wanted? Would he actually strike at Poland? Would he take his revenge on France like he talked about? Who knew? And if that were the case, why didn't I just up and leave? Why didn't I just retreat back across the Atlantic and hibernate through the winter cold? Or would the war reach out and eventually engulf the frozen north too?

Instead of a mouse, I had an overweight cat curled up on my bed but it too got bored with my rambling and, after awhile, it simply fell asleep. A bad case of nasal congestion caused it to snore and, since I didn't have the heart to throw it out, I got up, pulled on a robe I found in the closet and strolled out to the gardens. From the dining room, I could hear music and raucous laughter but out on the lawn it was cool and tranquil and I welcomed the night air. One of the problems, I knew, was that I hadn't saved enough. Traudl was right. That lousy seven hundred marks was all I had in the world and it was all too easy to look around and envy Siegfried his comfort. Easy and deceptive.

* * *

I don't know if Siegfried slept that night but he was apparently downstairs at some time close to dawn placing a call to Berlin.

"Morning, Traudl."

She was still asleep. "Who the hell…"

"It's Siegfried."

"What time is it?"

"Early. Listen, Traudl, I need you to tell me something."

"Siegfried?"

"Traudl, wake up, all right? If you can't open your eyes, then open your ears and listen. I need some information."

"What information? I don't have any information."

"Manfred Vollbrecht. Where is he?"

"Who?"

"Your client. I need to know where he is. Ed's here and I need to give him a push."

"Ed? You mean Edmund? He's there with you?"

"Yes, he's here."

"But he's not like you... is he?"

"No, no, it's nothing like that. He wants to know where Vollbrecht is. Which hospital?"

"Manfred? Manfred's not in a hospital. Who told you that?"

"So where is he?"

"He's here in Berlin."

"Where in Berlin?"

"Where he always is, at the Kaiserhof."

"You're sure about that?"

"Am I sure? Of course, I'm sure. I've got an appointment with him this afternoon."

"I thought he had a heart attack."

"He did."

"And you've still got an appointment?"

"Why wouldn't I?"

"I don't know, I just thought..."

"Men are men, Siegfried, even after a heart attack."

"Yes, well... I wouldn't know about that."

"You should try it some time. With a woman, I mean."

"I don't think so but thanks for the offer."

"You're welcome."

"What time will you be finished?"

"What?"

"With Vollbrecht."

"I don't know. My appointment's at three."

"Good, I'll send Ed there at four, all right? Is an hour enough for you?"

"Sometimes yes, sometimes no. I'm not the one who's got the problem, if you know what I mean."

"Well, let's say four anyway. Will you let him know?"

"If you like."

"Thanks, Traudl. Sorry I woke you."

"No, you're not, you don't give a damn about my beauty sleep. Wait... Siegfried?"

"Yes?"

"The money... I just wanted to say it was nice of you."

"No problem. Sweet dreams."

"It's been a long time since *my* dreams were sweet."

* * *

By the time I arrived downstairs, the previous evening's guests had all disappeared and Siegfried was alone, quietly eating breakfast and reading his paper as if he'd gone to bed early with a good book. I never quite knew how he did it. I hadn't partied at all but I felt terrible.

"Good morning," I said, trying my best to sound breezy. But it didn't work too well.

"You look like you need coffee."

"Just a couple of litres. Then I'll be fine."

"Eggs? Bacon?"

"No, thank you."

He folded up his paper and sat back in his chair as I sipped the coffee gratefully. "I have some news for you," he said quietly.

"Already? You've been busy."

"He's at the Kaiserhof."

"Who, Vollbrecht? What's he doing in Berlin?"

"Convalescing, I presume."

"At the Kaiserhof? Very nice too."

"I should say so. Even I don't stay there."

"So what now? Do I make an appointment or what?"

"Already done, dear boy. Today at four. That suit you?"

He expected me to be glad but I wasn't sure. How can you be

glad when you're knowingly walking into a trap set by the SS for reasons you can't begin to work out? And I still hadn't decided where Siegfried himself fit in.

"Thank you, Siegfried," I replied. It was as far as my gratitude would stretch.

"Well, don't thank me too soon. We may yet meet at Dachau."

"That's not funny."

"No," he agreed thoughtfully, "probably not."

I gazed across at him and, for some reason, recollections of my late night conversation with his cat came creeping back. "Siegfried, what are you still doing here?"

"What, in Magdeburg?"

"No, in Germany. You don't need to be here, your business is international. You could live anywhere."

"In theory, I suppose. Where would you suggest?"

"How about England? You seem to like it well enough."

His mouth was full of toast so he just shook his head until he was ready to speak. "Can't take the weather," he said.

"It's no worse than here."

"No, but it feels like it is."

"Okay, so somewhere warmer. How about Greece?"

"Hate the food."

"Switzerland then. Zurich. The weather and food are just like here. You could open your own bank."

"And pay myself interest? What a creative idea." He smiled at his own humour. But he still hadn't answered my question and nor did he have any intention of doing so. "You know what I've been thinking, Eddie?"

"What's that?"

"I've been sitting here thinking that you really do seem to have gone head over heels for this Vollbrecht woman. At first, I didn't believe it but now... I can see now that it might just be true."

"Is that so? And I suppose you're going to give me the same advice as Traudl."

"What advice is that?"

"Steal her money and run."

"No, I'd never tell you a thing like that."

"So what *would* you tell me?"

A smile but, this time, far more genuine. "Hard as it may be for you to believe, Ed, I take the business of emotion very seriously. What I think is that you should follow your heart."

"Follow my heart?" It was a strange expression coming from him and I smiled. I couldn't help it. "Bit of a cliché, Siegfried."

"Perhaps, dear boy. But clichés are only clichés because they're true."

"And if I do follow my heart, what then? Weren't you the one to suggest that Katharina might be part of the trap? What if following my heart kills me in the process?"

"So what if it does? What nobler cause can we die for?"

"Thanks a lot."

"All right, so why not look on the bright side? Remember what Nietzsche said... 'What doesn't kill me only makes me stronger.'"

"Which means?"

"Which means, dear boy, you're going to see Herr Vollbrecht this afternoon at four whether you want to or not. And no matter what you tell yourself, it won't be the SS making you do it. It'll be your own emotions."

I thought about it but I was hardly in a position to argue. He was right once again and we both knew it. Whatever I was walking into, I was doing it of my own volition. Then a disconcerting thought flashed through my mind: "Didn't Nietzsche end up in an asylum?" I asked him.

15

Siegfried was not only right about me, he was also right about Katharina. I just didn't know it yet. So that same morning, while I was on my way to save her from the vile clutches of Heinrich Himmler, the lady herself was being welcomed very graciously into the man's own office.

It seems that after she left me at Horcher's, she was escorted north to the estate in Schleswig-Holstein where she stayed with her father until his sudden heart attack. At that point, all plans were put on hold as the medical necessities took over. The local doctors responded well enough to the emergency but, as soon as her father was able to travel, she arranged his transfer to Berlin so he could rest up at the Kaiserhof under the personal care of his own specialist, one of the top men in all Europe. By the time Katharina arrived at Prinz Albrecht Strasse that morning, her father was well on the way to recovery.

"Fräulein!" said Himmler, greeting her as if she were part of his own family. "I was pleased to hear about your father. His resilience is a lesson to us all."

"Thank you, Reichsführer. He sends his greetings."

"Please sit down. Some coffee? Herbal tea, perhaps? I have a very fine blend."

"No, thank you."

"I appreciate your coming over. I wouldn't trouble you at such a time, except…" He didn't finish the sentence, he just gave that busy man's shrug, as if to explain the pressure of events.

"That's all right, Reichsführer. Now that my father's more alert, he's anxious to be of service."

Himmler got up from his chair and walked over to the window, his hands behind him. For a long time, he just stood looking out as Katharina waited. It was an unpleasant silence but she was determined to be as restrained as possible. The more she knew about this little game of his, the more she disliked it. She'd only become involved in the first place because of her father's insistent urging. It was important for the family, he'd told her. It was important for Uncle Erwin.

Himmler, meanwhile, was cleaning his spectacles with his pocket handkerchief. When he was done, he turned back to face her. "You know," he said, "sometimes we're faced with difficult challenges. Sometimes, for the general good, we're forced into doing things that, personally, we might otherwise shy away from. Your initial reluctance to take on this task was a good example and, believe me, I understand your hesitation. You're a very attractive young lady... full of the promise of tomorrow... You really shouldn't be mixed up in all this."

Katharina listened to all this with some distaste. She knew perfectly well that Himmler's view of women was identical to Hitler's - that they should be at home, breeding blond children for the thousand year Reich. But she didn't say anything.

"I wish I could avoid it," Himmler was saying. "I wish I could find another way but the simple truth is that I can't. Our task hasn't changed and I must ask you if you'll allow it to continue."

Katharina noted the word "our," as if she had some kind of ownership in all this. "My father has already said that he's ready and willing."

"Yes, Fräulein, but this much I know about him... You're his entire world and he'll only do it if you're in complete agreement."

She smiled politely. "With the greatest respect, Reichsführer," she said, "I find it difficult to believe that the mighty SS so desperately needs the services of a female art dealer and a sick old man to further its cause."

Himmler managed to resist chiding her sarcasm. "When duty calls," he replied, "it calls on everybody, the young and the old, the sick and the healthy alike."

"I appreciate that. But just for the sake of argument, what would happen if I *refused* to allow it?"

Himmler turned his head so he could stare out once again at the gray skies above. "Then," he said softly, "I'm afraid we would have a problem."

Katharina felt the chill. She was neither the first nor the last to feel it but it was the opinion of many that it was the Reichsführer's very normality that heightened the terror of his power.

"So what happens now?" she said with some weariness.

She watched Himmler walk back over to his chair and sit down at his desk, his hands now clasped in front of him. In another life, she felt, he might have been a parish priest or perhaps a local schoolteacher.

"What happens now," he replied, "is that Herr Schaeffer goes to see your father, as planned. In the meantime, you will be escorted elsewhere. I don't mind where, that will be up to you, but it must be far enough removed that there's no chance of his accidentally bumping into you on the street. He must still believe we are holding you. This is essential."

"Will I have freedom of movement? Of communications? I have a business to run."

He looked across his desk at her. "Fräulein... if I may have your word as a Vollbrecht that you will not try to contact Herr Schaeffer or do anything else to obstruct the course of events, then you can run your business. Do I have it?"

She thought about it carefully but there was really nothing to think about. "You have it."

"Thank you."

"And what if he doesn't show up to see my father? What then?"

"He'll show up."

"You think so?"

"Well, if he doesn't, we'll have to consider forcing the issue. But if I'm any judge of character, I can assure you that such a course of action will hardly be necessary. He'll come of his own accord because he's completely taken with you, Fräulein. And that's exactly how we want him to be. That's how we obtain not just his compliance but his commitment. Trust me, when a man thinks he's doing something for a woman, there's no greater commitment in the world."

"And does that knowledge come from your own experience, Reichsführer?"

The question was the height of impertinence but he accepted it because it came from an elegant young woman sitting in his office - a young woman who was also doing him a big personal favour. So all he did in response was smile placidly before standing up. The meeting was over.

"Thank you for your cooperation, Fräulein. It's much appreciated. And please be sure to give my best wishes to your father. Tell him he can call me at any time on this matter."

She nodded once and then took her leave, resenting the fact that they could conspire to place her in such an impossible position. All her life, the name Vollbrecht had been an advantage. It had opened every door. But there was a price to pay and that price was loyalty. To her family. To her father. It was both a demand and an expectation and, in many ways, she regretted not having the courage to rebel against it.

16

The train back from Magdeburg was delayed and I arrived back in town with little time to spare for my appointment. For once, however, I was lucky enough to find a competent taxi driver and, at exactly three minutes to four, I was standing in the ancient lobby of the Kaiserhof.

At one time, this had been Berlin's most respected hotel, the premier establishment of its kind. Emperors, czars, chancellors and all manner of other potentates had, at some time or other, been ushered through its doors. In that building they'd declared war, signed treaties and planned ever more conquests. And once they'd finished discussing how to rape the colonies, they usually moved in on the housemaids. It wasn't large as hotels go but it was certainly grandiose. On every floor, original paintings lined the public areas and curtains of rich velvet framed the windows. There was wrought iron on the banisters, gilt on the ceilings and solid silverware gracing every table. Even the chamber pots were of the finest Dresden porcelain.

At the reception desk, they informed me that Herr Vollbrecht was lodged in the Hapsburg suite on the second floor and that I was indeed expected. When I arrived, I was greeted in the outer hallway by his aging valet who told me that Herr Vollbrecht wished to convey his apologies. Apparently, the business meeting was taking a little longer than expected and would I care to wait in the salon? I told him I understood completely.

* * *

Of course, while I was in the salon reading an old copy of

the *Berliner Zeitung*, Herr Vollbrecht was in the master bedroom being entertained in a very different way.

My good friend Traudl was there in all her glory.

In other words, she was sitting astride him, dressed in a corseted bodice tied in the back with a drawstring, flimsy red underwear, sheer silk stockings and silver high heels. The mighty breasts, for which she was justifiably famous, were supported only by the most delicate black lace and each time she leaned forward, they fell out a little more, so it wasn't long before they were free and loose and living a rollicking life of their own. It was all part of the performance. But sadly, despite all her experience and expertise, she still couldn't get any kind of a rise out of him. Nothing. That didn't stop her trying though, encouraging him with endless compliments and giving out enough throaty groans to make him believe, or at least *pretend* to believe, that he was as virile as any of the stallions he once put out to stud.

Never mind that he'd just had a major heart attack and that the doctors had advised against any strenuous activity: he'd been enjoying these sessions with Traudl every month for many years and he refused to give them up. He didn't wish to suffer another bout, however, so he compromised by just lying there on his back, almost inert, as he watched her through watery eyes, grateful for what she was trying to do.

She was the only one he ever called and he always looked forward to her visits here at the Kaiserhof, caring for her in the sentimental way that only a rich old man ever could. The hotel management knew what these visits were all about, naturally, but he was a valued customer with a venerable name, so they chose to remain discrete. Officially, she was his private secretary while he was here in town and the story was that she came to the premises in order to take important dictation and deliver urgent mail. As such, they informed their staff that under no circumstances was Herr Vollbrecht to be disturbed on these occasions.

It was only because the "secretary" herself remembered to inform them of my appointment that I was even allowed entry.

* * *

It was forty minutes before the door opened and Traudl emerged, fully dressed with her coat on and ready to leave. Unlike our meeting in the Tiergarten, this time she didn't run over to hug me. She just gave me a simple, flat greeting, almost as if she were disappointed to see me.

"Hello, Edmund."

I looked straight at her. "You could have just told me the truth, Traudl. There was no need for all this."

She was about to reply but then thought better of it. Instead, she just shrugged and walked right past me with a sad look in her eyes. But before she passed through to the hallway, she turned back for a moment. The valet had gone into the bedroom to help Vollbrecht, so we were alone and she took the opportunity to whisper across to me.

"Edmund, take care. You're..."

"I'm what, Traudl?"

She hesitated a moment before making up her mind. "You're expendable," she said, her voice so low it was almost inaudible. Then, without saying anything else, she was gone.

Expendable... It was an ominous word, especially since I still had no clue what was going on or why I was even here.

That's when I heard the old man tapping his way slowly into the salon, leaning heavily on his walking stick. He'd taken the trouble to get dressed but not formally. Although his pants were perfectly creased and his tie tightly knotted, he was wearing a comfortable smoking jacket of Oriental design, a gift from the Japanese ambassador.

"Ah, Herr Schaeffer. I do apologize. Work, you know. Don't seem to be able to get through it like I used to."

I decided to accept the charade without saying anything. His affair with Traudl was none of my business anyway, so I adopted a sympathetic expression and shook the hand that was offered. It was trembling slightly and he seemed frail. Perhaps the strain of the past hour's activity had been too much.

Once he'd been helped into a chair, Vollbrecht ushered away the valet. "Pathetic, don't you think?" he said to me.

I sat down opposite him. "Not at all," I replied. "For a man who's just been through a heart attack, you're doing very well."

He tried to laugh but even that was too much for him and he became short of breath. "I'm beginning to understand what my daughter sees in you," he said as soon as he was capable of speaking again. He pointed his cane at the chair on which I was sitting. "Can't you bring that any closer? I can't shout."

I obliged by shuffling forward. "Look, Herr Vollbrecht..." I began, but he interrupted me.

"Are you in love with my daughter, Herr Schaeffer?"

I didn't know how to answer that question. Or maybe I did and I just didn't want to. I looked at him, at the lines on his face and the fatigue in those weak blue eyes. "I didn't really get that far," I said, "I didn't get the chance." It was an outright lie but then why would I tell him the truth?

"Then if you don't mind, just what is your relationship? I think a father has the right to know."

"Enough that I'm concerned for her welfare," I replied and saw him nod, suggesting I'd said the right thing. "Herr Vollbrecht, do you have any idea how she is, how she's being treated?"

"I've been given assurances that she's safe for the time being."

"For the time being?"

There must have been an edge in my voice because he gazed at me for some time. "I'm a respected citizen," he said defensively. "And, if I may say so, that respect is deserved. My family have been landowners in Prussia for... well, what does it matter? But the fact is, Herr Schaeffer, I'm a loyal patriot. Always have been, always will be, no matter who's in power, do you understand?" He didn't wait for a reply. "I lost two brothers in the war and I've a third in an asylum. I have nothing to be ashamed of... *Nothing!*" He began coughing again. "But... a man has certain obligations, do you know what I'm saying?"

Actually, I had no idea what he was saying but I let him go on.

I was hoping he'd come to the point eventually.

"I got to know Herr Himmler when I joined the 'Friends of the SS' and, because of my participation, the Reichsführer is doing me a certain favour. Now it's time for me to return that favour... but what he doesn't understand is that I'm a sick man."

He paused and I waited but he'd lapsed into silence. I heard the valet doing something in the next room. Then all of a sudden, he launched into a coughing spasm and I had to wait for a minute or two.

"What's he asking you to do?" I said.

He looked up from the white handkerchief he was holding. "Herr Schaeffer, how much do you earn?"

I was unprepared for the sudden change. "Excuse me?"

"You're a journalist, I'm told. You work for yourself. Am I right?"

"Yes..."

"So my question is simple. How much do you earn in a year... approximately?"

"Well, it depends." I replied. I didn't feel like answering until I knew where this was leading.

He waved a hand at my reluctance. "All right, no matter. However much it is... what would you say if I gave you an amount, let's say the equivalent of five years' income?"

I'm not sure what kind of expression was showing on my face. All I remember was trying to recover as fast as possible. "I'd say nothing is ever given away, Herr Vollbrecht."

"Very good, Herr Schaeffer. That's perfectly correct. You'd have to earn every pfennig. On the other hand, how many times do you even get such a chance?"

He had a point but I was becoming impatient. The money interested me, of course it did, but I resented his rich man's approach to whatever it was we were doing. He was maneuvering me, setting me up. He wanted to buy me and I didn't like it because it was so obvious.

"What does all this have to do with Katharina?" I asked him.

"Everything," he replied. "Have I not explained it well enough?"

"No, you haven't. So far you've told me nothing at all."

He glared at me and for a moment I glimpsed a flash of reproach, the Prussian landowner with a wayward peasant employee. But then just as quickly, it faded and he reverted once again to being just an infirm old man. It was like he was trying hard to be his former self without having the actual spirit to sustain it.

"My wife didn't live very long," he said hoarsely. "Died giving birth just two years after we were married. Two of the most peaceful years... You must understand, Herr Schaeffer... Katharina was our only child, just like Erwin is my only brother, and what the Reichsführer wants..." He came to a halt and just shook his head, as if in recognition that he was rambling. "What I'm asking, Herr Schaeffer, is that I'd like you to help me."

"Help you? For money?"

"The money is just an incentive. Take it or leave it, I don't care. I didn't mean to offend you."

"I'm not offended by money. I'm just offended by what we're doing here. Now please, what does the Reichsführer want you to do? A straight answer, if you don't mind, Herr Vollbrecht."

Another silence, as if he wasn't sure whether to cough or not. He held his handkerchief at the ready. "The Reichsführer wants me to blackmail one of his Gruppenführers."

"Blackmail?" I said, just in case I hadn't heard him right.

"That's right. And I want *you* to do it for me."

To say I was stunned has to be an over-simplification. Maybe my mouth was open, I don't know. "Me?"

"Yes."

"One of his Gruppenführers."

"Correct."

"May I ask which one?"

"His name is Reinhard Heydrich."

Heydrich, I thought, head of the Reich central security office. I knew his name and I also knew his reputation: perhaps the most ruthless man in Germany, if the stories I heard about him were true. I couldn't believe what I was hearing. It was outrageous and I closed my eyes for a second, trying to work it out. In the back of my mind, I could still hear Traudl's voice telling me I was expendable. Yet the strange thing was that Vollbrecht hadn't threatened me in any way. Not so far. He'd offered me money instead of retribution, the carrot instead of the stick, but I still had to know what the negative would be just for my own self-protection.

"What if I don't accept?" I said to him. "What if I refuse and just walk away? What then?"

He took a slow breath and looked down for a moment, as if I'd somehow failed him. It was an effective ploy and he did it very well. "Then, Herr Schaeffer, I very much fear for my daughter."

17

Over at the Abwehr, Wilhelm Canaris hadn't heard anything from Himmler since he'd handed over the dossier. However, on the same day I met with Vollbrecht, he happened to uncover a telltale piece of evidence that raised considerable doubt in his mind.

It came to light through his associate, Hans Pieckenbrock, whose brother-in-law had recently been dismissed from a senior position as one of the Berlin district fire chiefs. Apparently there'd been some kind of SS purge in the department and he was wondering whether it might be possible to gain entry into the Abwehr.

"He's bright," Pieckenbrock assured his boss. "Brought about several reforms in his sector. Cut the response time down by twenty-seven percent."

"Yes, very impressive," said Canaris, only half listening as he continued peering at a sheaf of reports. "I'm sure he's a worthy candidate." But then something in the conversation registered with him and he looked up. "What kind of SS purge?" he asked.

"I don't know, it's all fairly vague. But according to what he heard, it came directly from the office of the Reichsführer SS."

"Himmler? Why would Himmler concern himself with the fire service?"

"They say it's because of the false alarm."

"False alarm?" said Canaris. "What false alarm?"

"At Prinz Albrecht Strasse last week. You didn't hear?"

"No, I was in Hamburg last week, remember? What happened?"

"Well, like I said, there was a fire alarm and the building was evacuated. It turned out to be nothing but by all accounts, the Reichsführer was furious, just screaming for blood."

By that time, Canaris had put down the papers and was giving this subject his undivided attention. "Was the *entire* building evacuated? Including Himmler's office?"

"Actually, yes. He claimed something had been stolen so, of course, everybody had to suffer, even those who were only trying to help. Typical of the SS if you ask me, bunch of morons…"

But Canaris had stopped listening and was already on his feet, pacing around impatiently. He didn't know what it all meant but he had some very strong suspicions. Who else could it have been but Reinhard? "Don't you have some work you should be doing?" he said to Pieckenbrock.

"What about my brother-in-law?"

"Yes, yes, later. Now please, I have to make a call."

It was surprisingly abrupt for the Admiral but, because such behaviour was so unusual, Pieckenbrock chose not to take offense and left. He'd hardly closed the door behind him when Canaris had the phone in his hand.

"Office of the Reichsführer SS," he demanded. "Yes, of course it's damn well urgent."

* * *

At Prinz Albrecht Strasse, Heinrich Himmler was in the middle of a meeting with another Wilhelm - the Reich Minister of the Interior, Wilhelm Frick.

However, when the call came through and he heard it was Admiral Canaris on the line, he decided somewhat reluctantly to take it. "Herr Frick," he said, holding one hand over the mouthpiece. "I apologize, I really must take this call. Frau Jürgens has refreshments outside, if you'll just give me a few minutes…"

"Yes…" said Frick, "yes, of course." Even the Minister of the Interior bowed to the wishes of the SS.

Once he was gone, Himmler put the receiver to his ear. "Yes, Admiral," he said. "To what do I owe this honour?"

"Good afternoon, Herr Reichsführer. We're both busy men so I'll come right to the point if I may."

"Please."

"I heard some rather disturbing news recently."

"Really? About what, may I ask?"

"Well, it was all a little vague. Something about a fire alarm at your office? Would that be right?"

Himmler wasn't sure what to answer but he could hardly deny it. No report had ever been released to the press but, then again, neither was it any state secret. The entire building had been evacuated on to the street. "We experienced a minor incident. Nothing serious. Why do you ask?"

"Forgive me, Reichsführer, but I also heard something was stolen. From your own office in fact. From your safe."

Himmler tried to maintain an air of calm. "I see. And who was it told you that?"

"Is it true?"

"I can assure you, Admiral, everything here is as it should be."

"So nothing was stolen?"

"Admiral, I'm really not sure what all the fuss is about. It was just a fire alarm. It happens every day. In this case, several people were found to be incompetent and I've dealt with them."

"So I have your assurance?"

"My assurance? There's nothing you need my assurance about. Now, is there anything else? I'm in a meeting."

"No, thank you, Reichsführer. I'm sorry to have troubled you. Thank you for putting my mind at ease."

"Not at all. Goodbye, Admiral."

Himmler put the phone down but he didn't call his visitor back in. Not just yet. First he had to figure out what Canaris did or didn't know. The whole affair with the Gruppenführer was becoming aggravating indeed and although he had a solution in the works, the initiative with the Vollbrechts, it was making painfully slow progress.

* * *

The next person to receive a call from Canaris was the Gruppenführer's wife, Lina Heydrich, but it wasn't until the following morning, just as she was preparing to face the day. She'd had a fitful night's sleep and the early gray light struck her face with a certain savagery. Swollen eyes, furrowed lines, features she didn't even recognize any more. She felt old. More than old, used.

Her husband hadn't come home that night. It had become a frequent occurrence and she was getting tired of it. She knew her husband's propensity for carousing and whoring, knew it well, and she herself had already suffered from his sadistic perversions. Even *that* she was prepared to forgive up to a point. After all, their marriage was one of convenience and she herself had also indulged in the occasional side event, the most recent being Walter Schellenberg. But still, she didn't abuse the freedom like her husband. She didn't stay out all night. There was a line between convenience and neglect.

Eight years, she thought, as she stared into the bathroom mirror. Married eight years and for what? For the chance of an entry ticket into the Chancellery? For the chance to have that sycophantic Japanese ambassador bow before her? For the chance to have some fat Middle Eastern tyrant kiss her hand? Was it even worth the effort? She took a sip from the small tumbler of gin that stood on the dresser beside her.

Somewhere in the house she heard the phone ring but it didn't bother her. One of the servants would get it. And if it was her husband calling, she didn't want to know. She stripped off her nightdress and stood looking at herself naked, full frame. Not just at her face this time but at her thin shoulders, her pale breasts and hips. At one time she'd been able to arouse him despite their mutual dislike but even that small consolation had disappeared. They were in limbo, sexually and every other way, and who knew how long it could all last?

There was a tap at the door. "Frau Heydrich?" It was Hedda, her maid.

"Not now," she yelled back.

"I'm sorry but..."

"What is it?"

"He says it's urgent, *meine Frau.*"

"What are you talking about?"

"Admiral Canaris, *meine Frau*. He says it's urgent."

Lina Heydrich hadn't seen Willi Canaris in weeks. "What does he want?"

"He needs to meet with you, *meine Frau*. This morning."

"What for?"

"He didn't say."

"Tell him I'm busy. No, wait, ask him what he wants. No, wait, tell him I can't see him before eleven. Tell him he can buy me a pastry at the Café Schön. Tell him with lots of cream so I can get fat and ugly. No, wait, don't tell him that. Just tell him to meet me there at eleven."

"Yes, *meine Frau*."

Lina Heydrich was still looking in the mirror but she couldn't stand the sight of herself any more. Why not waste a morning with Willi, she said to herself? What else did she have to do that day?

* * *

During the late twenties, there'd been something of a café society in Berlin but, in recent years, it had almost ceased to exist. Superficially, things were the same - the older patrons still tried to feign elegance with their fur collars and their cigarette holders, and the waiters still served their gooey concoctions and maintained their pretense - but nothing was like it once was.

Amongst such faded establishments, the Café Schön was a prime example. Situated directly on the Linden, it had once been a permanent fixture on the social agenda with an eclectic mix of politicians, industrialists, impresarios and artists. On any given day, a factory deal could be signed at one table, while a popular musician wrote a score at the next and a Dada sculptor sketched feverishly at a third. But like so much in Berlin, its heyday was long past. Gone were the intellectuals and the dreamers. Gone were the days of free thought.

Nevertheless, Lina Heydrich still enjoyed it - or, to be more accurate, she still enjoyed the nostalgic memories it brought back.

A provincial girl herself, she could still recall vividly the first time she arrived in the city and was taken there by her dashing young husband. Despite believing fervently in the Führer's concept of a wholesome Aryan "*Volk*" life, she couldn't help being enthralled by the romance and sophistication that the Café Schön evoked and she actually wrote pages in her diary trying to reconcile her feelings.

"Frau Heydrich!" said the ancient waiter as she walked in the door. "Yes it *is* you! You haven't changed a bit."

"Hello, Konstantin," she said. She was genuinely glad to see him. "I can't believe you're still here."

"And where else would I be?" He helped her with her coat. "Would you like your old table?"

"If it's available."

"I'm sure something can be arranged. And will we have the pleasure of your husband's company today?"

"My husband? No, not today," she replied and left it at that.

She was already done with her first coffee by the time the Admiral arrived. He was looking a little harried but at least, she noted, he was wearing a jacket and tie for the occasion. Not exactly his naval uniform but nor was it his usual disgusting old sweater either and that was something to be thankful for. Unfortunately, he spoiled the effect by bringing his dogs in with him.

He kissed her lightly on the cheek and murmured apologies for his tardiness while the dachshunds flopped themselves down by his feet.

"How's Erika?" she asked him.

"Oh, she's fine. Sends her regards."

"We don't see the two of you any more."

"No," he said, not sure how to reply. "You know how it is."

She turned to the hovering waiter. "Konstantin, this is my good friend, the Admiral. Bring him a schnapps, would you?"

Canaris waved away the offer. "No, thank you. Far too early for me. Coffee will do nicely... and some of your very best pastries," he added. Then he touched Konstantin's sleeve. "And make sure they're fresh."

"Of course, Herr Admiral, of course." For Konstantin, the return of such prestigious guests to the café was a welcome sign.

Canaris watched the man leave, then said: "Nothing worse than a stale pastry."

"I agree," she said, "except maybe a young scotch." They shared the laugh. "So, Willi, how's life treating you?"

"Life..." he replied. "It blows us here, it blows us there. Who knows where we'll all end up?"

"Still off on those exciting missions or do you have other people doing that for you now?"

"No, I still go, but exciting is the last adjective I'd use to describe them. Tiring, perhaps, or boring."

"Been to Spain recently?" she asked him.

"Yes, I was there not too long ago."

"And how do you think we're doing?"

She was referring to Germany's Kondor Legion, fighting on the side of Franco's fascists. A year or so earlier, they'd staggered the international community with their first use of open civilian bombing at Guernica.

"I think we'll have it wrapped up fairly soon," he replied.

"Good," she said. "Once Spain's settled, we can move on."

Canaris smiled some kind of agreement but he wasn't interested in discussing either military or political affairs with Lina Heydrich. "And how about you?" he asked her. "What have you been doing with yourself?"

"Me? Not much. Trying to survive. Most nights I just wait for my husband to come home."

He acknowledged the unusual confession. "That bad?"

"You know Reinhard."

"Yes," he agreed, "I certainly do know Reinhard."

Konstantin brought the coffee, aromatic and frothy, plus a huge tray of Viennese-style pastries. Enormous cream meringues, liqueur-soaked sponges and rich chocolate gâteaux. All very expensive. They pointed out what they wanted and chuckled together at their indulgent complicity, a brave show by both of them under the circumstances.

When the old waiter had gone, Lina said: "Willi, why did you call me today?"

Canaris tasted a little cream with his finger and then took a sip of his coffee as a way to delay the answer. Having been eager to set up this meeting, he wasn't at all sure how to proceed. "I wanted to ask you a question," he said intriguingly as he watched her take her own mouthful.

"Fine," she said. "Ask."

He wiped his lip with the napkin and glanced around. The question was critical. "Do you know about the dossier?" he said very softly.

"And what dossier would that be?" she replied, matching his tone but still managing to make light of it.

Her response was akin to a denial and, although he knew it was false, he decided to go through the motions anyway. It gave him some direction and would allow him to gauge how to play it out. "Somewhere," he said, "there's an unmarked file with Reinhard's picture inside it. I take it you haven't seen it?"

"Not me, Willi. Is it worth seeing?"

"Some people might say so."

"Why? What's in it?"

"Everything."

"Everything?"

"All the proof anyone would ever need."

She stopped eating for a moment, then tried to cover it by reaching for her napkin. "And who put this file together?" she said more hesitantly. "Was it you, Willi?"

"What if I said no?"

"Then I'm not sure whether I'd believe you."

Underneath the table, the dogs were panting and Canaris made himself busy by pouring mineral water into a spare tumbler so that each of them could splash their tongues in it. In doing so, he noticed that the water happened to be a brand owned by the SS, one of the profitable business sidelines that few people knew about. When he was done, he heard Lina speaking again.

"This file," she said. "You said it was 'somewhere.' Does that mean you don't know where it is?"

"Well, I thought I did."

She was becoming a little frustrated with the conversation. To her it was like they were just dancing around. "Willi, are you going to tell me what you really want?"

"I don't want anything."

"So why are we here?"

"To enjoy the morning." He smiled, then put down his fork and decided she was right. It was time to get down to business. "The point is, Lina, I was under the impression that the dossier was at Prinz Albrecht Strasse, safely tucked away in the Reichsführer's office. But something happened... there was an incident... and now I'm not sure it's there any more."

"Where do you think it is?"

"I don't know."

"No, Willi, listen carefully. Where do you *think* it is?"

Again, he looked around but the few customers present on that Wednesday morning were fully engaged in their own affairs. Nobody was paying any attention to two people talking quietly who might well be having some kind of liaison for all they knew, despite the difference in their ages.

"What I think," he said, "is that Reinhard's got it. In fact, I'm almost certain."

"How certain? Twenty-five percent? Fifty?"

"I'd say about ninety-nine."

She did nothing for a moment. Her face was empty. Then slowly and in a very controlled way, she folded her napkin and placed it carefully at the side of her plate. "Thank you for the pastry, Willi. It was delicious." At that point, she pushed her chair back from the table, got up and walked purposefully away.

Old Konstantin hurried after her, worried in case there was a problem with either the food or the service, but she was in no mood for small-talk, not any more, and disappeared through the revolving door. The waiter threw his hands up in frustration.

18

"Do you have it?" she screamed.

It was after midday but her husband was still asleep on the bed, fully dressed, when she stormed into the house.

He opened his eyes very slightly to see what the commotion was about. "Do I have what?" he mumbled.

She stood in the centre of the room looking at him. His shirt was torn at the collar and he had some sort of red stain on the sleeve. His boots on the floor were muddy but at least he'd taken them off.

"The dossier," she said coldly. "Do you have it?" It was a much lower level of fury. More restrained but also more menacing.

Her husband just closed his eyes again. "I'm trying to sleep."

"And I'm trying to get a goddamn answer. Do you have it?"

He turned over on his side, away from her. "Leave me alone."

She continued looking at him for a moment, then glanced around the room. Almost immediately, she spotted his black leather briefcase over on the chair. Normally, it never left his side. She hurried over and immediately her thumbs were busy with the latches. It wasn't locked and she lifted up the lid.

Inside were perhaps a dozen or more file folders, plus some coded reports and several detailed maps - all the essential documents that he invariably carried around with him. Unlike the Reichsführer, he wasn't in the habit of trusting safes.

Her fingers began scanning the files until a firm, cool hand locked onto her left forearm, gripping her tightly, the fingers digging harshly into her flesh. The pressure made her wince. She hadn't heard him approach and she stood very still, not even daring to look round.

Then she heard the voice speaking delicately in her ear.

"If you ever open my case again, I'll kill you where you stand."

She still didn't move. She was afraid that if she moved even slightly, he'd break her arm without even thinking about it. Yet somehow she found the means to take a breath. "I want to know," she said, "whether you have it or not."

He pulled her arm away from the case, causing her to swivel around. Then, with his eyes fixed on her, he shut the lid with his spare hand and fastened the clasps. At that point, he let her go and for a few long seconds they just stood looking at one another before he went back to the bed and lay down again. Such was the threat that he didn't even need to lock the case.

"You do, don't you?" she said. "You have it! You took it from Himmler's office. From his safe."

He was on his back, looking at nothing but a point in mid-air. Then without bothering to reply, he closed his eyes again.

* * *

Lina Heydrich left the house but she didn't take her usual car and driver. Instead, she called a taxi and headed back across town, first to a private club where she drank her way through the greater part of the afternoon, then to her hairdresser and then to an exclusive apartment building on the edge of the Tiergarten.

She rang the doorbell, not really knowing whether he'd be there at that time. It was about six in the evening. She waited and was just about to turn away when, sure enough, she heard the sound of the deadbolt being released.

"Yes?" said the voice behind the door.

"Walter? It's me."

"Lina?"

The latch was unfastened and Walter Schellenberg ushered her in quickly. Then, just before he closed the door, he peered out into the corridor to check if anyone had seen them. It appeared to be clear.

"You shouldn't have come here," he said. Normally they met at a small hotel in Reinickensdorf near the Tegelsee.

"I'm sorry…" she said, throwing off her coat. It was then that she realized he was in full dress uniform: black tunic, oak leaves, dagger and all.

"I was just on my way out," he said by way of explanation. "I just came back to change."

"Anywhere interesting?"

"Charity concert. Wagner."

"It's always Wagner."

"I thought you liked Wagner."

"Going on your own?"

"No, with the others."

"Others?"

"Daluege, Pohl, Müller… the usual crowd."

"Is my husband going?"

"Not as far as I know."

She sat down on the broad leather sofa, ignoring the fact that he might be anxious to leave. "Do you have anything to drink?"

He nodded and went over to a mirrored cabinet by the wall. "You look pale," he said, as he mixed a couple of martinis.

No sooner did she have the glass in her hand than she gulped half of it down.

"What happened?" he asked her.

He sat down beside her but, by that time, she'd already finished her drink and had started unbuttoning her dress, revealing the white cleavage. Tonight, the blue veins were just about visible. He looked at her and the moment he did so, she grabbed on to him, pulling him towards her. Her tongue found his and her hand reached down automatically towards his black serge pants.

But he held her hand instead of allowing it to continue, a momentary reminder of her husband. It was more than she could take. This time there were no commands issued like at Webelsberg, no play-acting at all. This time, she just stopped what she was doing.

"What happened?" he said again.

"There's a file... a dossier..." she said. Then she pushed him away so she could go refill her glass. Her hair was already disheveled and her dress was half open but she didn't care and, as if to prove it, she kicked off her shoes angrily. "Why didn't he tell me?" she said as she poured out too much gin. It spilled over the edge of the glass. "Why the hell didn't he tell me?"

"I'm sure there must be a million details he doesn't tell you."

"Details? You think this is a *detail*?"

He didn't answer. But there was something unusual about the silence that caused her to try and focus. Then slowly, the revelation appeared in her eyes.

"You," she said pointing at him.

He shook his head. "What about me?"

"You're in this with him, aren't you?"

"What are you talking about?"

"You didn't even ask me what kind of file. You didn't ask me what's in it. That's because you know, don't you? You're in this with him."

"I'm not *in* anything."

"Liar!"

"Why would I lie? I hate his guts."

She just laughed. "I know, that's what's so funny. You hate him, he hates me and now I hate you. The perfect triangle, don't you think? What is it the French call it? *'Un ménage à trois?'*"

"Lina, listen..."

"Is there anybody else involved while we're about it? You may as well tell me. Your friend Daluege maybe? Or Pohl? Or that Gestapo swine, Müller? Is he involved?"

She'd been standing there with the full glass of gin in one hand and the bottle in the other but, at that point, she began moving towards him, not caring how much more she spilled. Then she held her arms out and began singing her own version of the national anthem: "Heydrich, Heydrich, über alles..."

He stood up to try and take the bottle from her but she was still singing and laughing and she turned around, refusing to let him have it. As she did so, the thin-stemmed glass broke in her hand.

Blood began to trickle down her arm and that's when the laughter stopped.

For a long moment, she just stood there looking at it. Her own blood. Then she ran for the door, holding tight onto the bottle but leaving her coat and her shoes behind.

* * *

She wasn't sure how long she spent wandering the cold, rain-washed streets in her bare feet before she found a cab.

She thought that maybe an ordinary policeman, a Schupo, helped her but she wasn't certain. If so, she was fortunate to get away with it because she was still half undressed and he could have easily taken her into custody. For someone in her position, it would have been more than a little embarrassing.

She dimly recalled that she almost gave the taxi driver her home address until she realized it was the last place she wanted to go. So, instead, she directed him to Betazeile in the district of Zehlendorf. To the home of Willi and Erika Canaris.

* * *

Walter Schellenberg arrived late at the Theatre am Vollendorfplatz and shuffled his way along to the reserved seat on the third row which was still vacant.

Above him on stage, the well-known pianist, Backhaus, was pounding out Wagner's prelude to Parsifal under the cultur-ally approved baton of Maestro Furtwängler. It was a rendition acclaimed only in Germany, however, as Backhaus had somehow managed to convert any subtleties the piece may have had into a kind of bombastic stridence.

While pretending to move his head to the ebb and flow of the music, Schellenberg gave in to the mental anguish that had been crowding his mind. The unexpected visit of Lina Heydrich had disturbed him. A woman like that, he thought to himself - naturally intelligent but emotionally unstable - she could ruin everything.

What had she been thinking, to come to his apartment? He'd had no choice about starting an affair with her. That was her decision and, because of the unspoken threat of retribution, he'd been obliged to go along with whatever little fantasies she came up with to entertain herself. But even then, he assumed that she'd act with some sort of discretion, if only for reasons of self-preservation. Now he wasn't even sure about that any more.

The real question, however, was how much she knew about the dossier and that was difficult to estimate. Had she searched through her husband's belongings while he was out? Had she actually found the damn thing? Was it perhaps in her possession?

As the music rose to its uninspired climax, the ambiguities and contradictions circled all around him and the various scenarios seemed to play themselves out to infinity without reaching any kind of resolve. He'd be number two in any new order, the Gruppenführer had told him so directly, but there were no guarantees. There were never any guarantees about anything.

* * *

At the Canaris residence, a new valet answered the door and for a full second they just looked at each other: Lina because she was expecting to see Otto and the valet because of the shocking state she was in.

"Are they home?" she said.

"Are you acquainted with the Admiral, Frau…"

"Von Osten," she said, deliberately avoiding the name Heydrich out of pure spite. "Frau Lina Mathilde von Osten… and yes, of course I'm acquainted with the Admiral or I wouldn't damn well be here."

She pushed her way past him and he retreated after her hurriedly. He was new here but he wasn't inexperienced and he just wasn't used to having his position challenged like that. He caught up with her in the hallway.

"Please wait here," he said to her firmly.

But as soon as he disappeared from view, she found her way

through to the study on her own and lowered herself into a chair. She closed her eyes, just thankful for the opportunity to rest. When she heard voices, she called out: "I'm in here."

It was Erika who answered. "Lina? What a surprise." She was casually dressed for an evening at home. Just a loose skirt, light sweater and carpet slippers.

"I'm sorry Erika, I had nowhere else..." She stopped in mid-sentence, realizing how she sounded. It would be better to act normal, to start a normal conversation. But that's when Erika saw the blood.

"My God, you're hurt!" She looked around for the valet. "Helmut, go and fetch the medical kit. Hurry."

"It's nothing," said Lina, "really."

But Erika wouldn't hear of it and the fuss continued until Helmut brought in the box with gauze, bandage and saline solution. Then she dismissed him and began treating the wound herself. The cut wasn't that deep but better to be on the safe side, she kept saying. It may become infected.

The saline stung slightly and Lina winced. "Where's Otto?" she said.

"He's... not here any more."

"You fired him?"

Erika continued to work. "No, we didn't fire him. It was something else. He's... dead."

"Dead?"

Erika refused to elaborate because she was certain it was Reinhard who'd given the order. Worse yet, it had happened in this very room. But that's when her husband appeared in the doorway.

"Hello, Lina," he said in that dry tone of his. "Long time, no see. What happened to you?"

"Nothing really, a small accident. Some glass. Nothing."

Wilhelm Canaris looked at her but, like his wife, he decided not to probe. Whether he believed it was an accident, however, was another matter entirely. For all he knew, it might even have been Reinhard who'd injured her.

Once the first aid had been applied, Erika sat back in her chair and that's when Lina's tears began to flow. It was no dramatic weeping but a muffled release, intense and tortured. Meanwhile, Willi Canaris just stood there, not really knowing what to do. Neither he nor his wife had ever seen her cry before - nor show any real emotion at all, come to that.

"Something to drink?" he offered. "Scotch? Gin?"

Lina shook her head. Far too much already.

"Coffee then?" suggested Erika.

"If it's no trouble."

"Not at all. I'll go see to it."

In fact, it was Erika's diplomatic way of leaving the two of them to talk and she tapped her husband gently on the shoulder as she went by. She knew they'd met earlier that day and she also knew what the topic had been.

"Want to tell me?" he said to Lina, once Erika had gone.

She breathed deeply to try and regain some composure. She felt sick to her stomach. "Reinhard..." she began.

"What about Reinhard?"

She took another breath. She was finding it difficult but she had to say it. Without her even realizing it, the whole afternoon had been building to this point, pushing her towards it.

"Reinhard is going to kill Himmler," she said.

At first, Canaris didn't blink, didn't react at all. Then, slowly, he said: "Are you sure?"

"He always said he would. As soon as he had the dossier."

"Did you see it, the dossier?"

"No... but I know he's got it... from what he said, the way he reacted. You were right, Willi. You were absolutely right."

Canaris nodded to himself. "Do you know who he's working with?"

That was a question she didn't want to answer. She thought about it but the silence dragged out and in the end, she let it be.

"Doesn't matter," he said. "Reinhard's the only one who counts."

She nodded, almost imperceptibly, to signify her agreement on that score.

He sat there just looking at her for some time. "You realize," he said eventually, "that if he succeeds, he may well become..." He came to a halt.

"The next Führer of Germany? Is that what you were going to say?"

"Well, yes."

She laughed out loud, even while the moisture still streaked her face. "My dearest Willi, that's all I realize. That's all I've ever realized."

Canaris sat back in his chair with an audible sigh. "Do you remember back in Kiel?" he said. "That evening in June we had dinner together? Remember that? At the French restaurant. What was its name?"

"Chez Antoine."

"That's right, Chez Antoine. The foie gras was excellent."

"The veal was atrocious."

"What do the French know about veal?" He smiled faintly at the memory. "Do you also recall our conversation by any chance?"

"Yes, of course."

"It was all a pack of lies."

She turned towards him. "What was a pack of lies?"

"The whole thing."

"I don't understand."

"Lina, I was the one who..." He lapsed into a strange limbo and it was a few seconds before he could speak the words.

"You were the one who *what*?"

"I was the one who had Reinhard dismissed from the navy."

"You?"

"I was the one who approved the charges. Of course, Reinhard made it easy with that attitude of his but when the tribunal decided to kick him out, all I had to do was agree. I could have protested but I didn't. I simply agreed. One nod of the head and it was done. My opinion carried a lot of weight back then."

"I'm sure it did."

"I needed someone in Munich, at the centre of the party," he explained, making it sound almost like an apology. "And you know, I don't think it turned out so badly... not from Reinhard's point-of-view anyway. For him it was probably the best thing that could have happened. For you too, in fact."

She thought about it for a few moments but chose not to respond. Instead, she said: "Is that when you gave Himmler the dossier?"

"No... Actually that was not until very recently. Not until I found out about Johannes Utz."

He was about to say more but he saw her looking at him - and that's when he decided he'd said enough. Despite all that had happened, he still didn't know where her true loyalties lay. As far as he knew, she was still a committed Nazi and still believed in it all. The Führer. The master race. The thousand year Reich. There was no reason to believe her opinions had changed, in spite of her marital breakdown.

When Erika returned with the coffee, Lina took a cup, sipped a little and, as if reading both their minds, she said: "I really would like to be the wife of the next Führer, you know." Then she smiled wistfully before adding: "I'm just sorry it has to be Reinhard."

Neither of them smiled back and there was a momentary silence.

"Of course," said the Admiral, taking up the conversation, "even if Reinhard does overcome Himmler, it's not certain the Führer will name him as successor. It could still be Göring or Hess, so why would he risk it?"

"Why?" Lina replied. "I'll tell you why. Because it's damn well worth the risk, that's why." She was beginning to feel a little better. Her hand wasn't throbbing so much and the warmth of the coffee was beginning to penetrate. She looked at him closely. "You still don't understand, do you, Willi? With all your foreign agents and your secret missions, you still don't understand..."

"Don't understand what?"

"You still don't understand who Reinhard really is. Or *what* he is. He can't stop, Willi. Normal reason has no place in his brain. He can't stop even if he wants to."

"I'm not sure what you're saying."

She took on an air of exasperation and turned towards Erika for help but the face was as blank as her husband's. Lina just shook her head. "I can't believe it," she said. "I just can't believe you're so naive, even after all this time. You still don't understand that as soon as he's finished with Himmler, he'll go after Hitler. Reinhard doesn't *need* to be named successor. He doesn't need anyone's permission to do anything. Once he's taken the SS, he'll just seize power and declare *himself* Führer."

19

At the Kaiserhof, Manfred Vollbrecht had told me to wait for further instructions about the best way of approaching Gruppenführer Heydrich and I didn't need telling twice. I wasn't exactly anxious to carry out such a foolhardy mission and besides, I'd been assured that Katharina was being treated well and in good health. If I look back now, I think I was still kind of hoping it would sort itself out, that it would all somehow come to nothing.

As a result, I'd turned to other matters, like earning a living for example, and on the same evening that Lina Heydrich visited the Canaris home, the evening of November 2nd, I returned to my apartment after a day of honest toil. I'd already eaten at Werner's but it was still early, so I took my checkbook and went downstairs to see my landlord, Asher Feldstein. I owed him a month's rent but I think that was just an excuse. What I really wanted was the company.

My metabolism had changed since I met Katharina and I just didn't want to be alone. She invaded my thoughts during every spare moment. The fact that I couldn't make contact didn't allow me to forget her more easily. It just made the whole thing worse.

When I knocked on the Feldsteins' door, I was glad that it was Asher who answered and not his wife, Rivka, who was still out shopping. On a personal level I think she liked me, especially since I'd helped her son, but there was an unmistakable feeling of mistrust towards non-Jews in general and, as a rule, she preferred to keep them at a safe distance. It was understandable. Asher himself, however, greeted me with a good shake of my hand and invited me in. We hadn't spoken in some time.

His hair was gray and disheveled, but it was difficult to

estimate his age. Fifty-five? Sixty? Who could tell? He seemed to have all the worries of the world etched on his face and he shuffled around with stooped shoulders as if he were carrying an immense burden. His clothes were old, usually a collarless white shirt and a frayed sweater with dark, baggy pants. And, because he was always buried in a book or a newspaper, he wore a permanent pair of half-spectacles on his nose. In another context, he could have been an eccentric academic.

Somehow, his apartment always seemed smaller than mine, despite the fact that, as owner of the building, he had the largest one in the place. It just felt more cramped because it was full of all that heavy furniture, which had been in his family for generations. There was a massive table, a carved sideboard, a chest-of-drawers, as well as sofas and chairs enough to seat an army - and, taking pride of place along the end wall, a high, glass-fronted cabinet where Rivka Feldstein kept her silver, a gleaming collection of dishes and festival artifacts that were always kept immaculately polished.

"Would you care for some tea?" he asked me. "I just made it fresh."

"Sure, thanks," I replied and accompanied him through to the back. I knew that, in Jewish homes, an invitation to the kitchen was the highest compliment a guest could be paid. It meant I was welcome, almost a part of the family.

I took a seat and glanced at the Yiddish newspaper that was lying there. It's basically a Germanic language, so I could just about understand the spoken dialect, but the written form uses the traditional Hebrew alphabet and I wondered briefly what the head-lines were saying.

Feldstein made himself busy with a large urn that stood near the stove. He placed a glass under the spout, pulled on the lever and the steaming amber liquid began trickling down. Then he placed the glass into a metal holder and passed it across to me, together with a small bowl of sugar. But that was a special treat, an expensive luxury just for my benefit. I knew that, normally, he drank his tea unsweetened.

"Some fruitcake?" he said. "Rivka just made it today."

"No, thank you. I just ate."

He took it out anyway, with side plates and a large knife. "She always needs compliments," he explained. "Here, you be the brave one and try it first."

He handed me a slice and I obliged him by tasting a small amount. It was a little dry. "Very good," I said.

"Really?" he replied. "Usually it's a little dry."

I smiled. "Where's your son today?" I asked. "Still at school?"

Feldstein took a seat opposite and sipped his tea. "Tuesdays and Thursdays he takes an extra class. Now they're trying to teach him woodwork but the only thing that interests him are the motorbikes. That's all he understands."

"Well, that's not bad. He'll make a living at least."

He looked at me like I was from another planet. "Herr Schaeffer," he said. "Tell me something. How many Jewish mechanics do you know? You think maybe BMW will hire him?"

He had a point. The German trade guilds had all been barred to Jews and I should have understood. I was embarrassed and there was nothing I could say.

Then he tilted his head and nodded in the direction of the Yiddish paper. "Doom and gloom," he said, "that's all we ever read about. Just doom and gloom." Then he looked straight at me. "Do you know what's going to happen, Herr Schaeffer? Tell me the truth."

"How do you mean?"

"How do I mean? You're a journalist. You read English, all the foreign papers. You've got connections abroad. Is there nobody willing to stop this madman?"

I shrugged. What could I tell him? I had no more insight than the rest of the world and, for the most part, they all kept getting it wrong. "If you're talking about Britain and France, they seem desperate to keep the peace at any price."

His expression was one of disgust. "Are you telling me there's nobody there in those places who can see what's going on over here? Nobody at all? All those educated people in London, in Paris?"

"Well, sure, a few. In London, there's a man called Churchill making a nuisance of himself." At the time, Winston Churchill was still in the British parliamentary back-benches and pretty much isolated in his opposition to what he called "Hitlerism." It would be two long years before he actually became Prime Minister.

"And this Churchill person," Feldstein was saying, "he can't do anything?"

"He can make speeches."

"Speeches..." he replied. "Anybody can make speeches. Even Hitler can make speeches. Ranting and raving. And what about the Wehrmacht? People say the Wehrmacht doesn't like him. They say the generals will stop him."

"People can say what they like... but nothing's stopped him yet."

He sighed, long and deep. A gesture of sadness, bitterness and resignation, all rolled into one. I suppose, looking back, I should have tried to be a bit more encouraging but I remember thinking I didn't want to give him false hope. I respected him too much to insult him like that.

"So how about you, Herr Schaeffer? You're still a foreign national. How come you don't leave? How come you don't escape all this while you can?"

It was the same question I'd asked Siegfried and now I threw it right back at Asher Feldstein. "I might ask you the same question," I said to him.

"Me? You're asking me why *I* don't leave?" He gave a short laugh. "Because I'm not like you. I've got no other citizenship. I wish I did, believe me. I don't even have German citizenship any more."

It was true. German Jews had been deprived of all social standing and it seemed to be getting worse every day. The latest disaster in the eternal story of Jewish persecution. Slavery, exodus, the crusades, the inquisition, the pogroms - and now "*Untermenschen*" as the Nazis called them. Subhumans.

"You can still emigrate," I said.

"I can? And where do you suggest I go? Who'll give me a visa? England? America? Australia? You think I haven't tried already? They've all shut down, it's like magic. They're not accepting Jews, none of them. Amazing, don't you think? All the great democracies with all that space and they've all just shut down. No room left for Jews, not a single square kilometre."

"Did you try Canada?" I suggested. I should have known better.

"Worst of them all," he replied. "They wouldn't even let me fill out an application form. The man at the embassy was nice enough but he said his hands were tied. National policy. You know what he told me? He heard they're maybe accepting people in Shanghai, that I should try there."

"In China?"

"I know, *meshugah*, right?"

The word "*meshugah*" I understood. It meant crazy. "How about Palestine?" I said. The British ran it as a colony but they were facing insurrection on all sides and I knew that many Jews were leaving Europe to smuggle their way in and join the fight. For them it was more than their ancient home, it was the land God promised to Moses, the last bastion in a hostile world. Better, perhaps, to die there for a reason than to wait here and suffer the consequences of doing nothing.

"Ah, now, Palestine..." he replied. "That's something else." This time, there was some longing in the voice.

"Would you go?" I asked him.

"Me? Yes, I'd go, even with all the risks. I'd be willing to try. But Rivka... Rivka wants to go where she's got family. In Manchester, in Philadelphia, she's got cousins. Distant cousins but cousins nonetheless. In Palestine, who've we got? Nobody. And to go and dig swamps on a kibbutz with the Arabs all around? She's not so sure. Every year at Passover we say 'Next year in Jerusalem.' It's like a prayer... 'Next year in Jerusalem.' But for Rivka, next year is always next year. You see how it is."

It sounded to me like one of those endless squabbles that form part of any marriage, the only problem being that this one could have major consequences. I gave him a sympathetic look but it wasn't my place to say anything, so I decided to avoid the issue. Whether I was right or wrong, I'm still not sure.

"I owe you some rent," I told him, taking out the checkbook.

He appeared not to have heard me, his head still stuck over there in Palestine. "The British and the Arabs together can't be as bad as the swine here," he was saying. "Do you have any idea what it's like for us, Herr Schaeffer? You live in our neighbourhood, you live here in my building, but do you really have any idea what it's like?"

I signed the rent check and passed it across the table just as we heard a key in the door. Then a woman's voice in Yiddish. "Asher, you there? Come help me with the bags... Asher?"

Feldstein put his tea glass on the table, looked at me knowingly and then went to help his wife. I got up too and I noticed that she was immediately uneasy when she saw me.

"Rent," I said, brandishing the checkbook. "Thank you for the tea, Herr Feldstein, but I have to be going. Say hello to your son for me."

I left without waiting for a reply but, as soon as the door closed, I heard the makings of an argument.

* * *

Early the following morning, the man who would eventually seal the fate of the Feldsteins was at home preparing for a trip to Munich. While his valet ferried bags down to the car, it was Reinhard Heydrich himself who carefully organized his business affairs. He had a thick wad of documents to read on the journey and several reports to write.

From across the bedroom, his wife Lina watched him, her hand still bandaged. She hadn't long come in.

"I'm sorry about last night," she said, trying to make it sound casual. She wanted it to seem as if she'd had a little too much to drink, cut her hand and wound up at the Canaris home where, for the sake of convenience, she'd stayed the night. It was basically the truth, even if it did leave out a few key details.

"How's Willi?" he said to her.

"Willi? He's fine. Sends you his regards."

Her husband smiled at the notion. "No, he doesn't." The brief-case was complete and he locked it shut. Then he walked over to the dresser mirror in order to straighten his tie.

"Staying at the usual place?" she queried.

He just continued what he was doing. "I'll be very busy. It would be better if you didn't try to reach me." Then he glanced at her. "What did you tell him?"

"Who, Willi? I told him nothing. What do you take me for?"

He didn't answer. He just picked up a clothes brush and passed it across the shoulders and sleeves of his tunic. "It'll all be over soon anyway," he said.

"Soon? How soon?"

"We have word there may be an attempt on the Reichsführer's life in Munich."

"What kind of attempt?"

"A Jewish plot," he replied with a straight face. It was a complete fabrication, a cover for his own plans, but he didn't want his wife to know that - or anyone else for that matter. The official story would be that it was a Jewish plot and that's what the public would believe.

After one last look in the mirror, he put the brush down, took the briefcase and walked out, calling for the maid as he went down-stairs. "Hedda!"

She came hurrying out from the kitchen and began helping him with his coat. "Yes, *mein Herr.*"

"Hedda," he said quietly, "I want you to give my wife a message after I've gone, would you do that?"

"Yes, of course."

"I want you to tell her that if she tries to leave the house, she'll be followed. Do you understand?" When there was no answer, he reached out and held her face up so that she had no choice but to look at him. "Do you understand, Hedda?"

"Yes, *mein Herr*." In fact, the word she used was "*jawohl*," which means more than just a simple yes. It's what a soldier says to an officer after he's been given an order.

"That's better," he said quietly. He then released his grip and strode out to the car where the driver and the valet were already waiting.

She didn't like it because she'd be damned one way by him or damned the other by his wife but there was nothing she could do. That was how it was at the Heydrich household.

* * *

By six that evening, Reinhard Heydrich was standing by the window in the Kommandant's office at the Dachau concentration camp, situated just northwest of Munich.

Outside, in the vast yard known as the *Appellsatz*, he could see about four hundred emaciated male prisoners dressed only in rough shirts and pants. Their heads were shaved and they were standing rigidly to attention in the freezing rain, watched over by two bored-looking SS men. To one side stretched the Lagerstrasse, the central alley of the camp that led to the seventeen barrack houses, the infirmary, the morgue and the disinfection hut for new arrivals, while over on the other side was the long rectangular building called the *Wirtschaftgebäude*. That's where the kitchens, laundry and latrines were located, as well as the punishment block. Surrounding the entire area was a grass "no-man's-land" where prisoners could be shot if they trespassed and beyond that lay a ditch and an electrified wire fence. Then, finally, there was a ten-metre brick wall with machine gun towers. The only functions outside the wall, apart from the SS barracks, were the burial pits, leading to the often repeated joke: "It's easy to get out of Dachau. All you have to do is die."

"Good evening, Gruppenführer," said a voice from behind. "Sorry to have kept you waiting."

Heydrich knew the voice belonged to the camp Kommandant, Theodor Eicke, and didn't bother turning around. He just continued looking out at the camp, watching the prisoners. But they didn't appear to be doing anything. "Kommandant, perhaps you can tell me something. How long have those prisoners been standing there like that?"

Eicke walked over to join him by the window. He was a solid, gruff-looking man, a couple of centimetres shorter than Heydrich. He was balding on top but carried an almost permanent stubble on his chin. "About two hours," he replied.

"And how long will they stay there?"

"There's no fixed measure of time. It depends on the circumstances."

"In this case?"

"I couldn't say. It's at the duty officer's discretion. I could call him in if you wish."

Heydrich shook his head but it was more a gesture of incomprehension. "I don't understand the point of it," he said.

"The point of what?"

"Having them just stand there like that."

Eicke was well used to explaining his methods to visitors and dignitaries of all kinds. Especially those who came down from Berlin. "It's called discipline," he said as patiently as he could.

Heydrich gave him a sharp glance in reaction to the patronizing tone. "That's exactly what I don't understand," he said. "Why do they need discipline? Why not just put them to work? If they work well, they live. If not, they die. That's the incentive. It's very simple."

"Your point, Gruppenführer?"

"My point, Kommandant, is that it's a waste of the Reich's manpower to have them standing there like that. It's unproductive. I've seen two collapse just in the time I've been watching."

Eicke breathed a sigh and moved from the window over to his desk. "Psychology is an intricate science," he replied as he sat himself down in the wooden chair. "You can't apply the laws of economics to every situation." He took out a cigarette and lit it with the ornate gold lighter he'd obtained from one of the prisoners.

In theory, Eicke was not subordinate to Heydrich, not according to the organization chart. As Inspektor of camps and head of the Totenkopfverbände, the "Death's Head" camp guards, he'd been awarded the full rank of Gruppenführer in his own right and was therefore not required to justify his methods. He was the one who'd organized the "Kz" camp system and he was the one who'd created the slogan *"Arbeit macht frei"* (Work brings freedom). He was even the one who'd personally developed the identification scheme of coloured triangles for the different classes of prisoners. Red for politicals, green for criminals, black for anti-socials, pink for homosexuals. And because Jews could fit into any one of these categories, their symbol was a yellow upside-down triangle that could be imposed on any of the others, thus cleverly forming a six-pointed Star of David. Yet despite such credentials, the fact was that departmental rank never counted for much in the predatory hierarchy of the SS. Gruppenführer Eicke may have been head of the camp system but his visitor was head of Reich security and that was more than enough to give Heydrich the edge.

Meanwhile, Eicke was still waiting for the other man to turn around. "If you'd like a full inspection," he said, "I'd be happy to give you a personal tour. I'm sure a few punishments could be arranged in your honour."

Heydrich finally looked at him. He wasn't interested in a tour and he didn't have time to waste watching punishments. Not today, anyway. "Will you be ready?" was all he said.

Eicke knew what that was about. He'd been told to expect up to twenty thousand new prisoners over the next few days, a large proportion of which would need to be housed right here at the Dachau complex. "Yes," he said flatly, "I'll be ready."

"Are you sure?"

"Do you doubt my capabilities?"

"I doubt everyone's capabilities," came the reply, "until I see that the job's been done. Then I begin doubting their capabilities all over again."

"I see. And does anyone ever doubt *your* capabilities, Herr Gruppenführer?"

Heydrich remained calm, well in control. "You have a reputation for details," he said to Eicke. "So let me advise you that if anything goes wrong, even the smallest of those details, then you will be held responsible. No matter whose fault it is, you personally will be held responsible."

"I don't report to you."

"Yes, you do. As of noon yesterday, a directive was issued on behalf of the Führer and countersigned by Reich Ministers Goebbels and Frick to the effect that I am in overall charge of this operation. Would you care to call the Chancellery and confirm it?" There was no answer. "I have also nominated Müller to act as my coordinator, so you'll not only take orders from me, you'll take them from him too. Is that understood?"

In the face of such an official onslaught, Eicke wisely chose to back down from the confrontation. "I told you I'd be ready and I will," he replied. "What more do you want?"

Outside, a more senior guard had joined the other two. An order was called and, after doing nothing for two hours, all four hundred prisoners instantly began the exercise known as "*Sachsengrüss*" or knee jerks. After just a short time, a dozen fell face down on the wet gravel, exhausted from the exertion. Of those twelve, four couldn't get up again. They would face punishment later for "taking a rest" which, in their weakened state, they probably wouldn't survive.

"How long does *this* activity last?" said Heydrich, looking out again.

"Who knows?"

"Total waste of time."

* * *

Reinhard Heydrich was not the kind of man to go to a common beer hall. He preferred to do his drinking late at night in the heavy, smoky atmosphere of a nightclub, where there was liquor and music and a backroom of girls. Yet when he left the Dachau camp, he told his driver to take him across Munich to the Bürgerbräukeller on the other side of the River Isar.

When he arrived, he found the place already crowded, even

though it was the largest such place in the city with a cavernous main hall that could hold over two thousand patrons. The reason was an entire week of activities celebrating Martyr's Day, with people coming in from all over Germany. The Bürgerbräu itself was a popular destination because of its historical significance as the place from which Hitler had launched his ill-fated putsch attempt. This had been the gathering point before the so-called "martyrs" had been scythed down by a volley of police bullets.

Heydrich eased himself through the crush and found his way over to a more subdued corner on the other side. Although he was still wearing his black tunic, he'd pulled on a neutral-coloured raincoat over the top in order to make himself less conspicuous. After a few minutes, he managed to catch the waiter's eye and ordered a large stein, just like everyone else.

He waited exactly thirty minutes. Then he put down his unfinished beer and left the same way he'd arrived. Out in the car park, he found his driver standing by the Mercedes and received a brief nod of confirmation.

Satisfied, he climbed into the back of the car and they drove away, back across the Ludwigsbrücke towards the handsome Vier Jahreszeiten hotel on Munich's central Maximilian Strasse. He knew that in the trunk of the car was a sealed package - and that inside the package was the explosive device that, in two days' time, would be used to finish off SS Reichsführer Heinrich Himmler once and for all.

* * *

The man who'd delivered the package steered his small van out of Munich, heading southeast towards the Austrian border, as per the orders he'd been given.

His name was Kurt Auer and it seems he was a fairly well-known criminal in southern Bavaria with an income derived mainly from smuggling. He was an ordinary-looking individual, the kind who could fit into any disguise and get lost in any crowd. According to his reputation, he could also supply any item in any quantity if the price was right - including enough weapons-grade TNT to blow up, for example, a seven-litre Mercedes.

It was somewhere in the Hofoldinger Forest that he met the two SS men who were supposed to pay him for the delivery. They were waiting for him as arranged and, as he got out of his van, they walked across the road to greet him. They even waved. Then one of them reached inside his coat but, instead of the expected parcel of cash, he drew his Walther pistol.

I don't know if Auer ever suspected anything but they couldn't have been more than a metre away when he took the two bullets, one in the heart, one in the head. He groaned, staggered backwards and finally fell silent on the ground, the thin rain diffusing the streams of blood that poured from his wounds. Then, just to make him unrecognizable, the man who fired put the muzzle to Auer's dead face and discharged another round. The SS were nothing if not thorough.

Then the two men strolled across to their own car and headed back towards Munich to rejoin the festivities.

* * *

When Heydrich arrived at the hotel, he made a few phone calls, then took a hot bath and slept for an hour. When he woke up, he put on a fresh shirt and sauntered down to the dining room where he found his aide, Karlheinz Oehring, already waiting for him at a private table near the back wall.

Oehring had brought more files down from Berlin and, while they ordered, Heydrich went through a whole raft of papers, signing some and questioning others. He was a well-known margin-scribbler, accepting nothing if he had the slightest doubt about the veracity of its information or the direction of its conclusions.

The waiter brought bread, wine and several plates of starters which they devoured as they worked. The hotel was famous for its French cuisine so, when the main course arrived, Heydrich decided to concentrate on his plate - boeuf bourgignon in a red wine sauce, a specialty of Provence, with sautéed mushrooms and asparagus, all accompanied by fresh, crusty baguette and a robust Bordeaux.

Then, about half way through the meal, he said: "Have you got the list?"

Oehring put down his fork and reached down into his briefcase for a brown envelope. He handed it to the Gruppenführer and then continued with his own food.

Inside were six folded sheets that had been clipped together, each containing the details of a specific individual, and Heydrich glanced at each in turn. The criteria for assembling such a list had been simple enough. Each person had to be a Jewish male living in the Munich area, aged between sixteen and thirty years of age, and each had to have some kind of criminal record, even if it was only the result of a schoolyard scuffle.

"Is this all?" he said. "Just six?"

"That's all we could collect in the time we had. Another week and we'd have had double the number. It's not easy when you consider..."

Heydrich wasn't interested in excuses. "All right, all right."

"Should we round them up?"

"No, not yet. Just keep an eye on them."

"Very good, Gruppenführer."

Heydrich put the papers back in the envelope, which he then placed in his own inside pocket. "If these people cause any trouble this week, any trouble at all, you'll be held responsible."

"I understand."

Heydrich appeared to be satisfied and continued with his meal. Later, when the waiter came with the dessert menu, he invited his adjutant to indulge. "Go ahead," he encouraged, "I recommend the *poire-hélène*."

He seemed to be in fine spirits. The operation was finally underway and the sequence of events had been set in motion. First, a seventeen-year-old Jew in Paris would be provided with a pistol and encouraged to assassinate a German Embassy official, preferably someone of minor importance. That had already been arranged by Joseph Goebbels and his agents in France. Then, supposedly in response to the assassination, hundreds of thousands of brown-shirts would be dispatched into the streets of Germany in plain clothes to loot and burn Jewish property. It would be made to look like a spontaneous outburst of anti-Semitism and was being organized primarily by Müller and his team at the Gestapo. Next, up to twenty thousand Jews would be sent to the camps and detained while their possessions were officially confiscated. That was being handled by Eicke, amongst others, who Heydrich met this morning. All well and good. All according to the Martyr's Day plan as approved by the Führer himself.

But what the Führer didn't know, however, was that there was also going to be a fourth step that would appear unplanned by anyone. It would merely look as if things got a little too far out of hand. That step consisted of yet a further act of retribution in which one of the six Jewish troublemakers, as identified by Oehring here in Munich, would appear to have placed a homemade bomb under the hood of the Reichsführer's car. That same Jew would also, conveniently, have sent a note to the *Beobachter* claiming responsibility. He would then be promptly arrested and Oehring, unfortunately, would be blamed for gross negligence.

Naturally, the death of Heinrich Himmler would be seen as a tragic loss for the Reich. The nation would mourn. Flags everywhere would be lowered. But then, after the state funeral, the Führer would have to nominate a new leader of the SS and there was only one worthy candidate - the ever-reliable, ever-capable head of Reich security, Gruppenführer Reinhard Tristan Eugen Heydrich. The man with the iron heart.

20

The story first appeared on the morning of November 8th and was presented in sensational fashion. The headline in the *Beobachter* was in massive type:

"JEWISH MURDER ATTEMPT IN PARIS." And under it: "Member of German Embassy staff critically wounded by 17-year-old Jew."

It was not exactly subtle and, since all the papers said virtually the same thing, it was evident that Goebbels' Ministry of Propaganda had been busy. Editorials were already condemning the event and calling for revenge on Jews everywhere and I sensed it might mean the start of serious trouble for my neighbourhood community.

But nothing had happened yet, so after reading several of the editions over breakfast at Werner's, I left on my pre-arranged workaday schedule. In the morning, I took a press trip out to the military airfield at Staaken to see the new Messerschmidt fighter, then in the afternoon, I conducted an interview at the Polish Embassy to seek their views on the current situation. After that, I was supposed to go for a drink with a bunch of car executives from Detroit, over here in Germany to inspect the new Volkswagen vehicle, but I didn't get the chance. In fact, I was just on my way out when my doorbell rang.

It was Siegfried, large as life. He had the Bentley outside with Alois at the wheel and a reservation at some secret spot that he wouldn't divulge. I thought about it for all of five seconds before making my decision. The guys from Detroit could go party on their own.

The restaurant turned out to be a small place with bare wooden floors and Expressionist murals just off Dorotheen Strasse, which Siegfried told me was half-owned by a Russian friend of his, a Muscovite called Igor. What I didn't find out until later was that Siegfried himself owned the other half. So we sat down to borscht, blinis with sour cream, Black Sea caviar and mighty bowls of goulash, all washed down by flagons of raw vodka, while a poor soul dressed gamely like a Cossack tried to pluck out melodies from the Steppes on a badly tuned balalaika. I must say I enjoyed the experience but, by the end, I was glad to take up Siegfried's more civilized suggestion of coffee and cognac back at his hotel, the Adlon.

At some time around eleven, we found ourselves sitting more or less alone in a corner of the beautifully appointed bar. We'd been warmed by several hours of meandering conversation and a large quantity of alcohol. We'd discussed the morning headlines, the cost of living, the survival of European monarchy and sundry other random topics, and it was only when we'd exhausted all of these that Siegfried finally got around to my ongoing adventure. He wanted to know how much progress I'd made and whether I'd heard from Katharina.

I evaded the issue for a while, just in case he really had been setting me up, but then I told myself I was just being paranoid. Surely no conspiracy could be that complex. Besides, I had to trust someone and Siegfried was probably the closest friend I had in the world at that moment, so I began to talk, describing in some detail my meeting with Manfred Vollbrecht and the blackmail mission I'd been assigned.

Siegfried seemed amused. "There are probably easier ways to commit suicide," he said.

"Wait a minute, weren't you the one who said I had to follow my heart?"

"No, what I said was that you had *no choice* in the matter, so you might as well follow your heart anyway. There's a difference. I also said that if you die in the process..."

"What nobler way could there be? Yes, I remember."

"Now, now. You can't blame someone else because *you* got involved."

Maybe it was the booze, I don't know, but that's when I began to lose patience. "Listen, Siegfried, you're such a smart-ass, tell me this... Have *you* never felt that way about someone? And don't tell me no because I won't believe it."

At Siegfried's signal, the barman brought us two more cognacs. It was turning into quite an evening. Siegfried sniffed the glass and swirled it around but since this was already his third, it all looked a bit pretentious even for him, but I guess he had his ways. Plus I was still waiting for him to answer. A minute passed, then two, and I was beginning to think he'd shut down for the night.

"He was an English boy," he said quietly. "His name was Sebastian."

It took me a moment before I caught on. "How long ago?" I asked.

"Before I knew you."

"Here in Berlin?"

"No, over in London. We were staying at the same hotel, the Savoy. It overlooks the river, you know. Superb kitchen. Menu composed by Escoffier himself."

"Never had the pleasure."

"He was married."

"Who? Escoffier?"

"No, Sebastian."

"To a woman?"

"I'm afraid so."

"What happened? She found out?"

He shook his head gravely. "She not only found out, she jumped from the window."

"Into the river?"

"No..." he said, exaggerating his impatience. "She jumped five floors to the street and broke her spine. Spent six months in traction... surgeons, physicians, physiotherapists... But it was clear she'd never walk again. Confined to a wheelchair with Sebastian pushing her around. He was so taken with guilt, he devoted his life to it. You know, the strange thing is that in his own funny way, I think he actually loved her. He loved both of us."

"And you? How did *you* feel?"

"I felt like jumping from the room too but I couldn't do that to him. Hard to push *two* wheelchairs around."

"So what did you do?"

"Nothing. Absolutely nothing. We wrote for a while, until she was out of hospital anyway, but we didn't see each other and we haven't since. Well, that's not strictly true. I saw him once in Harrod's. He was still wheeling his wife and I didn't have the heart to disturb them."

His voice trailed off and there was another long silence.

"You never told me that story," I said.

"I never told anybody. You're the first."

For some reason, I felt honoured. That's when I noticed something about him that I'd missed for all those years, even though it had been there all the time. The only word for it was grief, a kind of personal inner grief that stayed with him despite all the high living.

"You never found anyone else?" I asked him.

"Oh, I've had a fling every now and then, as well you know, but it was never the same." He actually used the English word "fling." It was very like Siegfried to do that.

I nodded my understanding. Another layer of the onion.

"Love is a form of insanity," he was saying. He'd returned to philosophical mode, speaking like he was some kind of oracle who possessed the wisdom of the ages. "Nothing but a chemical imbalance in the brain. We tell ourselves that it's wonderful because they all sing and dance about it so much, but it's not, it's insanity."

I thought about that for a while. "Well, you could say it's insanity," I said. "On the other hand, you could also say there's nothing more natural."

"Natural? Excuse me? You're proposing to blackmail an SS Gruppenführer, quite possibly the most dangerous man in all of Germany, just for the sake of a woman. And you say it's not insanity, it's natural? My God, you spent one evening together, not even that. And now you're pining after her like some schoolboy with a crush. If that's not insanity, I don't know what is."

His comments stung but he was only telling me what I already knew. I looked at him and decided it was time to call it a day. "Let's go for a walk, clear our heads," I suggested. "What do you think?"

He agreed it was an excellent suggestion so we retrieved our coats, told the half-asleep Alois what we were up to and then strode off into the night, heading east past the familiar buildings of the Linden, all the way down beyond the university towards the old imperial palace where Kaiser Wilhelm Strasse crossed the Spree. It was a long walk taken in complete silence and, when we got to the river, we stood for some time staring down into the inky-black depths, each of us still wrapped up in our own thoughts.

We made a strange and lonely pair.

21

If I was hung over the following morning, Lina Heydrich was in even worse shape.

At some time in the early hours, she gulped down a large sleeping draught, not really caring about the quantity. On top of about a litre of gin, it was just too much. Her system couldn't handle it and she collapsed on the floor of the bedroom, lucky not to have cracked her head open.

She stayed there until they found her, unconscious and completely naked. It was the maid, Hedda, who discovered her first and wrapped her in a blanket before calling in the other staff. Then, together, they lifted her back on to the bed. The doctor who was summoned prescribed a mild sedative and advised rest - but the moment his car left the driveway, Lina Heydrich was up and struggling to get herself dressed. She knew she had to get out of there or the next time they found her, she'd be dead, not by her husband's hand but by her own, and that would be even worse. She had to escape.

In just a few minutes, she was ready, even if she was still a little unsteady. She put through one private call, packed a small bag and then made her way carefully downstairs to the front door.

"You'll be followed," Hedda told her in the hallway.

"Let them try," came the reply.

* * *

Right across the street from the front gates was the omnipresent black Opel, stationed there on the direct orders of Gruppenführer Heydrich. It looked very incongruent in this placid suburban setting of large houses and mature trees but nobody around the neighbourhood questioned it because a uniformed SS Oberführer sat behind the wheel.

This morning, he was relieving his boredom by flipping through a lurid tabloid, *Der Stürmer,* run by the well-known fanatic, Julius Streicher. Like every other newspaper, its front page featured yet more giant headlines about the embassy shooting in Paris. Plus, today, there was a large photo of the culprit in custody, a wide-eyed Jewish boy named Herschel Grynszpan. The officer was more interested in sports, however, and he was half way through a long article about his favourite team, FC Schalke, when he saw her emerge: Lina Heydrich, the Gruppenführer's own wife, the subject he was required to keep under close observation. Reluctantly, he folded the paper.

With her husband away, Frau Heydrich had use of the official limousine and he watched her climb in the back. Once the door was closed behind her, he saw the driver give him a brief nod, a pre-arranged signal which meant that the two cars would travel in tandem. The Oberführer responded by bringing his own engine to life.

* * *

Lina Heydrich knew perfectly well what was happening. The conspiracy around her was more than evident and, even in her current mental state, she could see that the two drivers weren't even bothering to hide their complicity. Each time she looked around, the Opel was there, sometimes ten metres away, sometimes a hundred, but always there.

Any other time, she might have been furious but, by this stage, it was just a minor irritation, nothing more. She had a plan to deal with it. Calmly, she took the mirror from her purse and began inspecting her makeup.

They were held up for a while on Gertrauden Strasse but the limo driver knew the city well and cut back through a small alley just before the Mühldamm. The destination she'd requested was an old-style department store called the Kaufhaus Hermann Tietz, situated on the Alexanderplatz. Like the nearby Wertheim, it was an older establishment but still a good place for certain personal items and she was a frequent customer.

The driver pulled to a halt and Lina Heydrich stepped out on to the sidewalk. There were a few glances, as always, from people wondering which celebrity could possibly be arriving in such a fine automobile but she paid no attention to them, just as she tried to ignore the Opel that was still stuck in traffic half way down the street.

She was feeling a little better but, nevertheless, paused to steady herself. What she was about to do would take a high level of energy and she was hoping she'd be up to it.

The department store's liveried doorman saluted smartly as she entered and then immediately summoned one of the floorwalkers to assist her with her purchases. But the young woman had hardly approached before Lina Heydrich dismissed her with a wave of her hand. She had no time for niceties.

As she reached the elevator, she risked a quick look behind. The Oberführer had just entered and had already spotted her, so instead of waiting for the slow contraption, she took the stairs all the way to the lingerie department on the third floor. The store managers hadn't changed the layout in ten years and she knew her way around, even if she was a little dizzy by the time she arrived.

In front of her were all manner of nightgowns, pajamas, slips and corsets - "the very latest from Paris and New York," as they claimed in their publicity. Just like on the main fashion floors, sculpted female mannequins displayed some of the garments but, because of their more explicit nature, it was a general rule that gentlemen be restricted from wandering that particular department.

The Oberführer knew the etiquette and, as he came bounding up the stairs, he slowed to a halt. On the one hand, his orders were not to let her out of his sight but, on the other, there was no point making such a scene that he'd attract the attention of store security. Of course, there'd be nothing they could do against the SS but it would be enough to divert his focus. He therefore decided that his best tactic would be to hang around by the elevator lobby as if waiting for his wife or girlfriend. That way, he figured, he could hardly miss her, no matter which way she left.

By that time, Lina Heydrich was being shown into the changing rooms by one of the lingerie department assistants, who'd been trained to wait just outside the area in case there were any further demands. Ten minutes went by. The girl checked her watch and wondered what to do. Then another five minutes. Finally, she called out to ask if everything was all right but received no answer. She didn't know it but her customer had already disappeared through the back of the changing rooms and the emergency exit beyond.

Hurriedly, Lina made her way down the narrow iron staircase that served as a fire escape. Her shoes clashed on the painted metal like badly tuned percussion instruments and she was obliged to slow down a little in case she slipped.

To avoid the limousine driver who was still waiting out front, she descended all the way to the basement. There she emerged into a corridor that ran between a large storage room and the staff cafeteria. The whole area smelled of cooked carrots. From there, she found her way past the mailroom towards the staff exit. A few people passed her as she slipped through but they didn't seem to notice her. It was a large enterprise and all kinds of activities went on behind the scenes that didn't concern them.

Directly behind the building was a loading dock for the store's large vans. One of the workers whistled at her and, despite her prickly sweat and racing heartbeat, she found a moment to smile to herself.

She crossed the yard and saw a low black coupe parked in the back street. A quick blast on the horn told her it was the right one and she ran across the cobbles as rapidly as her heels would allow. Even before she'd managed to slam the door behind her, the car was moving away, its tires spinning to find a grip on the uneven surface. As they turned onto the Alexanderplatz, she ducked her head below the wooden dash so as not to be seen by her limo driver but, before long, they filtered into the anonymous traffic of Königstrasse and she was able to sit upright.

Only then did she look over at Walter Schellenberg. He was dressed in civilian clothes and had a golfer's flat cap pulled down low over his forehead. She burst out laughing, then saw his responding grin and, for the first time, she realized she was actually enjoying herself. No more dizziness, no more headache. The chase, the escape and her total success in pulling it off had brought her back to life.

22

Wilhelm Canaris was at the Abwehr that afternoon, delivering a lecture to a group of senior officers from the OKW high command.

The subject was a speciality of his, the port-by-port tracking of foreign navy vessels, and was always popular with the officers. When he unveiled the map of Europe showing in precise detail where the ships were, he invariably received a round of applause. It was no coincidence that he liked to put on that particular presentation around budget time.

Afterwards, he stood at the door shaking the hands of the attendees as they left, then returned to the privacy of his office. Just as he entered, the phone rang.

"Yes," he said impatiently.

"I'm sorry, Admiral. I know you're just on your way out…"

"Yes, yes, what is it?"

"I have an officer of the SS on the line. He says it's extremely urgent."

"The SS?" His thoughts went immediately to Reinhard. "What's his name?"

"He wouldn't say, Admiral. Just that it was extremely urgent."

"All right, put him through if you must." He heard the line click. "Canaris here," he barked. He was pressed for time.

"Good afternoon, Admiral… Walter Schellenberg, Ausland SD."

It was something of a surprise. Canaris knew Brigadeführer Schellenberg as Heydrich's own protégé but he'd never had many dealings with him, just the occasional greeting at a mutual event. He certainly had no idea that it was Schellenberg himself who'd invaded his home and murdered his valet, Otto, in the personal sanctuary of his own study.

"Good afternoon, Brigadeführer," replied Canaris, trying to hurry it along. "What can I do for you?"

"Well, it's a little difficult to explain on the phone. Is there any chance we could meet?"

"Yes, of course. When do you suggest?"

"This afternoon. Right now, if possible."

"I'm sorry, out of the question." He glanced at the agenda that lay open on his desk. "The earliest opportunity would be one week from today."

"No, I'm sorry, Admiral. By then it will be too late. It has to be today."

"Well, I'm sorry too, but I have a flight to catch. So if you'll excuse me…"

"With all due respect, Admiral, I really think this is something you should know."

Canaris looked at his watch. "Can you give me some idea of what it's about?" There was a pause. "Brigadeführer?"

"Yes, I'm here. I was thinking. There's really very little I can say on an open line."

"I see. Well, as I said…"

"Admiral, this is urgent."

"So is my trip."

There was a second or two of hesitation and Canaris was just about to put the phone down when Schellenberg came back.

"There's a certain female," he said, "whose spouse has a certain plan."

Suddenly, the Admiral was all attention. "And?" he replied.

"And there've been some developments. I would say *crucial* developments."

"All right, I understand. Don't say any more. What I suggest is this. My flight is due to leave at six but I'm told the departure's been delayed, so we can perhaps talk at Tempelhof. How does that sound? Can you meet me there?"

Schellenberg didn't like the idea. Tempelhof was at the opposite end of the city from Reinickendorf, a journey of two hours at the very least. He'd have to leave immediately and drive like the devil.

"That's the only chance?"

"I'm afraid so, Brigadeführer. A decision if you don't mind."

"Fine... Fine, I'll be there. I appreciate your involvement."

"Yes, well, if you must know, I'd rather not be involved at all. Now I really have to go. And so do you if you're going to meet me."

"Of course, Admiral, I'll see you soon. Heil Hitler."

"Yes, yes, Heil Hitler."

* * *

If the Anhalter rail terminus was noisy and chaotic, the airport at Tempelhof always seemed eerily quiet. The flights were not all that frequent and the winds that constantly whipped across the vast, grassy expanse tended to drown out the dull drone of the engines.

The other major difference was that flying was still prohibitively expensive and the terminal facilities were designed for the upper class passengers who used them: modern lounges, luxurious bars, comfortable armchairs; plus, on the walls, a wide array of poster art featuring all manner of romantic locations.

Today, however, the Admiral's destination was somewhat less than romantic. While much of the Nazi faithful would be at the festivities in Munich, he was flying in the opposite direction to the industrial port of Rotterdam. He'd made good time to Tempelhof but there was still no word about the aircraft, a Junkers 90, which had some minor problems with instrumentation. When he arrived, he could see the engineers still working on it through the terminal window. Beyond, he could make out a Marchetti of the Italian airline, Ala Littoria, and farther away, an Imperial Airways Electra. Although his true expertise was shipping, he always made a point of keeping up with the newest facets of aircraft design.

He was still in the uniform he'd worn for the presentation, in contrast to the ever-stylish Hans Pieckenbrock who was traveling with him today and sporting exactly the right kind of tweed clothing for such a trip. So far, Canaris hadn't told his colleague about the rendezvous with Schellenberg and, as they sat in the lounge, Pieckenbrock couldn't help wondering why the Admiral kept looking at his watch.

Five o'clock came and went. Then five-thirty. Eventually, at five-forty, the flight was called, right back on schedule, and the two Abwehr officers followed eighteen other passengers out into the evening chill. Even then, Canaris was inclined to dawdle. The more he thought about the call from the Brigadeführer, the more he wondered if he shouldn't have made an effort to be more accommodating. He could still avoid taking the flight, of course, but that would be a little drastic. His excursion to Rotterdam was also important. It was in the Netherlands that German naval technicians were secretly developing their U-boat fleet, banned by international treaty but long considered one of the OKK's highest priorities.

With Pieckenbrock at his side, Canaris walked out to the aircraft and climbed up the small staircase into the narrow confines of the fuselage. Back then, even major airliners sat on their tail wheels, which made the boarding process an uphill struggle, especially for passengers up front in the first class cabin. Within a few minutes, the heavy door was closed and the big motors were roaring loudly but then, without any warning, they were cut back. The passenger door was re-opened and the purser came to whisper something in Canaris' ear. The Admiral nodded briefly in response, then as he got up to leave, he told the curious Pieckenbrock that he wouldn't be more than a few minutes.

The stairs had been wheeled back into position and, next to the aircraft, no more than ten metres away, was a black coupe, silhouetted against the twilight sky. The car's headlights flashed twice and Canaris struggled his way through the propeller wash to reach it. Finally, he got into the passenger's seat and pulled the door shut to drown out the noise.

"Good evening, Brigadeführer."

"Herr Admiral."

"I think you just made a plane-load of people very upset."

"This shouldn't take long."

"What is it that's so urgent?"

Schellenberg glanced at him, still not too enthusiastic about committing himself, even after all this effort. He began cautiously. "I'm not sure how much Frau Heydrich told you about her husband's intentions…"

"Enough."

"So you're aware of the operation he's preparing?"

Canaris was impatient. He just wanted to get on with it. "Against the Reichsführer, yes, yes… but you mentioned crucial developments."

"That's right… It seems the operation may well take place within the next few days."

"In Munich?"

"I believe so."

"And who's involved in this… this *operation*?"

"In planning, just the Gruppenführer. As far as carrying it out, I couldn't say."

Canaris glanced at the younger man. He could see the boyish face now taut with anxiety. "How about you, Brigadeführer?" he asked. "Are *you* involved?"

"No, Admiral, just the Gruppenführer."

"You see, I need to be sure."

"With respect, Admiral, if I were involved, would I be here telling you about it?"

"I don't know. You might be just writing your own insurance policy."

"I'm sorry?"

"Really, Brigadeführer. Do I need to explain it? If the Gruppenführer succeeds, you also succeed, isn't that right? What has he offered you? A senior position? His deputy perhaps? And if the operation fails, then you can always demand my support because here you are warning me about it."

Schellenberg's only reaction was to smile gently. "Very good, Herr Admiral. But even if all that's true, the fact remains that I'm here and I'm speaking frankly, which means a great deal of risk on my part, wouldn't you say?"

Canaris grunted. He had to acknowledge the point. If Reinhard even suspected what they discussing here tonight, Schellenberg's life would certainly be at risk. "How reliable do you think this new information is?" Canaris asked.

"Well, emotionally, I think Frau Heydrich is in a bad way."

Canaris nodded his head as recollections of the previous evening came flooding back. "Which means?"

"You've known her a long time, Herr Admiral. Longer than I have. But what I think it means is that we'd be wise to take her seriously. If she were in a better frame of mind, I doubt she'd be as forthcoming."

"And *your* interest, Brigadeführer? Specifically?"

"Let's say I play the role of confidant," he said, "both to the Gruppenführer and to his wife."

"A delicate role, to be sure."

"As you say."

Canaris looked at him again but decided not to press the issue of any extra-marital relationship. He didn't need the sordid details. All he wanted was to get back on board the aircraft and try to get some sleep. "All right," he said at last. "What happens now?"

"I'm not sure. Maybe that's why I need your advice."

"I see. All right, well let's start with what you know for certain."

"For certain? Not that much, to be honest. All I know is what Frau Heydrich has told me. The rest I've pieced together myself."

"All right, so tell me what you believe."

Schellenberg took a moment to think. "Herr Admiral... do you know anything about the Goebbels initiative?"

"The little Doktor has many initiatives. Which one in particular?"

"The one concerning the young Jew in Paris."

"I only know what I read in the papers."

"Well, apparently, it's just an excuse to start an action against the Jews."

"Yes, Brigadeführer, thank you. Even I'd figured that one out."

"Sorry, Herr Admiral. But I'm not sure you're aware of the scale. They're preparing for twenty thousand new arrivals at the camps."

Canaris found it difficult to absorb such a number. "As many as that?"

"The Gruppenführer is in direct contact with Kommandant Eicke. That figure may even be a conservative estimate."

"Go on."

"Well, here's where it gets a little more vague. But from what I can make out, the Gruppenführer is planning to take it all further than anyone realizes."

"That sounds like the Reinhard we know. In what way?"

"Himmler's death will be made to look like an act of revenge for the pogrom. A bomb or a bullet, I don't know. But however it happens, the finger will be pointed at the Munich Jews. As a matter of fact, I think a few of them are already under observation."

"No doubt they'll be tortured into confession after the fact."

"No doubt."

"And you say Lina told you all this?"

"Some of it she told me, some I already knew."

"Where is she now?"

A hesitation. "At a place I know."

"And does the Gruppenführer... What I mean is, do you think he suspects anything?"

Another long pause. "You have to understand, Admiral. Their marriage is built on ambition."

"You don't have to tell me that."

"No... so let's just say that it's... well, it's a more *open* marriage than usual."

"Has she left him?"

"Temporarily."

"Which implies she'll go back."

"Yes... Yes, I actually think she will."

"Even after all this?"

"What she's doing now... Like I said, I think she's a little emotional. Unstable. Drinking too much. She's not sure how much she trusts him any more."

"Yet you say she'll go back."

"For the sake of their ambition, yes. She's invested too heavily in their marriage to do otherwise."

Canaris nodded slowly. It made a certain kind of sense. "And will that be the end of it, do you think? Between you and her?"

It was the first time it had been spelled out and Schellenberg's instinct was to deny it point blank but he gave it some more thought. "I can assure you," he said slowly, "that whatever exists was not my idea. I had little control over the start and I'm sure I'll have even less control over the conclusion."

"I understand, Brigadeführer. But that doesn't answer my question."

"That's because there *is* no answer. It may depend on the outcome of the operation."

"Yes... the operation," said Canaris. "It all comes back to the operation."

"Do you think we should warn the Reichsführer?"

"I suppose so. But it's difficult to know what to warn him *against.*"

"We could tell him not to stay in Munich."

Canaris shook his head. "When the Führer's in Munich, Himmler must also be there. You think Reinhard doesn't know that?"

"So what do you suggest?" Schellenberg waited for a response but it didn't come. Outside, the aircraft engines had been completely switched off so as not to waste fuel. A mere captain of Lufthansa had no authority over either the Abwehr or the SS. All he could do was sit and wait - just like Schellenberg whose fingers had begun drumming on the steering wheel. "Herr Admiral?"

But Canaris had retreated into his own thoughts. The pressure was all around him, closing in, demanding a solution that just didn't seem to be there. The mission to Rotterdam was essential as far as his military masters were concerned. It would be difficult to explain why he hadn't made the trip. Yet what could be more important than the future of Germany?

After a few more minutes, he pulled himself together. Somehow or other, he had to make a decision.

* * *

That evening found Reinhard Heydrich mingling in Munich with the rest of the Nazi faithful, expecting the momentary arrival of the Führer.

They were at the Brown House, the party's official Munich headquarters situated on Brenner Strasse between the Karolienenplatz and the Königsplatz, and by seven it was packed to capacity. For the staff who worked there, the mood was jubilant and the excitement intense. Since becoming Chancellor, Hitler only ever returned once each year during Martyr's Week.

Architecturally, it was an impressive structure, a former palace that, for many years, had been occupied by the Italian Legation to the Royal Court of Bavaria. In 1930, it was purchased by Bormann on behalf of the party for a million and a half and then renovated by Troost for the same amount again. While some questioned the expense, Hitler begrudged nothing. He felt he needed a building of style and quality to impress the capitalist fundraisers as well as to reassure the public that both he and his ideas were to be taken seriously.

In fact, it was not long after the re-opening that Heydrich started working there. His party number was 544916, his SS number was 10120 and his mandate from Himmler was to set up a security division, which became known as the SD, the Sicherheitsdienst. His first goal was to reorganize and expand the files, a job that confined him to the steel clad basement for long periods of each day. To the ordinary rank and file, it seemed like an arduous chore but he was skilled enough to understand that it would become a real base of power. With the files came the secrets and, in a short space of time, he knew more things about more people than anyone else in the party.

Strange that now, seven years later, it was a file that was making him vulnerable and he was well aware of the irony.

It was there, too, that he and Lina began to develop their primal ambition. As a party member in her own right, she had occasion to visit the Brown House and once, while waiting for her husband, she happened to meet Hitler himself. It was a brief moment but it became the turning point in her life as she found herself wondering what kind of man it took to wield such power. What began as fascination then grew into an obsession as her husband rose in importance; and it was the sheer force of that ambition which maintained their relationship even when there was little else.

The memories passed through Heydrich's mind, back and forth, until the noise level increased and the guest of honour arrived. As the Führer strode in at the head of his entourage, he was instantly mobbed by well-wishers and it took him half-an-hour just to cross the lobby and climb the staircase. Heydrich stood patiently near the top, a position which gave him an excellent vantage of the Führer's progress and a central point at which to greet him.

Sure enough, as Hitler finally approached, the alert eyes picked out Heydrich and sparkled in recognition. "So, Gruppenführer," he said, reaching out. "How's my security today?"

Heydrich grasped the firm, dry hand. "Every time I see you so fit and healthy, mein Führer, I know our security is good."

Hitler smiled appreciatively, then clapped his favourite SS man on the shoulder before moving on. Upstairs there were more friends and the adulation continued right through the evening but, as far as Heydrich was concerned, it was mission accomplished. He'd been there, he'd been seen and his devotion had been reconfirmed. He, too, could move on.

23

I think it was a combination of the weather, the stress and the alcohol intake from my evening with Siegfried but, when I came home that evening, my hangover headache had worsened. I was feeling hot and clammy and I suspected I was running a fever.

I warmed up a bowl of stew and tried to eat but it only served to turn my stomach, so in the end I just dumped a shot of rum and some sugar into a tall glass of hot milk and went to bed.

Thoughts were swirling around in my head and, after a while, I drifted towards that strange, hard-to-define point someplace between sleep and delirium. One moment I saw Katharina laughing at one of my jokes and the next, her chair was empty and she was gone. Then I thought I spotted my mouse but that didn't stay long either. Siegfried's marmalade cat chased it away. Other characters put in cameo appearances too but they became disjointed and blurred and I couldn't tell one from another.

Hours rolled by and it was dark when I eventually awoke. I managed to get up, wrap my old bathrobe around me and change the sweat-soaked sheets but the effort almost finished me and I was forced to slump down in an armchair to recuperate.

It was then that my conversation with Siegfried came back to haunt me. Especially the part about leaving the country. In all honesty, I was beginning to doubt that journalism was a sufficient reason to keep me here. I was tired of Germany. Tired of what it had become. Tired of the tension, of the risk, of the ugliness. I didn't want to watch any more fanatics on the march or see any more vulgar graffiti or hear any more whispered stories about the camps. And what was I even thinking to imagine I could black-mail the Satan of the SS and get away with it? How did I expect to survive? Was Vollbrecht crazy? Was Himmler? Why was I still here? It certainly wasn't the money, even if I did still harbour the distant notion of a house on Île-Saint-Louis. No, Siegfried was right. I was doing it for a woman - but not just any woman. This was the goddess Katharina and I'd fallen for her to the point of risking my own self-destruction. That's when the image returned and, once again, she was there right in front of me, just beyond my reach, talking, smiling, laughing. I even saw her rising to dance with me and it was clear that she was now the one and only reason I stayed.

It doesn't make much sense, I know, but that's what I went through before I finally staggered back to bed. It was as if the very thought of her helped chase the demons from my brain and I immediately fell into a heavy sleep.

* * *

I was woken by a loud, incessant banging at my door. My fumbling fingers found the lamp switch and my watch told me it was just after one in the morning. Someone, a woman, was yelling "Herr Schaeffer! Herr Schaeffer!" But I was still heavy with sleep and I just wanted it to stop.

"Herr Schaeffer! Please, Herr Schaeffer! Wake up!"

Again, I struggled into my bathrobe. Why wouldn't they all just leave me alone? I opened the door to find Rivka Feldstein standing there, also in her bathrobe. Her face was pale and she looked very frightened, on the verge of panic.

"Oh, thank God," she said as soon as she saw me. "Please, Herr Schaeffer, come, come. They're going to kill him, my Yossel."

"What? Who?"

"Just come, please, please…" Her pleading was becoming a frenzy, so I shuffled into my ragtag carpet slippers and followed her downstairs. She was trying to hurry so much, she almost fell down the entire flight.

It wasn't until we were down near the front door of the building that I began to hear the commotion outside. There was the sound of glass breaking, interrupted by men's voices, shouting and swearing. Some were even laughing. As I opened the front door, the shock of the cold, damp air hit me hard, forcing my eyes to register the vivid scene in front of me.

There must have been seven or eight of them and, even though the only uniform they were wearing was an armband, I knew instinctively they were brown-shirts. One was standing behind Asher Feldstein, holding him by the arms, while others were milling around the ground floor stores. The plate glass windows were shattered, hundreds of shards all over the sidewalk, and they were also smashing everything else they could find - phonograph records, cigar boxes, furniture, everything. And the damage was not confined to our building, either. It was happening all over the street. In the distance, I could even make out the glow of fires burning. How I'd slept through all that, I don't know.

Then I saw young Yossel. He was lying there in the middle of all the glass, bruised and bleeding. He wasn't moving but I could tell he was still breathing, so I knew he wasn't dead. Not yet.

I took all this in with one sweep of my head before they even noticed me and, even then, it was only Rivka's cry of horror at seeing her son that made them turn around. As she waded through the glass to try to reach him, I yelled out: "What the hell is going on?" It was a dumb thing to say since it was all too evident what was happening.

I saw the one nearest Rivka grab her arm and throw her to the ground, so that she too was down in the jagged mess, and he was the one I went for. He turned to face me with a pick-ax handle at the ready but he never got the chance to use it. Even as he raised the weapon, I was ploughing into him with enough momentum that he staggered backwards. Then, without even realizing what I was doing, I had my left hand at his throat, pinning him to the brick wall, while my right fist was smashing into his face. I don't know what got into me but by the time they pulled me off him, he was covered in his own blood and my knuckles were scraped bare.

Then it was my turn. An arm flashed in front of me and I felt a sharp pain in my abdomen that doubled me over. The next blows I didn't see at all. They were just explosions of coloured light. One was on my left shoulder and the other smashed into my kidneys. I could feel my legs collapsing beneath me but someone was holding me up. Then something blunt and heavy hit the back of my neck and I didn't know any more.

* * *

When I regained consciousness, I felt cold water being sponged onto my face. It hurt like all hell. My ears were ringing and my body felt like a lump of pulverized meat. I cursed loudly - German, English - I don't even remember what language I was speaking.

"Welcome back," said a voice. "Glad to see you're awake."

He was speaking German, definitely German, so I knew I must be still in Berlin. Gradually, as my eyes opened, I realized I was back in my own apartment, lying on my own ancient sofa. I could sense there were two of them. The one next to me handed me a cold compress. The other seemed older somehow but he was beyond my immediate range of vision.

"What the Christ happened?" I said. "Who are you people? Where are the Feldsteins?" I coughed a little and tried to sit up but my entire body was one swollen, aching mass and I couldn't make it. I couldn't even grimace without hurting.

"Which question would you like me to answer first?"

It was the older one who spoke, his voice calm and reasonable. I didn't like it and I refused to respond. That's when his head appeared above the back of the sofa. I stared up at the white hair but I couldn't figure out who he was.

"Canaris," he said, introducing himself. "This is Pieckenbrock."

I vaguely recognized the name Canaris but couldn't quite place it. "What time is it?"

"Two-ten. You were out for over an hour."

I nodded and gradually my mind began to relive the situation. The street. The broken glass. The fight. "How are the Feldsteins?" I asked him.

"The people downstairs? They're back in their apartment. A little shaken up but they'll be all right."

"The boy. What about the boy?"

"Yes, the boy. He was in worse shape but I think he'll live."

"You *think*?" I yelled at him, the anger coming back. I tried to sit up but, again, I failed. My kidneys were throbbing too much. The other man helped by placing a cushion behind my back but I didn't bother to thank him.

"You really shouldn't try to move just yet," said Canaris.

"Were those *your* goons down there?"

"Don't be ridiculous."

"Did you try to stop them?"

"Our arrival drove them away, if that's what you mean."

"So you did nothing."

"Herr Schaeffer, are you Jewish in any way? Perhaps one of your parents? Your grandparents? Forgive me, but I'm just wondering why you live here."

"What business is that of yours?"

"You're right, it's not. I was just wondering, that's all."

I didn't just object to the question, it was also the tone. Even more than that, it was the context, everything I'd just witnessed. "What are you doing here anyway?" I said to him. "What do you want?"

"We were looking for you, as a matter of fact. I believe we have one or two things to discuss."

"We do?"

"Yes, if you're up to it."

"What if I say no?"

"Herr Schaeffer, we probably just saved your life. I really think you might be a little more accommodating." He then nodded to Pieckenbrock who got up and walked towards the door.

"Where's he going?" I asked.

"He'll be outside the door," said Canaris. "Just in case there's any further disturbance."

"I hope he has better luck than I did."

That's when I first noticed the carbine rifle leaning against the wall. Pieckenbrock picked it up as if he knew what he was doing, clicked the safety catch a couple of times and left.

Canaris pulled up a chair opposite me. "So... Herr Schaeffer."

"So... Herr Canaris."

"Actually, it's Admiral Canaris. I'm with the Abwehr. We're a branch of..."

"I know what the Abwehr is."

"Yes, well, I'm sure you do. So what's all this I've been hearing?"

"About what?"

"About you and Katharina Vollbrecht."

I just looked at him. "How do you know about that? From her father?"

"No, as a matter of fact, it came from a friend of yours."

A friend? I couldn't imagine who he meant. I didn't have any friends left. At least none that I'd confided in. Except one, of course. For a moment, I tossed it around in my mind, or as much as my mind would allow. But then I realized it was the only possible answer. Siegfried. Even in *my* state, I could see how it made perfect sense. In his position, he must have made it his business to know all kinds of prominent people - including members of the elite like Canaris. No doubt it was the only way someone like him could survive in such a hostile environment.

"Does he work for you?" I asked quietly.

"No, I wouldn't say he works for me as such. Not in the strict sense. But he travels around, visits certain locations. Occasionally he's been known to act as my courier."

"Did he tell you everything?"

"He told me enough."

"And when *was* this? Yesterday by any chance?"

"Yes, as it happens."

"So that's why he came to town. Some friend he turned out to be."

"Oh, I wouldn't be too hard on him if I were you. Believe it or not, he was looking out for your interests. He does care, you know."

"Cares for himself, more like."

"Yes, that too."

I squeezed the compress on my neck and felt the water dribbling down my back. The pain was sending a burning sensation all the way across to my temples and I really didn't feel like talking any more, especially not to this man. "All right, let's get to the point, shall we? Thank you for saving my life but either tell me what you want or get the hell out."

I saw the calculations taking place behind those cautious blue eyes. I saw the wheels spinning and the numbers drop into place. Then I watched him undo the buttons of his overcoat to reveal layers of woolen sweaters.

"I'm here," he said, "because it seems likely that Reichsführer Himmler won't survive the next forty-eight hours."

"Is that right? And why should I care?"

"Why? Because right now your lovely lady is still safe. She's been detained by the SS but she's under Himmler's protection. Once he's no longer around..." He left the sentenced unfinished.

"So what are you telling me? That Himmler's now her guardian angel? That if he dies, she'll die too? This is getting stranger by the minute."

"I don't disagree. That's why we need to accelerate the schedule."

"What schedule?"

"For you to meet the Gruppenführer."

So that's what this was all about, I thought to myself. Reinhard Heydrich. It was all coming back to haunt me. "I was supposed to wait for instructions from Vollbrecht."

"We don't have time for Vollbrecht. You'll have to do it tonight."

"Tonight? Spitting blood like this? You're out of your mind. I can't even stand up under my own power."

He wasn't listening. "They're all in Munich," he continued. "If we leave right now, we can be there by first light."

"I'm not going anywhere."

"Herr Schaeffer... I think you may be under the impression that this is a debate."

"So what is it, a threat?"

"We're all under threat. Especially, I might remind you, Fräulein Vollbrecht."

And there it was. It was like I couldn't escape. Once again, it all came back to Katharina and I was forced to acquiesce. What else could I do? "First I need some answers," I said.

He looked at his watch. "What kind of answers?"

"Oh, nothing too tough. Just maybe what this whole damn thing is about."

He ignored my sarcasm. "Vollbrecht didn't tell you?"

"He told me that it would be my job to blackmail Heydrich. He didn't say how or why."

"I see."

"So?"

"Yes, well, it's basically very simple," he said. "The Gruppenführer has a file in his possession, a dossier. He stole it and now we need to get it back."

"Who's *we*?"

"Everybody."

"So what's the problem? If he stole it, why doesn't somebody just arrest him?"

"Yes, Herr Schaeffer, good idea. I wonder why *we* didn't think of that." It was his turn for sarcasm.

"Okay, I get it. Too many connections at the top, right?" Even in my condition, it wasn't hard to work out. "That's why you want *me* to do your dirty work, isn't it? Because I'm expendable."

"Your word, not mine."

Actually, it was Traudl's word but I didn't mention that. "And what's in this precious dossier?"

"You don't need to know that."

"Not good enough."

"Well, I'm afraid it's going to have to be. In fact, if we're being totally honest, you don't need to know anything at all, Herr

Schaeffer. All you have to understand is that you need to do as your told. It's perfectly straightforward. If you don't, you'll have to accept the consequences, for yourself as well as for the Fräulein and that's all there is to it. The choice is yours. You have ten seconds."

I looked at him but I didn't need his ten seconds. I made a concerted effort to get to my feet and struggle across the room. I wanted him to think he'd won but when I got as far as the small side cabinet, I paused to open the drawer. Then, as calmly as I could, I lifted out the small, snub-nosed pistol, swiveled awkwardly and leveled the thing at him. It was an old souvenir from my days in Asia and the barrel was fused shut, so it was useless as a weapon. But, of course, he didn't have to know that. From a few paces, it looked convincing enough.

He didn't react much to the sudden move but, then again, what was I expecting? He was a military man, a war veteran. Guns didn't surprise him any more, in any shape or form. Instead, he just looked at me steadily.

"Hans is just outside," he said, "in case you may have forgotten."

By way of an answer, I stretched out both arms to the classic marksman's position, so that the weapon was aimed straight at the centre of his chest. "Before you make that kind of mistake," I said, "let me tell you what happens. You call out for Hans. Then I shoot you. Then Hans comes running in with his rifle at the ready and he's perfectly framed against the doorway. I know where he is but he doesn't know where I am, so I beat him to the draw and shoot him too. Result? Schaeffer two, Abwehr nothing. And when they come to arrest me, I blame it on the goons downstairs."

"You seem to have it all worked out."

"No, actually, I'm making it all up as I go along, just like everyone else."

"All right, Herr Schaeffer…" There was weariness in the voice. "Whatever you want, let's get on with it, shall we? Time's passing."

I allowed myself the briefest of smiles. I couldn't believe such a fool maneuver might be working. "I already told you what I want,"

I replied. "What I want is the whole story. What's in the dossier? Why is it so goddamn important to everybody? I want the whole thing and the faster you tell me, the faster we can go save your dear Reichsführer Himmler."

Canaris sat back, crossed his legs and just looked at me, as if making up his mind. Then he seemed to come to a decision. It may well have been the simple desire to move things along - or he may even have been as tired of it all as I was.

"Gruppenführer Heydrich has been accused of being part Jewish."

"What?"

"You heard me."

"You're telling me the head of security for the entire Third Reich is part Jewish?"

"No, what I'm telling you is that those are the accusations. It's only a suspicion and even then, it's only by SS technicality. Any Jewish genes he might possess came through his paternal line and the Jews themselves only accept the maternal."

"You mean he's only Jewish by SS definition but now he's stuck with it? Hoisted on his own petard. It's almost comical."

"I can assure you it's not comical at all."

"But how did he get into the SS in the first place? What about all the racial requirements? Wouldn't that make him a little impure?"

"What it makes him is controllable. Or it did, once upon a time. His fear of being exposed put a check on his ambitions. But recently, the Gruppenführer has been able to… let's say, he's been able to eradicate any living testimony. The dossier was the only thing remaining and now he has that, too."

"So now Himmler has a problem."

"Now we *all* have a problem."

"And how do you know Heydrich hasn't destroyed it by now? How do you know he didn't just set a match to this precious dossier the moment he got hold of it?"

"I don't think he'd do that."

"Why not?"

"Because I know him. Instead of destroying the documents,

he'll use them to his own advantage, to clear his name. He'll have them forged so they'll say... Well, never mind what they'll say."

"No, tell me."

"We don't have time."

"We'll make the time. I need the details, Herr Admiral. You want me to go face him? I need to know as much as possible."

He breathed in deeply. "All right, very briefly. Reinhard Heydrich grew up in the city of Halle where his father, Bruno, ran a music academy. There were many competitors and somehow they learned that the name on Bruno's mother's grave is Süss."

"A Jewish name."

"Correct. But Süss was the name of her *second* husband. That's why she was buried with that name. The name of her first husband was Heydrich."

"And that was Bruno's father? So what's the problem? If Bruno's in the clear, then so's his son, Reinhard."

"No, it's a little more complex than that. Apparently, the woman entered a relationship with Süss while she was still married to Heydrich."

"Did she indeed? Well, good for her. So Bruno was the product of which union, the first or the second?"

"Our Gruppenführer would claim it was the first."

"And you think it was the second? That his paternal grandfather was Süss?"

An empty smile. "What *I* think doesn't matter. The fact is that the dossier contains signed witness testimony and *they* all say it was Süss."

"And how do you know all this?"

"How? Because for many years, I was the one who held the dossier. Then I gave it to Himmler. And then my good friend Reinhard stole it from his office."

"He stole it? From Himmler's own office?"

"No snide comments, Herr Schaeffer, if you please. We don't have time. It was careless, I know, but that's what happened."

"So now your friend Reinhard's got it back, he can change the documents, clear his name and move against Himmler."

"That's right. But not necessarily in that order."

"You're saying he'll move against Himmler first?"

"Yes, in Munich. Our information suggests he's going to use tonight's anti-Semitic violence as camouflage. His plan, we believe, is to eliminate the Reichsführer and blame it on the Jews, as an act of revenge on their part. Then, once Himmler's out of the way, Heydrich will no doubt take over as head of the SS... and after that, who knows where it will end?"

"You mean Heydrich as the next Führer?"

"Anything is possible, Herr Schaeffer."

"But there's one thing doesn't make sense."

He gave out with a sigh and I could tell he was losing patience. This couldn't go on for much longer. "Just one?" he said cynically.

"Why doesn't Himmler just tell Hitler the truth? Why doesn't he just reveal the fact that Heydrich may be part Jewish and have done with it?"

"Because it wouldn't work. Heydrich can't be touched."

"I don't understand."

"No, obviously not. Heydrich can't be touched for the simple reason that the Führer doesn't *want* him touched... and Himmler would never go against the Führer's wishes."

"Loyalty to a fault, right? So why doesn't Himmler just kill Heydrich first? Isn't that how they do things in the SS? Dog eat dog? Wouldn't that solve the problem for everyone?"

"Didn't you hear what I just said? The Führer doesn't want him touched. Heydrich is more knowledgeable, more intelligent and more ruthless than anyone else in the party. That makes him a very valuable asset."

"Also very dangerous."

"Yes, Herr Schaeffer, that's exactly right. Also very dangerous."

By that time, my head was really beginning to throb. The whole thing was becoming outlandish, like something from Faust, but somehow I'd landed right in the middle of it all and I had to come to terms with it. "So what happens now?" I asked him.

A simple shrug. "We drive to Munich," he said. "You inform Heydrich that unless he gives the dossier back to Himmler and ceases all further action in this regard, you'll expose his Jewish secret to the western press, which will cause him major embarrassment. Worse, it will also cause the Führer embarrassment and nobody wants that... least of all Heydrich."

"And if Himmler gets the dossier back, Katharina will be released?"

"That's the understanding. You'll both be free to do as you please. Everybody wins except the Gruppenführer... and even he gets to keep his job. It's a good solution, Herr Schaeffer, and all *you* have to do is make it work. For Fräulein Vollbrecht's sake, if for nothing else. Now, please, put down that gun or it'll be too late to do anything."

I felt him looking at me, his gaze long and hard, and I knew that was it. There'd be no more conversation. I'd found out as much as I could. Wearily, I lowered the useless piece of metal I was holding, placed it back in the drawer and tried to summon up the strength to get dressed and follow him out.

All I had to do now was confront the most ruthless man in all of Nazi Germany. And for what? For a woman who once asked me to dance.

* * *

The street was littered with pieces of furniture and ruined merchandise, as well as fragments of glass that seemed to sparkle in a thousand different ways - an effect that would later suggest the name "Kristallnacht."

We climbed into the large Mercedes. Pieckenbrock settled into the driver's seat, the carbine next to him, with Canaris and myself in the back. From Prenzlauer Strasse we turned south onto Alexander Strasse but the jolting of the car wasn't doing me any good at all. My head was still pounding, my limbs were stiff from the earlier fever, my blood-stained knuckles were sore and the rest of my body felt like it was screaming in surrender. Yet I was beginning to see that others had suffered a lot worse on that night.

On Oranienburger Strasse, the landmark Neue Synagogue was burning furiously, with flames in the windows and thick smoke rising above the neighbourhood roofs. It was still dark but, as we passed by at speed, I caught sight of figures running in the street, although whether they were fighting the flames or fanning them I wasn't sure. The fire brigade had already arrived but they didn't appear to be doing anything. No hoses, no ladders, no activity at all. They were just standing around and I later learned that their official orders consisted of protecting non-Jewish property only.

Elsewhere, I witnessed more damage and at one point I glimpsed several people prone on the pavement. Were they alive? Were they dead? I couldn't make it out. "How widespread is this?" I asked Canaris.

"I see what you see," he replied flatly.

We continued in silence as we cruised through the wealthier districts of southeastern Berlin, eventually finding our way to the autobahn that would carry us the length of Germany. After we left the city, Pieckenbrock put his foot down, while I lay my head back on the leather seat and allowed my eyes to close. There was little to see anyway, except for our own headlights in front of us, and it was a welcome, if temporary, relief.

24

It was already dawn by the time we arrived in Munich, although you'd hardly have known it from the somber, overcast skies.

We entered the old part of the city through the familiar arches of the Siegestor and weaved our way through the narrow streets, passing right by Residenzstrasse with its magnificent royal palace. I was well acquainted with the Bavarian capital and, under normal circumstances, it was one of my favourite German cities. But on this occasion, I took no delight whatsoever. I was hurting and I don't mind admitting that I was also very afraid. It was a vicious combination.

At last, we arrived at the Vier Jahreszeiten hotel and pulled up outside. I tried to stretch my legs on the sidewalk for a moment before I was ushered in through the grand doors.

Breakfast was Canaris' suggestion and I was thankful, so while Pieckenbrock went out to make phone calls, we entered the large dining room. It was still early and there were few guests around but this was a deluxe establishment and the hotel's efficient staff was able to oblige us with coffee, eggs, ham, fresh-baked bread, home-made jam and anything else we might have desired. I was starting to feel a bit like a gladiator who's fed and fussed over, just before he enters the ring and is torn to pieces by the lion.

While we ate, Canaris outlined various options and strategies that I might care to employ against Heydrich but it was all so loose that it became meaningless. A confrontation like that could take so many different turns that the only way to approach it was to have a general idea of direction and then be sharp enough to react to each moment as it came. The only problem was that I didn't feel sharp at all. I just couldn't seem to get my brain in working order.

I was a bruised and swollen mess, yet he expected me to intimidate the head of Reich security? There wouldn't be any need, I was thinking. When Heydrich saw me, he'd probably just laugh himself to death and I'd be able to stroll out of the room with the dossier under my arm.

After about twenty minutes, Pieckenbrock returned to sit with us. Then, ten minutes after that, an imposing-looking SS officer came to join us, striding in with a purposeful air. But, as I found out, it wasn't Heydrich. It was his adjutant.

"This is Oberführer Oehring," said Canaris, handling the introductions. "He's with the Gruppenführer's office." Canaris turned to the new arrival. "Have you eaten?"

"Yes, thank you, Herr Admiral." All very polite, like it was just another day.

"Then if you don't mind, we'll just finish breakfast. We still have a few minutes' grace, I believe."

It was close to eight when we all finally stood up but it was only Oehring and I who made to leave. "You're not coming?" I said to Canaris.

"No…" he replied. "The Oberführer here will escort you." But just as we were leaving, he called over to me. "Herr Schaeffer…"

I turned to look at him.

"The Fräulein," he said quietly. "Remember the Fräulein."

I felt like telling him I'd been thinking of nothing else but what purpose would it have served? Instead, I just followed Oehring out of the dining room. But we didn't walk out to the car, we went towards the elevator. It hadn't occurred to me that Heydrich would be in the same building. We rode up to the sixth floor in silence.

The corridor was deserted as we walked along to the corner suite. When we arrived, Oehring knocked loudly on the door.

The voice from inside replied crisply: "Enter."

It was a broad, handsome room, the furnishings ornate and the decor refined. The man I'd come all this way to see was sitting over by the window reading the morning's *Beobachter*: Gruppenführer Reinhard Heydrich, as yet totally oblivious to my presence. In front of him, on a small round table, were the remains of his own breakfast. He was fully dressed apart from his tunic jacket, which was slung over the back of his chair.

Oehring snapped to attention. "Herr Schaeffer," he said, announcing me.

Heydrich glanced up, not with scorn but with disinterest, as if I were interrupting him. I wasn't sure if he even knew why I was here. Then he dismissed the adjutant with just a movement of his head.

"What can I do for you, Herr Schaeffer?" he said once the door was closed. He'd already turned back to his paper.

He hadn't yet invited me to sit down so I decided to throw him a little by inviting myself. I took the chair right opposite him and noticed his look of admonishment but he didn't say anything. I was hoping that I appeared more nonchalant than I felt.

"Well, Gruppenführer…" I replied. "I believe it's more a case of what *I* can do for *you*."

He didn't look up. "You sound like you're going to sell me something."

I pretended to be amused. "As a matter of fact," I said as pleasantly as I could, "I'm not going to *sell* you anything. I'm going to *give* you something."

Still no interest. "Just state your business."

"Actually, it's some advice. You might find it of some importance."

That's when he looked over at me a little more deliberately. He was obviously not impressed. "I agreed to see you," he said, "only because Admiral Canaris personally requested it. I strongly suggest you don't abuse the privilege." Then he flipped the page and began scanning the headlines.

"I know about your operation," I said.

"There are many operations," he replied casually.

"I'm talking about the one targeting your Reichsführer."

I didn't know what effect I was expecting but there was no reaction, not even a flicker.

"You have the wrong department. Rumours come under the Ministry of Propaganda."

"This rumour comes directly from the Abwehr."

"You're a fool," he replied. Then he lifted his head and called out: "Oehring!"

The man came in smartly. "Gruppenführer?"

"Show him out."

Oehring came over to my chair and I felt a big hand on my shoulder. I was about to lose the game before it had even started.

"I also know about your family," I said, hoping it might embarrass him a little in front of his subordinate. "I know about your grandfather and about the dossier."

It seemed to work. "Wait outside," he said to Oehring, then slowly folded his paper. When he was done, he looked at me directly, a penetrating stare from those cold blue eyes.

I tried to gather what remained of my resources. "I'm here today because I, too, am answering a request from the Admiral," I told him. "He asks that you do two things. The first is to discontinue your planned operation against the Reichsführer. The second is to return the dossier."

He leaned back in his chair and massaged his forehead with his middle finger. "Herr…"

"Schaeffer," I said.

"Yes, Herr Schaeffer. I feel there may be something else on your mind."

"Something else?"

"Some kind of threat perhaps? I don't know. You tell me. I don't think the good Admiral would have sent you in here without providing one, surely?"

"All right, fine. You want a threat, I'll give you one. If you don't accede to these requests, then I'll have no choice but to release a copy of the dossier to the international press. I'm sure I don't need to explain the fallout from something like that."

I waited but he said nothing. I had no idea how much damage I'd caused or whether I'd caused any at all. Then, very deliberately, he reached for a black leather sheath that was hanging on the back of his chair. I hadn't noticed it before because it had been hidden within the folds of his tunic.

"You know what this is?" he said, slowly drawing out the glistening blade. "This is a ceremonial dagger, presented to an SS man on induction. According to Reichsführer Himmler, it's his most valuable possession." He began fingering the lethal instrument, playing with it in his hand.

Normally, I can read people fairly well. I pride myself on it. But the Gruppenführer had all the makings of a psychopath and I had no idea what he was going to do. From less than two metres away, I could see the light gleaming on the blade and I felt the rush of fear attacking whatever was left of my composure. A cough, a sneeze, a smile... It wouldn't have taken much on my part, I'm sure, for him to have thrown the table aside and lunged towards me. I'd have struggled, naturally, but he was bigger, younger, fitter. Also uninjured, I might add. I'd have felt the slash of pain as the knife tore through my flesh, my nerves and my arteries. And then what? A quick death or a slow one? A sudden rush of black or a long fade to gray as I lingered on the carpet, twitching until the life oozed out of me?

I tried to speak but it was difficult. My throat was dry. Men are always taught that they shouldn't be ashamed of fear but they are. It's something innate and very primitive and, even to this day, I can still recall the terrifying paralysis of that moment.

Then something changed and, for the first time, I saw him smile. It wasn't exactly a warm or pleasant smile but it was there nonetheless. "What's the joke?" I said tentatively.

"The joke?" he replied. "The joke is on Canaris. The joke is on Himmler."

I shook my head. I didn't understand so he began to explain it to me slowly, as if he were talking to a kindergarten child.

"The file is not genuine," he said. "I was going to change it, to doctor it for my own purposes but I don't have to. The testimonies are false. The signatures are all forged. Believe me, I've examined them. The dossier's a complete fake and it always was. That's the joke."

My expression must have been something to see. But I couldn't allow myself the indulgence of being stunned. It seemed he no longer feared the dossier's exposure and, somehow, I had to pull myself together. I was certain that as soon as he composed himself, the farce would stop and my death sentence would be carried out.

That's when I saw the newspaper that still lay on the table and something clicked in my journalist's brain.

"You know what Doktor Goebbels does for a living?" I said. "He prints lies. All those stories he tells the press to print. They're all fake, just like the Admiral's dossier. Now ask yourself this. Does the fact that they're fake stop people from reading them? Does it stop them from believing them?"

His smile retreated slightly but he still had a semi-amused look on his face. Had I hit home or not? I couldn't tell, so I decided to pile it on while I had the chance.

"That's the beauty of my profession," I added. "We're just a bunch of whores. We can create any story we want and, as long as we present it right, people will accept it."

He said nothing so I kept going.

"Let me be honest, Gruppenführer. What you don't know is that, right now, a sealed copy of that file is sitting with an acquaintance of mine in Melbourne, Australia. He's the legal counsel for a major newspaper chain and if I don't call him by noon our time, he has instructions to open it and send its contents to the editorial department for publication. Now, what you should appreciate is that Australian newsmen are just like any others. They don't care if the dossier is fake or not. They don't even care if the facts are true. They're not interested. All they're interested in is scooping the world with a big story... and this is a very big story. The head of Nazi security is really a Jew. You see, where *they* live, it's kind of out of the way. They don't get too many chances like this. I worked there myself, so I know. Trust me, they'll be very excited by what's in the envelope and before you know it, they'll have sold the rights on every continent. It'll be front page news in every capital in the world."

He continued looking at me for some time. He was still holding the dagger but I felt I'd won a stay of execution, however brief. I sat back in the chair, not sure whether to breathe or not. Of course, nothing about my story was true. I'd never even *seen* the dossier, much less sent it to Australia, but he didn't know that. It was a bluff, just like the jammed gun back in my apartment, and I thought it was a pretty smart ploy under the circumstances. Unfortunately, I couldn't tell if he'd believed me or not. There wasn't a flicker on his face.

A full minute went by. Down below us, the morning traffic flowed on Maximilian Strasse and, from where I was sitting, I could see the streetcars crawling back and forth like ants building a nest.

Without saying a word, he stood up and paced thoughtfully around the room, tapping the blade of the dagger on his palm in time to his steps. When he arrived back at the window, he just stood there, gazing at a mid-point somewhere between the hotel and the buildings on the other side of the thoroughfare. Finally, the thin smile returned and he sat down in the same chair, placing the dagger on the table in front of him.

"It's all irrelevant anyway," he said. He looked at his watch. "In exactly forty-three minutes, the Jews intend to blow up the Reichsführer's car as he travels peacefully along the autobahn."

I was thrown for the moment. "You already placed a bomb in Himmler's car?"

"No, not me, the Jews."

I saw his smile broaden out and from the back of his throat came a short, high-pitched laugh. Meanwhile, I took the opportunity to check my own watch.

"What? You think you can stop it?" he said, still laughing to himself. "You and the Admiral? Go ahead, try, by all means. If you want to go chasing along the autobahn, you're welcome to do so. Be my guest."

"You realize that if we can't stop it, the dossier will be published anyway."

"The dossier…" His tone was derisive. "I'll just say it's a fake smear story put out by the international Jewish conspiracy."

"Nobody in the world's going to believe that."

"I don't care about the world, as long as Germany believes it.

You saw last night how the people really feel. There was no objection, no protest. Nobody stood up to help the Jews, the crowds just stood by and watched. Many even cheered. It was clear demonstration of how they feel. Everything changed last night. As a journalist, you should understand that."

"And how about the Führer? What will *he* say when the dossier's splattered all over the news?"

The smile suddenly vanished and he glared at me, his eyes as sharp as the dagger in front of him. "The Führer? You *dare* to mention the Führer? You just don't understand, do you? Any of you. Even now, even after all this. If I arrange it and Germany believes it, then the Führer will endorse it. It's as simple as that." Then he sat back, glanced at his watch again and said: "You now have forty-*two* minutes."

I had no idea what to do. Did I have the upper hand or did he? My brain was swirling around, my mind in chaos, but all that seemed to emerge from the debris was an image of Katharina, floating up in front of me - ethereal, angelic - and I succumbed to it. The clock was ticking on her life so I took the risk. I got up and made for the door, not even sure whether I'd get that far.

He could have killed me himself or ordered Oehring to do it. Either would have been easy. But instead he just said: "Give my regards to the Admiral."

And that was it. I walked out without looking back. I passed Oehring in the corridor and paced my way as calmly as I could to the elevator. When it arrived, I stepped hurriedly inside, shut the grille behind me, pulled back the lever and only once the cage was descending was I able to breathe.

What I couldn't work out was why he'd told me about the bomb. Or why he'd let me go. But then, somewhere between the third and second floors, it all became instantly clear. My subconscious had somehow managed to figure it out without any help from me.

Maybe he really *was* concerned about the story going out internationally, I thought to myself, and maybe he really *did* want us to try and stop the attempt. Maybe all the rest was just bravado.

25

I found Canaris and Pieckenbrock sitting in the lobby lounge, going through some papers as if nothing had happened.

"Let's go," I said and then, before they could ask me any questions: "I'll tell you in the car."

It took me over fifteen minutes to explain what had happened up there on the sixth floor because Canaris kept posing questions, trying to get an exact feel for what had taken place. Pieckenbrock, meanwhile, said nothing. I don't know how much he'd been told about any of it but he appeared to have no opinions and made no attempt to comment. He just kept driving, negotiating his way along Ludwigstrasse and then back the way we came. We assumed that the autobahn Heydrich had mentioned was the one that led back to Berlin because that was the only thing that made sense. Where else would the Reichsführer be going?

Once we were out on the open road, the speedometer flickered up towards the two hundred kilometre mark and I looked at my watch for the umpteenth time. Just a few more minutes before it was meant to happen. I peered ahead through the windshield, thinking I might even spot the distant explosion. My eyes tried to pierce the dim gray mist on the horizon for any signs of smoke.

The due time came and went, yet still nothing. Bombs can be notoriously unreliable, Canaris informed me, especially the home-made variety. But five minutes passed, then ten, and still nothing. We were hurtling along Fritz Todt's smooth, four-lane highway with no sign of anything amiss.

Then we rounded a long curve and we saw them. A convoy of three cars, traveling sedately up ahead at about half our speed. They were still a good kilometre away but we were closing fast.

It was at that point that I began wondering how much explosive can be packed into a car trunk? If we rolled up right next to them, would we also bear the brunt of the blast? Yes, it actually crossed my mind. Then we'd all die - Himmler, Canaris, Schaeffer and finally Katharina - all of us in one great and tragic ending. Another joke for Heydrich to enjoy.

We kept gaining, closer and closer. I felt the sweat begin to trickle down my collar.

"Which car is he in?" said Pieckenbrock.

"Centre," said Canaris, more familiar with SS protocol.

Pieckenbrock flashed his lights, then put his hand on the horn and left it there. It didn't help my headache.

We ate up the last few hundred metres and suddenly we were alongside and all four cars swerved to a halt at the edge of the road. We'd hardly stopped before the driver's door was flung open and Pieckenbrock was out, screaming and yelling at the top of his lungs. Gradually, the occupants of the other cars emerged to find out what all the fuss was about, including the SS Reichsführer himself, Heinrich Himmler, who was a little slower getting out.

Then the full realization set in and people were scrambling everywhere. Voices gave rapid orders and there was the sound of jackboots on asphalt as everyone was herded towards the adjacent field.

But still, no explosion. We waited expectantly but the minutes passed and there was nothing.

Eventually, someone was dispatched for help in Canaris' car, the only one they knew would be safe. But long before he returned, Himmler's adjutants had flagged down a police vehicle on the autobahn so that the Reichsführer could continue his journey. Meanwhile, the rest of us waited in the muddy cabbage field until a military truck arrived carrying a pair of sappers with all their bomb disposal equipment.

They carefully searched the Reichsführer's car before turning their attention to the other two but, in the end, they found no trace of any bomb. No sign at all. Was it a mistake? Or had it all been a deliberate hoax?

* * *

Reinhard Heydrich also returned to Berlin that day, flying his own small Focke-Wulf as he so often did, from Munich back to the military airfield at Staaken. By the time night fell, he was already celebrating at a seedy nightclub called "Der Anker," along with Walter Schellenberg, "Gestapo" Müller - and Heydrich's own wife, Lina.

The place was really nothing more than a hole-in-the-wall, the kind of dive where you could get almost anything you wanted - a girl, a game, a good cigar, even cocaine if you had the money - but for most people, booze was the drug of choice. In such bars, nothing was actually available on the premises for fear of a raid, especially if the bribery was in arrears. Yet customers could still obtain what they wanted by whispering in the ear of the right hostess who would gladly pass on the request to a runner in the alley. For a small commission, naturally.

On that particular evening, a raunchy, middle-aged woman with bleached hair and a silver-sequined gown was up on the small stage, doing her best with some blues lyrics, something about love and betrayal. But there weren't that many customers and her performance was mainly directed at the high-ranking party from the SS. They all seemed to be having a good time, laughing hysterically and ordering champagne by the magnum.

The topic was Heydrich's story of the day: about how he'd told some small-time foreign journalist that there was a bomb in the Reichsführer's car and how Himmler and his entire personal staff had been banished to a cabbage field, knee-deep in mud, in case the imaginary bomb exploded. It was hilarious and each new detail seemed funnier than the last.

Finally, at some time after midnight when they'd all had their fill, the Gruppenführer and his wife went home together, just like old times. Just as Schellenberg had predicted.

In the end, it was Lina who'd warned her husband that his bomb plot against the Reichsführer had been compromised and, although it had been necessary to abort the operation, he was highly appreciative of her loyalty. Despite their past differences, it was clear that she still recognized the true value of their relationship, as well as the ultimate vision they shared. Their marital alliance, it seemed, was back on track.

26

After spending a restless night on a camp bed at the Abwehr, I woke up and ate the minimal breakfast they served me. Dry black bread and a cup of weak coffee: not exactly the Vier Jahreszeiten hotel. I wasn't in handcuffs but I *was* in custody and the room had been locked from the outside. Canaris had told me I'd be free to go, free to do as I pleased, but that was evidently not the case. I'm not sure I'd ever really believed him anyway.

The real problem was that I'd also received no news of Katharina. I'd made persistent demands but so far, not a word. Had she been released? Was she still being detained? Had he also lied about her? I had no idea.

Promptly at eight, I was picked up by Hans Pieckenbrock, who was accompanied on this occasion by one of his more muscular aides. I was driven to my apartment on Prenzlauer Strasse, where I was instructed to collect my belongings, or at least everything I could carry. I was about to be deported, they informed me, by signed order of Reichsführer Himmler. It was for my own protection and the less fuss I made about it the better.

The neighbourhood streets were still a mess and it was a shock to see in broad daylight how much damage had been done. All across the country, Jewish property had been ransacked, synagogues had been burned, untold numbers of Jewish women and girls had been raped and over twenty thousand Jewish men were on their way to internment at Dachau, Buchenwald and other camps. There were also draconian new laws being passed in Göring's Reichstag that deprived them of even more rights. And all of it was supposedly justified by Goebbels as retribution for one confused seventeen-year-old taking an amateurish pot-shot at a third-grade embassy official in Paris.

As we left the building, I looked for the Feldsteins but Pieckenbrock's man refused to let me even knock on their door. He kept hurrying me along down the stairs and, since my incentive was the barrel of a Luger digging into in my still-bruised kidneys, I had little option but to comply.

I was driven to the Friedrichstrasse rail terminus, arriving just in time to catch the 11:15 departure for Cherbourg, change in Paris. Of course, I had a hundred questions, none of which they answered. Above all, I wanted to know about Katharina - but there comes a time when prudence takes over and, in the end, I just shut my mouth and allowed them to bundle me onto the train, praying to whatever God was up there that they were really letting me go.

Just to make sure I didn't jump off at some point along the track, Pieckenbrock assigned his colleague to accompany me all the way to the French border, instructing me in no uncertain terms that if I ever tried to re-enter Germany for any reason whatsoever, I would be immediately arrested.

* * *

After a long and tiring rail journey, I finally reached the Channel port of Cherbourg on the afternoon of Monday, November 14th, in good time for the ship's departure. It was due to sail the following morning on the early tide.

I stopped at a cheap bar near the wharf and tried to call Berlin. I wanted to speak to Siegfried Wachter or even Manfred Vollbrecht but I couldn't get through to anyone and, after several attempts, the operator told me that there were no lines available. It was a common occurrence with the antiquated French phone system but, nevertheless, I hung up in a thoroughly bad mood, convinced that I was still somehow being victimized. I'd done what they wanted, so where was Katharina?

Since I had little money left in my wallet for a hotel, I decided to board the ship that same evening. I was told there'd be a prepaid ticket waiting for me. It took some time to organize but, eventually, I was directed towards my reserved cabin - a noisy, third class closet over on the port side, close to the stern.

She was waiting for me inside. Katharina. Just sitting there on the bunk, cool and calm and leafing through a tourist magazine.

As I came in, she stood up and smiled at the look of total astonishment on my face. I didn't know how she got there, who authorized it or whether she, too, was being deported but I didn't care. Without thinking too much about it, the sheer surprise propelled me forward and I kissed her, not sweetly on the cheek but full on the lips. My arms were around her, my hands were in her long, chestnut hair and I could feel her fingers undoing my coat.

It was completely automatic, completely natural, because that's what happens when there are no prior questions, no thoughts, no ambiguities. Things just flow and feel right. My body was still in pain but I needed her warmth next to me, enveloping me. And she was wearing the same perfume, the one she'd worn at Horcher's, and I was losing myself in the vapours. We entwined and, with our eyes closed, spiraled down onto the bunk.

But it wasn't a wild, thrashing climax. It was rich and deep and I didn't want it to end. It was the answer to everything pent up inside me, all the stress and the tension and the fear, and I just wanted it to go on and on, to lose myself forever in the moment.

* * *

I was woken by a soft tap on the door and it took me several seconds to work out where I was and what I was doing here. I put on some pants and eased open the cabin door, only to be faced by a young man in uniform.

"Good evening, sir," he said.

The language was English, the accent was Cockney and, much to my relief, the uniform was white, not black. He was just a steward but he represented final confirmation that I wasn't still in Berlin and that I was, in fact, on board the Cunard steamship "Lancastria" bound for Québec City via Southampton. He'd put my baggage down by the door and was waiting for his tip.

"Just a minute," I replied and went back inside. I saw that she was awake and smiling as I fished out some loose change. Then, once he was gone, I undressed before slipping back down under the covers and, once again, we wrapped ourselves around each other. But that's when it struck me - the steward had only brought one set of bags.

"Where's your luggage?" I asked her. "You're coming with me, aren't you?"

She was holding me gently and fingering my bruises delicately. They were the slim, gentle hands I'd thought about so often.

"I can't," she said very quietly. "Not right now."

"Why not? I'll book you a ticket. We'll find stuff for you on board. They must have stores or supplies or something..."

"No... No, my father's very sick. I have to go back. I can't leave him."

"But I can't go back to Germany. I'll be arrested."

"I know."

"You do? So what are we saying here? You can't stay with me and I can't stay with you?"

She looked at me, her face expressing what I was beginning to feel. "I'm sorry, Ed... I seem to have caused you a great deal of trouble."

It was a considerable understatement and I wasn't sure how to respond. Then something inside of me snapped. I needed to know what was going on. "Tell me the truth," I said. "Were you working for Himmler all along?"

"No," she replied, her voice still soft. "Not at first. Not when I accepted your invitation. That was real."

"How about Horcher's?"

"No, that was real too. Right up until..."

Her voice trailed off, so I finished it for her.

"Until the SS arrived. After that, it was all a show, right?"

"I'm afraid so."

"The detention, the story your father gave me, everything. It was all a set-up, wasn't it?"

"I'm sorry, Ed."

"But why? Why did you do it? Why did you *agree* to do it?"

My questions were almost plaintive and I could hear her breathing as she tried to formulate a reply. Her hair, I noticed, was all over the pillow forming intricate patterns, brown on white. Then she shook her head slightly and the patterns changed.

"I don't know," she said.

"You don't know?"

"What I mean is, I don't know exactly. Circumstances, I suppose. We sometimes have to do things... Ed, I'm sorry."

"Are you a Nazi?" It was a terrible thing to ask and I wish I hadn't said it but there it was.

"Some of us don't know what we are," she said.

Her entire conversation was a mass of uncertainty and I began to wonder: who was the real Katharina? Behind all that elegance and confidence, was she just as mixed-up as the rest of us?

I propped myself up on one elbow. I had an idea. "Hey, why don't we find ourselves a neutral country?" I suggested. "You could bring your father with you."

"Where?"

"Who cares? Switzerland... Sweden, maybe... Anywhere." I waited but there was no answer, so I lay back down again and stared at the rivets in the ceiling. "Why did you come here?" I asked her. "Was it guilt? Did you think you could apologize for everything you put me through?"

"No... I mean yes, but that's not the real reason."

"Then why?"

"I came because..."

"Because what?"

"I just wanted to see you again."

I didn't know how to reply. I felt her edge a little closer to me and that was when we began all over again, slower and deeper and even more intense. Afterwards, we just collapsed in sweaty exhaustion and drifted into sleep. This time, there was no steward to wake us up.

* * *

When I opened my eyes, it was close to dawn and, from the dim light of the porthole, I could just about make out her profile. She was already sitting up with her back against the wall, staring into the darkness with a blanket wrapped around her. She looked at me and I could see the faint radiance in her eyes. She still seemed so remote, even after we'd been as physically intimate as any two people can be.

"Tell me about it," I said softly.

She didn't move. "About what?"

"Everything. Tell me the whole story."

"I'm not sure…"

"You're not sure I want to hear it? Yes I do."

It took her some time but finally she began to open up. About her father and how he was so worried about his brother in the mental institution. About how she was recruited by Himmler himself and how, little by little, she was drawn further into his scheme, much further than she ever wanted to be. They said it was for the good of the country, that's what they kept saying. Except they didn't use the word "Reich." They used the word "Fatherland," which has a far more ancient and honorable appeal.

Then, towards the end of her discourse, she mentioned my sometime friend, Siegfried Wachter, and I was surprised to hear the name. "How do you know him?" I asked her.

"Siegfried? I've known him for ages. He works with Ribbentrop."

"Really? I thought he worked with Canaris."

"I think he does all kinds of work."

"My, my! Clever Siegfried."

"Speaks fluent Russian, did you know that? Ribbentrop finds it useful, sends him to Moscow quite frequently."

No, as it happened, I didn't know but I could well believe it, especially after that strange dinner we had at Igor's. But then she said something that totally floored me, something I wasn't expecting at all.

"Of course," she said, "that's how he obtained the dossier for Canaris."

"The dossier? The one about Reinhard Heydrich? Wait a minute, you're telling me it came from Moscow?"

"You didn't know?"

"No, I didn't know. Why would the Russians put together a file on Heydrich?"

"Because Stalin wanted it."

"Why?"

"It's very simple. Hitler thinks he's just a dumb Slav and that his people are inferior. It offends Stalin. So he thought if he could compromise the head of SS security, it would send a strong message."

"But it didn't work."

"Didn't it? So how come we're here talking about it? If *we* know about it, how many others do you think there are? The dossier may be a fake but Heydrich's secret is wide open. Himmler, Canaris, Göring... They all know. Even your friend Siegfried knows. How easy do you think it will be for Hitler to name Heydrich as his successor now?"

She had a good point and it crossed my mind that she'd make one hell of a journalist. But that raised another question in my mind about sources. What I still couldn't fathom was how someone like Katharina could possibly know all this. Who was providing the information? Did everyone in Europe confide in her?

"Who *are* you?" I asked her.

The laughter rang out and all of a sudden we were back to the first Katharina, the one I danced with at the restaurant. "I'm my father's daughter," she replied.

That's when a weak sun put in its first appearance above the horizon. The ship would soon be ready to sail.

"There aren't many left, you know," she said a little wistfully.

"Who?"

"The old guard. The old generation. The ones who believe in the old values."

"You mean like your father? But he belongs to the 'Friends of the SS,' doesn't he? I was told he runs the damn thing."

"He does but..."

"But what?"

"Things are not as simple as they might be. You have to understand. Yes, he belongs to it but he also despises it. And he's not alone. There are still a few of them left... working, believing. They have secret meetings to try and build support amongst the generals before it's too late, before we're dragged into a war that destroys all of Europe. They say that's the only hope left, the Wehrmacht."

"They're planning a coup against Hitler?"

"No... I mean, they like to think so but it's just a delusion."

"So why do they do it?"

"Why? Because they don't want to let the hope die. Once the hope dies, they'll all just die along with it."

"Including your father."

"Especially my father."

"So he sits out there on the family estate while you keep in touch with what's going on, right? You travel, you mix in the right circles, you talk to Ribbentrop, to Henderson, to whoever you can. You're his entire network, aren't you? You're his eyes and ears. A one-woman bureau."

She laughed again but she didn't deny it.

And that's when we were interrupted by a loud, clanging bell, followed immediately by an English voice: "All ashore who's going ashore!"

I sat up and she shared the blanket with me. I put my arm around her shoulders and let my fingers play with her hair. Suddenly I didn't care about politics or intrigue or anything else we'd been discussing. I only cared about her.

"Stay," I said.

"I can't."

"Would you, if you could?"

She kissed me very gently, then got to her feet and began picking her clothes from the floor. After a while, I couldn't even look at her any more.

We slowly got dressed and I walked with her up to the main deck. We said nothing. I heard the loud wash of the waves and felt them slap against the side - the tide that would soon carry me out, away from here - away from *her*. The ship was rolling slightly on its moorings and we stood there for a while, holding the handrail and breathing in the wintry ozone. Her hand reached for mine.

"What will happen..." I said, "when they find out you told me all this?"

"Hopefully, they won't." Then she leaned over, kissed me and put a single finger against my lips. "I trust you," she said softly.

And I immediately knew what that meant. It meant I had the scoop of a lifetime but I could never wire it out because she trusted me not to do so. Yet, somehow, it didn't matter. At that moment, I wasn't worried about stories, or bylines, or quotes, or any of the other things that filled my average day. I just wanted her more than I'd ever wanted anything. She'd captivated me, overwhelmed me, and it meant more to me than my career. I'd risked everything for her. I'd risked Dachau, I'd risked death... How much more could I do?

"Why can't you stay?" I said, almost pleading. "Why can't you just forget everything and stay?"

She just looked at me. "Ed..."

Her voice drifted away, lost in the wind, and already I was feeling the loneliness, the longing. And she was feeling the same, I could tell, but she was trying very hard to hold it all back, her face almost contorting with the effort.

"Be careful on the journey," she said, and then she was gone.

27

I stood at the stern of the Lancastria as it steamed out of Cherbourg and watched my life disappear into the distance.

I must confess that, for one brief moment, I actually considered climbing over the rail and I recall wondering how it would be just to let everything go - to say goodbye to the world, let the ocean fill my lungs and just sink into total oblivion. I stood like that for some time but, in the end, I couldn't do it. Maybe it was lack of courage or maybe it just wasn't my style but, having made up my mind that I would keep breathing, I was then faced with another problem.

I had to consider the fact that her final words were meant as more than just a parting shot. After all, she could have chosen to say anything. She could have even chosen to say goodbye, for pete's sake, but she didn't. Instead, she told me to be careful and she specifically said "on the journey." And the more I thought about it, the more I knew I had to stay alert. It's possible I'd developed a large dose of paranoia over the past few weeks but I became convinced they were going to come after me. Perhaps not Canaris, or even Himmler. But Heydrich was a psychopath. I'd faced him down with his own secret and tried to blackmail him with it - and now he'd had time to think about it. Would he just let such a confrontation go or would he consider it a challenge, an insult that had to be avenged?

I couldn't answer that question, so I forced myself be on guard every minute of the day and night. I couldn't relax. I couldn't enjoy the voyage. While I was strolling the decks, I was peering around every next corner. When I was in the salon or the dining room, I was busy analyzing the faces of the passengers. And the few conversations I struck up were mainly for the sake of probing further. "Hi, where are you folks from?" or "What brings you on board?"

There were about the same number of English citizens as French, most of the former having been picked up when we called in at Southampton for the day. There were also quite a few Belgians and Dutch plus, of course, a fair sized contingent of Canadians returning home.

And, yes, there were also seven Germans on board and I reserved my special attention for them. But it soon became very clear they could all be dismissed from suspicion. Three middle-aged ladies, one in a wheelchair. A pair of elderly businessmen, both with large paunches. And a single woman, a professional nanny, with a four-year-old who never stopped whining. It was almost inconceivable that any them could be SS assassins.

The Canadians on board seemed quiet in comparison to the others and, during a few precious moments, I allowed myself to relax a little in their company. It had been a long time. They were ordinary people for the most part and there was one family I especially liked, a couple from New Brunswick with their three teen boys. They'd been visiting relatives and were on their way home for Christmas. They were big people, with the oldest son towering over everyone on board. A promising defenseman, his dad told me proudly, apparently going for a try-out soon in Boston. We spoke knowledgably about the game of hockey and it brought back some of the more pleasant memories from my childhood.

It was selfish, I know, but when I met that particular family, it immediately occurred to me that I might call on them for extra muscle should the need arise. I wasn't proud of myself for thinking that way and I knew well enough that the last thing a nice family like that needed was trouble of my sort.

So I continued to skulk around, keeping only to well-lit areas and even sniffing my food whenever possible before I ate. At night, I tried to lock the cabin but it was an older ship and the mechanism didn't work too well. Since the furniture in the room was all bolted down, there was nothing I could push against the door. I did have one inspiration though and, on the second day out, I managed to smuggle a small metal table lamp from the salon. Every evening from then on, I pulled the lamp out from its hiding place in my locker and placed it right behind the door. It was a simple concept but it's probably why I'm alive today.

It happened on the last night of the voyage.

We'd reached the St. Lawrence estuary and were due to dock at Québec City the following afternoon. It was already snowing and I heard someone saying that there wouldn't be many more ships through here before the deep freeze.

Thus far on the journey, there'd been nothing untoward and perhaps I allowed myself to relax too much. The continuing tension plus the frigid Atlantic air had taken its toll and I was desperately tired. I'd already purchased a small bottle of rye from the on-board duty-free, partly as a homecoming gift to myself and partly as nostalgia for Horcher's. Anyway, whatever the reason, that night I allowed myself a couple of shots and fell into a deep sleep.

I don't know how long it was before I heard the lamp tip over, smashing the bulb. Never one for instant reflexes, I sat up in bed, startled. But that was only for a second. In my head, I'd already planned for this scenario a hundred times.

I jumped up but whoever it was had already gone. I reached for the door, grabbing the whiskey bottle as the first thing that came to hand, and stepped out just in time to see a shadow disappear around the far bulkhead. I was only in my shorts and it was bitterly cold but I gave chase like a lunatic.

I knew that the passageway he'd taken would lead him upstairs to the deck, so when I turned the corner, I was prepared for the climb. Ignoring my aches and pains, I bounded up the stairs, sure of my footing in my bare feet. But then, once I emerged outside, my skin was instantly in shock from the wet snow.

He turned and saw me and that was his undoing. As he tried to put on a spurt, he skidded on the slippery deck and went sprawling. He tried to get up but he fell again and by that time I was on him. He wasn't that powerful and I was able to push him over again easily. Thoughts of my battle with the brown-shirts resurfaced and

I half-expected several of his friends to assault me from behind but they never arrived. He was alone and I piled on to him. That's when I saw the flash of the weapon, a small knife. I was beginning to hate knives and all the SS fanatics who wielded them.

With all my planning, I hadn't planned for this: going head-to-head with an armed killer and me with just a bottle in my hand. Steel against glass. A professional SS assassin against an out-of-shape journalist. It should have been no contest but, for the moment, I was on top. He was down on the deck while I was still on my feet.

He slashed at me wildly from where he lay but I was able to avoid the strike by leaning backwards. Immediately, he swung again, cutting open my thigh. It was the worst thing he could have done. The sudden thrust of pain released the adrenalin inside me and all the pent-up emotion turned into violent aggression. There was no way I could stop myself. Before he could move again, the bottle came crashing down on the side of his skull, breaking his head open like a piece of ripe fruit. Before I knew it, there were streams of blood and fragments of bone all over the frozen white deck, staining it deep pink. The stench of whiskey was everywhere.

I knew he was dead and, for the moment, I just stood there breathing heavily in the freezing air, vaguely trying to work out who it was that I'd just killed. And then slowly, I began to recognize his face. I'd seen him around the ship, both in the dining room and out here on the deck. I'd assumed he was one of the Dutch contingent because he always seemed to be with them. Obviously, that assumption was wrong. It wouldn't be difficult for a German to pass as Dutch and I'd almost paid for the error in judgment with my life.

I don't know how long I remained there like that but when I finally looked up, I found myself staring into the face of a horrified young crewman.

* * *

Looking back, I've no idea what I might have done. Pushed the body over the side, probably, before returning to my cabin as if nothing had happened. I don't know. I wouldn't have had any scruples about doing it, that much was certain. He was SS and he'd come to my cabin to murder me, no doubt on Reinhard Heydrich's orders. As it was, I just stood there in front of the young crewman, numb from the cold and from the murder I'd just committed. I couldn't run because there's nowhere to run on a ship, so there was nothing for it but to wait for the kid to get his wits together and go for help.

I was brought before the British captain who listened politely and attentively to the story I concocted, something about a vicious thief breaking in to my cabin. He then informed me that, since the event happened in Canadian waters and we'd be docking that same afternoon, I would have to come under their jurisdiction. Meanwhile, the ship's medic dressed my thigh wound and the crewman they assigned as an escort treated me to a nice lunch in the mess room. Their civility under the circumstances was appreciated.

Yet I'd reckoned without the sobriety of Canadian justice. At first I'd lied to the captain and said the man was a thief because I was still traumatized and thought nobody would believe the real story. Then, when the Mounties came aboard to question me, they kept asking why I'd chased a mere thief half-way along the ship and then killed him, so I decided to tell the truth after all. But I was right in the first place. They just scoffed at the idea of an SS assassin and asked why, if I was so involved in international intrigue, my only weapon was a whiskey bottle. "What brand was it?" one of them asked, to which I myself very nearly laughed out loud.

I wasn't laughing, though, when the judge handed down his jail sentence. And I wasn't laughing too much either on that depressing February morning when they deposited me at the Kingston penitentiary. As they slammed the cell door shut, it seemed like the end - and in the terms of the tale I have to tell, it was. No last minute reprieves. No dramatic jail breaks. Not even a visitor, except for my cousins from Kitchener who came along to stare at me like I was some kind of zoo animal.

A sad finale, perhaps. But there was one bright side at least. However insecure I was, I knew for sure that even the most daring of Heydrich's hit squads couldn't get at me in the depths of the Kingston pen. And when hostilities ceased on that memorable day in 1945, I was cheering louder than anybody because it meant that all the Nazi scum I'd had to deal with during that last fateful autumn in Berlin were gone and I was the last man standing.

As far as I was concerned, I'd won.

E P I L O G U E

Barcelona, September 1951

In recognition of my good behaviour, and perhaps helped along by the spirit of benevolence that seemed to wash over Canada after VE Day, I was given an early parole. By VJ Day, I was out on the town, celebrating the end of hostilities along with everyone else.

With the little money I had left, I traveled back to Europe and saw the remains of wartime damage. Everywhere I went, I found bombed-out buildings and displaced persons trying to salvage whatever they could and rebuild their shattered lives. But even then, nothing could prepare me for the devastation I found in my old stomping ground of Berlin. Streets, landmarks, entire districts had just disappeared. The city was unrecognizable. It had been pounded and pulverized and it was now divided into four zones, each supervised by one of the major allies - US, British, French and Russian.

I arrived there in the spring of '46 and spent several weeks picking through the mounds of gray rubble, searching for information, clues, anything I could find about the people I once knew. Then I stayed on throughout the Nuremberg trials, paying my way as a translator while I tried to sort out where I belonged and what to do next.

Eventually, I began freelancing again, mostly for the newly emerging local press. They were free from Goebbels for the first time in twelve years and seemed to appreciate the western contacts and perspective I was able to provide. I made good progress and, when the Middle East conflict began to heat up towards the end of the British mandate, I volunteered for the assignment to cover it first-hand.

Was it still some weird fascination with the fate of the Jews, the same reason I remained on Prenzlauer Strasse when so many people advised me to move? Perhaps. Or was it just something I felt I owed the Feldsteins after I ducked out on them like that? I don't know. I'm still trying to figure it out.

At any rate, I did a pretty good job out there, all things considered. Then, one day, I was strolling through the souks of Jaffa the way I'd once sauntered around the Alexanderplatz when a grenade exploded not fifteen metres from where I was standing. Several small fragments lodged themselves in my spine and I spent six months in and out of a Tel-Aviv hospital trying to get some movement back into the lower half of my anatomy. It was a long, difficult recovery but it did give me time to come up with an idea.

I knew that the fledgling Israeli government of Ben Gurion dearly wanted to bring ex-members of the Nazi fraternity to justice, so I made a deal. I used a ministerial contact to gain access to the higher levels of the newly formed Mossad and told them that, for a modest bounty, I was prepared to identify their quarry as they tried to make good their escape. We settled on Barcelona as a location because Franco's Spain had become a well-used stopover on the route to South America.

And so, here I am; still here on the Ramblas, still sitting at José's sidewalk café watching the sun go down. I have a buzz in my head, a piece of shrapnel in my back and, some would say, a major chip on my shoulder. But before I drown in a deluge of self-pity, I think I should finish by revealing the rest of what I managed to find out. So here, in approximate order of appearance, is what happened to the people who together managed to carve such a big chunk out of my life back in Berlin…

Wilhelm Canaris, head of the Abwehr, was arrested by the Gestapo early in 1945, accused of treason against the Führer. He was imprisoned at Flossenburg and eventually hanged from a meat hook with a piano wire.

Erika Waag-Canaris, despite reports to the contrary, was living under an assumed name when I found her in Dortmund. She was very helpful in filling in a lot of gaps.

Reinhard Heydrich was promoted to the rank of SS Obergruppenführer. When the war began, he took charge of the

Einsatzgruppen death squads that followed the Wehrmacht across Europe, the first step in the mass murder of Jews, Gypsies and other "undesirables." Then, in January 1942, he organized the infamous Wannsee conference and took supreme personal charge of the "final solution" apparatus, including the extermination camps of Auschwitz-Birkenau, Treblinka and others. As a reward for his services, he was appointed Reich Protektor of Bohemia and Moravia but his elevation didn't last long. In March of that year, he was assassinated in Prague by Czech agents. At his funeral, Hitler mourned him as "the man with the iron heart" and, in retribution, ordered the entire Czech town of Lidice to be wiped out - the slaughter of over 15,000 men, women and children.

Lina von Osten-Heydrich survived the war and was eventually remarried to a Finn. I traced her back to her native island of Fehmarn in the Baltics, where she'd turned her family home into a small hotel. In a meandering conversation, she gave me her own unique interpretation of events but I found her account self-serving and questionable in many areas. Last I heard, she was still defending her late husband's activities to any journalist who came along. She still maintains he was a hero of the Reich.

Walter Schellenberg, head of the Ausland SD division of the SS, continued his habit of playing both sides right through to the end of the war. He finally made contact with the American OSS in Spain, as well as the Red Cross in Sweden, before he surrendered. In 1946, he gave evidence on behalf of the war crimes prosecution at Nuremburg, in return for which he received a relatively light sentence. He was recently released.

Hermann Göring remained a popular public figure and was nominated Hitler's deputy. He got the prize they all had fought over. As head of the Luftwaffe, Göring supervised the air component of the blitzkrieg against Poland, Norway, France and the Low Countries but failed to finish off the British at Dunkirk, his worst military disgrace. He finally surrendered himself to Eisenhower's forces and took cyanide in his cell at Nuremberg before he could be tried.

Emmy Sonnemann-Göring, the one-time film actress, I didn't

bother tracking. It's believed, however, that she was the one who passed her husband the fatal pill.

Nicholas Brent-Alderton, British Embassy attaché, was recalled to London and spent the war years keeping his head down along the ministerial corridors of Whitehall. I think he was on Anthony Eden's personal staff for a time. Where he is now, I don't know. Probably running some snooty pub back in Somerset.

Hans Pieckenbrock of the Abwehr was killed in an accidental air crash in 1942 while visiting the U-boat flotillas on the French Atlantic coast.

Heinrich Himmler, Reichsführer of the SS, expanded the service to include the Waffen SS military divisions, which fought alongside the Wehrmacht. He was captured by the British in 1945 and, in his final delusion, he actually thought he could negotiate an armistice. Like Göring, he took his own life before they could hang him.

Ingrid Jürgens (Himmler's personal secretary), I met in Berlin. She's now married. In return for her considerable help, I agreed not to print her real name.

My old friend, Traudl Lohse, was badly mauled by the invading Soviets. Like many women, she was held in a military cell and suffered mass rape for many months. She now resides in an institution near the Tegelsee. I don't know what happened to her younger sister, Gerda, or to Gerda's unborn child.

Siegfried Wachter, capitalist and double agent *par excellence*, survived the war handsomely by trading commodities and secrets to both sides. Today, he owns a thirty metre yacht and I still see him occasionally when he calls in here. In spite of everything that happened, I find it impossible to remain upset with him and we still enjoy a cognac together. As I always said, nobody knows how to live better than Siegfried.

Karlheinz Oehring (Heydrich's adjutant) was a good source of information as he passed through Barcelona not too long ago. I promised not to reveal his real name here either - but I had no scruples at all about passing it on to the Israelis. I'm not sure whether they ever caught him.

Theodor Eicke, the Kommandant at Dachau who pioneered the "Kz" concentration camp system, became supervisor of all the German based camps. He was killed on the eastern front in 1943.

Heinrich "Gestapo" Müller continued to run the Geheime Staatspolizei as a division of the RSHA, first under Heydrich and then Kaltenbrunner. In April 1945, he disappeared into the chaos of Berlin and was never found.

Herschel Grynszpan (the Jewish boy whose attack on the German embassy official in Paris became the excuse for Kristallnacht) was first jailed and then sent to the camps in 1940. Somehow, he survived the war and today he's back living in France.

Sadly, my landlord and his wife, Asher and Rivka Feldstcin, were not so fortunate. They were taken first to Buchenwald and from there transported by cattle car to Treblinka, where they suffered the same fate as six million others.

However, I'm glad to report that their son, Yossel, managed to escape. He stole a bike in Berlin and rode it as far as Silesia, where he crossed the Polish border and joined up with the partisan resistance. He's now married, a father of two and working as a qualified mechanic in Haifa, which was where I last saw him. We still correspond.

And there it is. All of it. Except for Katharina.

I searched, God knows I searched, but I could find nothing. Her father, Manfred Vollbrecht, finally died of heart disease in 1941, leaving the estate in trust for the nation - but what happened to her, I have no clue.

So here I sit, day after day, night after night, hoping that one of those faces passing by will be hers. In my mind, she'll look just the way she did the evening I took her to Horcher's. She'll still be wearing the same perfume as the night we made love in a third-class cabin on the Lancastria, she'll still open up that radiant smile - and, yes, she'll still laugh at my jokes.

AUTHOR'S AFTERWORD

A historical note

Although a work of fiction, much of this novel's groundwork is factual, based on information gleaned from a multitude of sources: official archives, witness testimonies, interviews, articles from the period and a whole library of authoritative volumes.

As such, the physical reality of the Third Reich was very much as described here, including major events like "Martyr's Day" and "Kristallnacht," as well as actual personalities like Canaris, Göring, Himmler, Schellenberg, Eicke, Müller and others. In particular, careful attention has been paid to the central theme of the story, the remarkable facts concerning the career and character of SS Gruppenführer Reinhard Heydrich.

It's difficult to overstate the impact of Heydrich's career, not just on Nazi Germany but on the psychology of the entire post-war world. Surviving transcripts and other well-substantiated records have proven that he was the prime instigator of the Holocaust, the calculated genocide that has been called the worst crime in the history of mankind. Hitler may have devised the broad racial theories but it was Heydrich himself who brought about the practical application on such a massive scale.

By all accounts, Heydrich was obsessively ambitious and many historians have concluded that he would indeed have been the most logical choice to become the next Führer. In Joachim Fest's esteemed volume, "The Face of the Third Reich," the author offers an entire chapter on Heydrich entitled "The Successor."

Also true, surprisingly, is the principal plot catalyst of this book - that Reinhard Heydrich was accused of being part Jewish through his paternal line and that this "racial stain," generating almost a self-hatred, played a major role in determining his motives.

But was there ever a real dossier, manufactured in Moscow

and then planted in Berlin? It's conceivable. There's no question that, before the war, the Nazis and the Soviets were in collaboration on many fronts and their respective security agencies knew a great deal about each other. Indeed, Himmler's SS was said to have been modeled on Beria's NKVD and concentration camps like Dachau, forerunners to the death camps, were versions of the Siberian gulags.

Yet, as Adolf Hitler stated in his personal manifesto "Mein Kampf," he always did consider the Slavic peoples to be beneath contempt - and Josef Stalin, a native Georgian, always did consider it a personal affront. For Stalin to make his point by compromising the head of Reich security would have been inherently feasible and very much in character.

Despite their alliance, Hitler finally proved his disdain by launching a surprise attack on Soviet territory in June 1941. The Red Army suffered massive losses, eventually making its stand in a bitter, frozen struggle at the symbolically named city of Stalingrad, and the resulting German defeat became one of the turning points of the war.

Leon Berger, Montréal, 2006